For Ann

Tuesday, October 4, 1994, 10:45am

1. Money Woes

"Where's your rent, Miss McCormick?" Kristi's building manager stood in her office doorway. He was a middle-aged man with thin, balding hair, and he had a big belly from pigging out on junk food while voraciously devouring everything on TV, from Vince McMahon's World Wrestling Federation to President Bill Clinton's recent military operation in Haiti.

Kristi pasted a polite smile on her face. "Good morning, Mr. Haddon."

She'd managed to avoid the gross guy for most of the month. It hadn't been easy, because he always kept his office door open during business hours, his TV blaring, and she had to pass by it to reach the stairs to her own office.

Haddon's bristly mustache twitched as he squinted at her through steel-rimmed glasses. "October rent was due yesterday."

"I was planning to drop the check off later today, after I go to the bank," she lied.

Truth was, her bank account was down to double digits. She put down the book she'd been reading and started stacking the empty notepads and manila folders on her desk, pretending to be busy.

Haddon came over, his cheap Nike knock-offs squeaking on the old linoleum floor. He picked up the book and glanced at its cover. "You ain't fooling me, kid. I bet you just spend your time in here reading crap like this. 'K is for Killer'." He rolled his eyes.

She glared at him but was dismayed by his accurate assessment. "It's Sue Grafton's latest. Have you read it?"

"Hell no. I've got more important things to do."

Like what, watch TV? Aloud, Kristi said, "Then don't badmouth her work."

"I don't give a rat's ass about any of that." Haddon dropped the book onto her desk with a resonant thud. "You're a day late on the rent. I'm here to collect it."

"I know. I'm sorry, but-," Kristi tried but failed to meet his eyes as she uttered the biggest whopper yet, "-my case load has been so heavy, I haven't had time to get to the bank."

Haddon's stared at her through the thick lenses of his glasses, his watery blue eyes skeptical. "You're lying."

Good PIs should be able to lie if necessary, she thought, but felt her face flame as she said, "I'm not lying. I'll have the money for you by the end of today."

Launching a PI business was turning out to be a lot tougher than she'd expected. At this rate, she was just going to have to swallow her pride and ask her dad for help. She pushed back her chair and stood up. "If you'll please excuse me, I've got to go now."

When she moved around the narrow space between the desk and the corner wall of the office, Haddon didn't step back. She smelled stale coffee on his breath as he crowded her with his bulky body and she grimaced.

He looked her up and down. "You're mighty young to be a detective."

"True, but it's the perfect cover." She spoke quickly as she slid sideways past him, the sharp edge of the desk pressing into the back of her jeans. "Being young and blond in Santa Barbara, no one notices me." She hurried to the office door.

He followed, close on her heels. "I notice you, Miss McCormick. I notice you everyday when you come to work, and when you leave. I've also noticed that no one has been up those stairs—" he gestured a the stairs outside her office door, "except you and me this past month."

Kristi's heart rate kicked upward at his calling her bluff, but she turned and made herself give him a wide-eyed look of innocence. "So?"

"So, you haven't fooled me one bit, kid. Where are all your clients, huh?" Haddon moved close again, invading her personal space.

No way was she going to let him intimidate her. Fighting the urge to either shove him away or move back, she stood her ground. "I told you, I'll pay you later today. Now, excuse me, but I need to get to work." She stepped aside and waved her hand out the door, signaling for him to leave.

Instead, he reached up and cupped her chin with an unpleasantly moist hand. "How's about we work out a deal, and I can give you another week to pay your rent?" His eyes dropped to her breasts. He released her chin and his hand started down toward her T-shirt.

She didn't give him the chance. "No thanks, Mr. Haddon. I'll pay you later today."

Remembering a martial arts move her younger sister, Izzy, had taught her, Kristi grabbed Haddon by the wrist and twisted, forcing him sideways and propelling him past her and through the door.

Haddon stumbled forward and almost collided into a tall man who had just reached the landing outside her office.

The man stepped quickly aside. "Excuse me."

The office manager didn't reply as he bumbled away from them and down the stairs.

2. Kristi's First Case

Kristi looked up at the tall stranger and forgot the building manager as her heart swelled with hope. Could this be a prospective client?

The man was a couple of years older than she, mid-twenties, and wore a dark gray business suit and carried a brown leather briefcase. Probably an attorney, she guessed. The whole getup reminded her of James, the assistant District Attorney she'd started seeing recently. Unlike James, however, this guy wasn't blond-haired or blue-eyed. The crisp white dress shirt contrasted sharply with the man's black hair and dark complexion.

She smiled at him in hopeful anticipation. "May I help you?"

"Kristi McCormick?" The guy had a deep, compelling voice and piercing eyes an unusual shade of light gray.

"That's me. Please come in." She followed him into her office, her heart ratcheting up a notch. Though the guy wasn't classically handsome like James, there was something about him. Despite his height, she didn't feel threatened by his size.

He took the chair across the desk from her. Removing a card from his coat pocket, he slid it across the desk to her. "I'm Brian Castillo, an attorney with Byers and Martin. I need some help on a case."

Kristi picked up the card and tried to hide her eagerness as she looked at it. Byers and Martin was one of the top law firms in Santa Barbara, and dollar signs started dancing in her head as she thought of the rate she could charge him. Maybe she wouldn't have to ask her dad for money, after all.

The guy held up a hand. "Look, it's pro bono. I won't be able to pay you much."

He must have picked up on what she was thinking, and Kristi had to give him credit for being astute. She toned down her expectations, her smile fading as she dropped the card onto the desk.

5

Anything was better than nothing. "That's OK. What's the case about?"

"Have you heard about the woman who was found dead at her home in Montecito last Thursday night?"

"There was something about it in the newspaper yesterday. I figured it was an accident or something because of her age." The brief article had stated that the body of Miss Catherine Cole, a woman in her early 70s, had been discovered at the bottom of the stairs inside her mansion.

"The cause of death hasn't been determined yet."

Kristi looked at him in surprise. "Could she have been murdered?"

The cheap vinyl chair creaked as the guy shifted his long frame in it. "The situation is more complicated than what's been publicly communicated." He caught her eye. "You will keep what I say completely confidential, right Miss McCormick?"

"Of course, but please call me Kristi." She made herself hold his gaze, despite the fact that his intense regard was making her feel self-conscious and nothing like the cool-headed PI she wanted to be.

"I'm Brian," he said, giving a quick nod, and then continued. "Miss Cole was supposed to be out of town the night she died. She'd hired a young woman named Rose Schmidt to house sit and look after the cats while she was away. Miss Schmidt discovered the body. When the police arrived on scene later that night, they found evidence that Miss Cole had been robbed."

"The newspaper didn't say anything about a house sitter or that Miss Cole had been robbed."

"The police have kept a tight lid on the case, probably because Miss Cole came from a prominent Santa Barbara family—"

"Wait, was she a Cole as in 'Cole Bank'?" Kristi looked at him in surprise. It was a well-known local Santa Barbara bank; Kristi's own family banked there.

"Indeed. The police are undoubtedly under pressure to move quickly. They will probably hold a press conference in the next day or so. I expect the story will blow wide open at that point.." Brian's mouth flattened. "The DA is already zeroing in on Miss Schmidt as the prime suspect. I'm proactively beginning to assemble her defense."

"You think she's innocent?"

His gray eyes met hers, serious. "That's immaterial. What matters is that Rose is entitled to adequate legal representation."

Spoken like a lawyer, Kristi thought, but she didn't disagree. Aloud, she said, "Why does the DA think Miss Schmidt is a suspect?"

Brian held up three fingers. "She was the first person to discover the body; she's struggling financially, and she has no alibi. The DA has good reason to suspect her of theft, at the very least. Rose has sworn to me, however, that she didn't kill Miss Cole and that she had no idea that any of Miss Cole's jewelry had been taken."

"Do you believe her?"

Brian shrugged. "I'd like to, but there's something she told me that complicates matters."

"What's that?"

"She says that the night Miss Cole died, there was an intruder in the house when she got there. The problem is, Rose doesn't want to tell the police about it, because she's afraid that if it gets out that she saw the intruder, the man will come after her."

"Did she recognize him?"

"She said she didn't get a good enough look." Brian's expression turned troubled and his gaze drifted away from her to the office window where the mid-morning sun shone through the dirty glass and promised another hot October day.

His strong features and bold chin were accentuated in profile, and when he abruptly turned back to her, Kristi hastily looked away, telling herself to focus on the case and not the guy. She picked up a pencil and tried to look professional, jotting down notes about what he'd said. Something occurred to her. "Could Rose have made up the intruder story to cover her own guilt?"

"It's possible, but if there was an intruder, it would be the key to clearing Rose." Brian rubbed a hand absently over his jaw, the rasping sound audible in the quiet room. "I have a feeling there's more to what happened the night Miss Cole died, but when I tried to push Rose for more details, she got upset and wouldn't say any more. It's my hope that if you talk to her she might be more open."

"Why do you think that?" Kristi hazarded a glance up from where she was scribbling notes.

"Because you're less intimidating than I am?" The whisper of a smile crossed Brian's face, transforming him from intimidating attorney to a suddenly very attractive guy.

Kristi jerked her eyes from his. "How do you know Rose?"

"Through a friend of my dad's. Rose used to be his English Language teacher. My dad asked me to take the case."

Kristi rolled her pencil between her fingers and considered the intruder angle. "Maybe the robbery was unrelated to Miss Cole's death. Isn't it possible that they could have happened at two separate times, and maybe Miss Cole's death was actually just an accidental fall and not murder?"

"That's not how the police or the DA see it." Brian frowned. "I don't want Rose railroaded by the legal system simply because she's poor and an easy target."

"Of course. I hope that everyone gets a fair trial in our town."

"Maybe, but I won't let Rose be unfairly prosecuted." Brian laid a hand on the desk for emphasis.

"Are the two of you involved?" The words were out of Kristi's mouth before she could stop them.

Brian's brows shot upward. "Of course not!"

"It's just that you seem awfully concerned about her." Kristi felt her face flush when she realized it wasn't simple professional curiosity driving her question.

"Miss McCormick—"

"Kristi, remember?"

"Kristi. The legal system doesn't always work the way it should. I care when anyone is treated unfairly by the law." His face was as earnest and serious as his words.

"I do, too." She smiled at the admirable sentiment, but why would someone from the powerhouse firm Byers and Martin want to hire a newbie like herself. "How did you hear about me?"

"Pete McCormick, a detective at the SBPD, recommended you."

"You know Pete?" She looked at him in surprise.

"We've worked a few cases together. He's a good guy."

Kristi found herself smiling again. It was another vote in Brian's favor that he liked her Uncle Pete.

She sat back in her chair and chewed her lip, considering everything he'd told her. The dead woman hadn't been just anybody, she'd been a member of the powerful Cole family. If it turned out Miss Cole had been murdered, the case would become high profile and the stakes would be huge. If Kristi screwed up her investigation, she could kiss her PI dreams goodbye. But, her rent was due, and this was the only case to come along. Besides, what if Rose was telling the truth? And Kristi agreed with everything Brian had said about fair legal treatment.

"OK, I'll talk to Rose." She pulled open the top drawer of her desk and took out a contract along with one of her business cards. She slid them across the desk. "I charge hourly plus expenses. Did Pete tell you that I'm still finishing the requirements for my PI license?"

"He mentioned it." Brian reviewed the contract.

Kristi watched him and realized that he probably couldn't pay top dollar on a pro bono case. Maybe that's why Pete had recommended her. Her rates were bottom-barrel, considering she was desperate.

Brian pointed to a paragraph in the contract. "I'm glad to see you have the standard confidentiality clauses, but that does mean you won't share details of the case with your uncle, right?"

Kristi tried not to sound insulted. "I'm a professional."

"Good." He pulled a checkbook and pen from the inside pocket of his coat.

Kristi's heart raced with anticipation as she watched him sign the contract and fill out the check. The money would buy more time to keep Eye Spy Private Eye going. She'd be able to get that horrid Mr. Haddon off her back for a while longer, and maybe now, her dad might start showing her career choice a little more respect.

Brian removed a file from his briefcase. "Here's all the information I have. Rose's contact information is in there, too, but she's hard to reach. The last few days have been pretty hard on her, and as I said, she seems quite emotionally fragile. All things considered, I'd like to arrange your interview with her and perform the introductions, if that's OK?"

"Sure." Kristi's eyes fell on the check, the contract, and the file. Excitement bubbled up. This was it, her first case!

Brian pocketed her business card and stood up. She jumped to her feet and came around the desk, aware again of how tall he was.

He looked down at her, his expression serious. "I realize you may be busy, but could you make Rose's case a priority?"

If he only knew! "Of course."

She stuck out her hand to seal the deal. His large hand enclosed hers in a warm embrace, his grip sure and strong, and caught her off-guard by the sudden physical intimacy. Her mouth went dry.

"Thanks," she managed to mumble.

"For what?" His expression was polite and impassive as he released her hand.

She cleared her throat and tried to stand taller. "For entrusting me with your case."

She knew that sounded lame, especially when what she really wanted to do was throw her arms around him and thank him for saving her dream of becoming a PI. Fortunately, he didn't seem to notice.

"I'll call you once I have an interview time with Rose." He gave her a brief smile and then turned and left the office.

3. The Investigation Begins

Kristi closed the door after Brian Castillo and leaned against it, listening to the footsteps of her first client fade away down the stairs. When she turned back to her office, it was like seeing it for the first time-the small wicker bookshelf across from the window with all her Sue Grafton mysteries and other paperbacks, the orange vinyl chair with its skinny metal legs, the desk a friend had scored from a curb in Isla Vista, and the tattered but still decent office chair she'd bought at the thrift shop on Milpas Street. Her office wasn't much, but it was hers, as long as she could pay the rent. She picked up K is for Killer and took it to the bookshelf where she tucked it in next to J is for Judgment.

Time to solve a real life mystery, she thought, as she crossed back over to her desk.

She flipped open the slim file Brian had given her. Thumbing through the pages, she noted that most of them were the hand-written notes he'd taken during his interview with Rose. Kristi sat down and started to read.

The first page in the file described Rose's background. She had grown up and attended college in the Midwest and then moved to Santa Barbara three years ago to teach English as a Second Language. She taught ESL at a private school for foreign students and in night classes held at the public high school to the town's large Spanish-speaking population. She supplemented her income with house-sitting gigs and met Catherine Cole a year ago through a student in one of her night classes, Eduardo Garcia. He had been Catherine's groundskeeper for the past five years, until he quit three months ago to care for his sick wife. Brian had added a note in the margin about Eduardo being his dad's friend and that he was the one who had asked for help on Rose's behalf.

Kristi turned to the next page in the file, where Rose had told Brian about Catherine. According to Rose, the Catherine was very reclusive and rarely left her large estate in Montecito. One of her cats developed a serious health problem a year ago, which was why she hired Rose to house sit when she went out of town. The only other resident on the property was the new groundskeeper, Tomas Silva, who lived in one of the outbuildings. Tomas maintained the extensive gardens and took care of Catherine's groceries as well as other matters pertaining to the operation of the property. As far as Rose knew, Catherine didn't have any enemies, never had any visitors, and only ever left the estate when she went on those mysterious trips every few months, their destination unknown to Rose. Rose also didn't know why Catherine came back early from her last trip. She insisted that, when Tomas came into the foyer immediately after her discovering Catherine's body, she was simply checking Catherine for a pulse. She reiterated that she never would have killed Catherine.

Kristi put the page down and imagined the scene in her mind's eye-Rose came back from work, found Catherine at the bottom of the stairs, and went to see if she was alive. Had Catherine's wrist still been warm? Kristi shuddered at the thought. Why had the poor woman come home that night? Had she interrupted a burglary?

Running a hand through her short curly hair, Kristi thought of more questions. If there had been an intruder, had Tomas seen the man? Why had Tomas gone into the house when he did? For that matter, why did Catherine need a house-sitter when she already had a groundskeeper? Couldn't Tomas look after the cats?

So many questions, it was time to make a list. Kristi grabbed her notepad and started writing. From what she knew so far, both Rose and Tomas had similar means and opportunity to kill Catherine. As far as motive, Rose was hard up for cash. What about Tomas? She'd definitely need to check him out.

Kristi turned to the last page of the file. It contained a single hand-written note scrawled by Brian about the fact that Catherine hadn't hired a security firm or used surveillance equipment, either of which might have revealed an intruder on the property the night she died. Kristi closed the file and sighed. So much for an easy way to prove Rose's claim.

The sun blazing against the window was making the office hot and stuffy. Kristi went over to open it for some fresh air but was met by a furnace blast of heat. She slid the window back down with irritation. She was getting pretty sick and tired of the October heat wave hitting Southern California. Plucking at her T-shirt where it stuck to her sweaty skin, she went back and sat down at her desk again. Her phone rang.

She picked up the receiver. "Eye Spy Private Eye."

"You sound so professional." It was one her oldest friends, Carla Deville.

Kristi grinned. "I should. I just scored my first case."

"Awesome! Does this mean your dad'll get off your back about not working for him?"

"I doubt it. He's still mad I don't want to keep working for him and learn the insurance business." Unlike the licensed PIs in town, she grimaced, none of whom had wanted to take her on as an apprentice. They'd all said she was too young, but she suspected that was just code for being female.

"Insurance." Carla faked yawn. "Ho hum! Being a PI is much more exciting."

"Yeah, right. The last month all I've been doing is reading mysteries and waiting for a real one to walk in the door."

"You wanna sneak out and go to the beach?"

"Now? It's not even lunchtime. Don't you need to keep the Magic Shop open?"

"Not if this heat wave is gonna kill me!"

"Drama queen!" Kristi laughed, but the thought of plunging into the cold ocean was tempting. Her office was starting to feel like an oven. "How about we meet up after work?"

Carla groaned. "If I'm still alive, but yeah. What time?"

"I'll swing by the Magic Shop a bit after five. OK?"

Kristi hung up and ran her fingers through her now damp hair, bringing her thoughts back to the first case. Maybe her uncle could offer some insights. At least she could thank him for sending work her way.

She picked up the phone again and dialed his extension at the Santa Barbara Police Department.

Pete answered, all business. "McCormick here."

"Hey, Uncle Pete."

"Krissy, what's shakin', bacon?" His voice held a smile in it.

She rocked back in her chair. "What can you tell me about Brian Castillo?"

"He came to see you?"

"Yeah. What's his story?"

"Castillo's one of the good ones. Cares about justice and doing what's right, especially for the under served. I respect that. We need more people like him."

Brian's serious face and earnest gray eyes flashed in her mind's eye, followed by a whisper of disappointment as something occurred to her. "Are you guys together?"

"No."

He didn't elaborate.

She was afraid to push for more details. President Clinton's attempt to liberalize attitudes at the federal level with a new "Don't Ask, Don't Tell" policy in the military didn't mean much in a conservative town like Santa Barbara. Her uncle's being gay was a carefully guarded secret, not only from the police department but also from her dad. She often wondered if their falling out was somehow connected. The two brothers hadn't spoken in years.

Kristi reminded herself that Brian was off-limits, regardless. He was a client, and of course there was James. After an awkward pause, she said, "Well, thanks for sending him my way. I've just taken the Rose Schmidt case."

"You're welcome, kiddo."

"Were you one of the detectives who questioned Rose?"

"Yep."

Kristi looked down at her list of questions on her notepad. "Do you think she's capable of murder?"

"Everyone is, given the right conditions."

"Sure, but in your professional opinion as a well-seasoned detective-"

Pete chuckled. "You make me sound like a piece of meat."

Kristi chuckled too, but then sobered, her mind moving back to the case. "Seriously, do you think she could've killed Catherine?"

"It's possible. All fingerprints from Cole's bedroom and the safe were wiped."

"Really?" That certainly sounded suspicious, but someone else could've done it. Kristi couldn't ask him point blank about the intruder, not if she wanted to maintain client confidentiality, so instead, she said, "What about other possible suspects? Other people had access to the house, like Tomas Silva, and maybe even the old groundskeeper who knew Rose and got her the house sitting gig at Catherine's in the first place. Have you talked to them?"

"We've talked to Silva."

"Does he have an alibi?"

"He claims he was in his apartment at the time of Cole's death."

"Can anyone corroborate that?"

"No."

"Couldn't he have stolen the jewelry and killed Catherine before Rose got there? Maybe he's framing Rose."

"Hold on, hotshot," Pete laughed. "There's no point throwing out theories, certainly not until we have the coroner's report. We don't even know for sure that we're dealing with a homicide."

"What about the lack of fingerprints in the bedroom?"

"Maybe she had a real thorough cleaning lady."

It was her turn to laugh. "Yeah, right. Do you know when the report will be out?"

"Unsure. Soon." She heard him shuffle papers on his end and sensed his attention starting to drift elsewhere.

"I'll let you get back to work, Uncle Pete. Thanks again for helping me get my first case. I just hope I can succeed."

"If you need my help, Krissy, you just let me know and I'll do what I can, OK?"

"Thanks, Pete." She hung up, a lump in her throat. Unlike her dad, her uncle had always supported her dream of becoming a PI.

She glanced at her watch and saw that it was time for lunch with James.

4. Trouble with James

On her way to lunch, Kristi stopped by the building manager's office. For once, Haddon wasn't there. She slipped a rent check under the door with a sense of satisfaction. It wasn't enough to cover the whole month, but at least it bought a couple more weeks to keep Eye Spy Private Eye's door open.

She set off down the street to meet James at an exclusive venue a few blocks from her office. He arrived just when she did.

"Let's get out of this heat," he said, giving her a quick kiss, and then leading her to an outdoor patio that was cooled by tall broad-leafed plants and a fountain that splashed nearby.

Kristi looked around the place in admiration. The restaurant was the kind of beautiful, upscale venue she'd only ever seen from the sidewalk before she started seeing James a month ago. That was right before she left her dad's company. James had come in to handle some details of his family's account and had asked her out.

As he took a seat across from her at the small table, Kristi was still surprised that someone as rich and powerful as he was interested in her. Not only was he a member of Santa Barbara's upper crust and one of Santa Barbara's youngest deputy district attorneys, but he was also model-gorgeous and always perfectly dressed. The linen suit he wore was just right for the hot weather. She felt like a slob in comparison, sweating across from him in her cotton T-shirt and jeans.

He brushed back his sun-bleached blond hair and smiled at her. "You surf, right?"

"A little," she said between bites of a perfectly prepared spinach quiche, the crust light and flaky. "It's been a while."

"That's OK." When his sky blue eyes met hers, her heart did a little flip in her chest. He was so incredibly good-looking.

"Some friends and I are going surfing next weekend. You wanna come?" He raised a glass of white wine to his classically molded lips.

It seemed kind of extravagant to drink wine during a workday, but he'd told her lawyers were expected to do such things. Kristi pulled her gaze from his mouth and focused on his words. He hadn't invited her to go surfing before and she was flattered. "Thanks, but I don't have a board anymore." She'd sold hers in high school to help pay for her car.

"No worries." He leaned sideways and studied her body around the edge of the table. "What are you, five two or three?"

She was impressed by his accuracy. It wasn't the kind of little detail she thought he'd noticed. "Five three."

"I've got a short board that should work."

"Cool." Despite being flattered, she felt a twinge of irritation. He'd turned down all of her offers to go swimming after work. Of course he was busy, but still. Swimming was her passion, besides mysteries. She took a sip of ice water and considered his offer. "When are you going?"

"Saturday. We're going to head out to Hollister Ranch. They're forecasting a good-sized swell off Point Conception. Don't worry, there's a beginner break there, too."

"Thanks." He'd misread her reticence. She wasn't the best of surfers, but truth was, she much preferred swimming. She loved the feel of being in the wave rather than on it, the feel of her body sliding unhindered through the water. She didn't bother to explain. Surfers never understood. "I think I can go unless something comes up with my first case."

James put down his fork and smiled. "Your first case? That's great news. Tell me about it."

"There's a woman named Rose Schmidt—"

"I know who she is." His smile faded. "Why did she hire you?"

"I'm sorry but I can't tell you."

"Client confidentiality, I get it." James' eyes turned cold as he took another long sip of white wine, the glass now heavily beaded with condensation.

Kristi didn't understand the negative look on his usually easygoing face. She'd waited until they were almost done eating before mentioning her news, wanting to save the best for last. "Aren't you happy for me?"

His expression softened. "Of course, but I just don't want you to fail your first case." He put the wineglass down and took her hand in his.

"What do you mean?"

"Schmidt's likely guilty, if not of murder then certainly of theft."

Kristi pulled her hand free from his cold, clammy hand and rubbed it dry on the leg of her jeans. "Why do you think that?"

"Because I'm a deputy district attorney and Catherine Cole's case is my top priority."

Kristi felt a sinking sensation in her stomach to think that James was now her adversary, but then she realized maybe she could use his position to her advantage. "What evidence do you have against Miss Schmidt?"

"Beyond the fact that she had the motive, means, and opportunity?" He gave Kristi an arch look.

"That's not the same as evidence," Kristi pointed out, taking another bite of quiche.

"Babe, you should drop the case and start with something less high profile. Build your reputation slowly, with more obtainable goals."

He was trying to be helpful and she knew he was right, but there was something about the casual way he said it that put her off. It wasn't as if she could be picky. No other clients had knocked on her door.

James drained his glass of wine. "My grandfather was great friends with Catherine Cole's father. He wants me to make sure justice is served regarding her death. I plan to see that it is." There was a challenge in his eyes.

Kristi's lunch turned to sawdust in her mouth. James' grandfather was a well-known judge and public figure in Santa Barbara. With a powerful man like that and his grandson the prosecuting attorney, both out for swift justice, what chance did someone like Rose Schmidt have? Or her? Kristi pushed the rest of her quiche away.

James continued. "I'm surprised Schmidt would seek you out. The woman has absolutely no money."

"She didn't." Kristi thought of the tall, dark, and serious man who'd come to her office.

"Who then?"

"An attorney taking her case pro bono, a guy named Brian Castillo."

"Castillo?" James waved a hand dismissively in the air. "I heard the guy's a hopeless do-gooder."

His naked condescension set her teeth on edge. "How can you say that? He's trying to help people less fortunate than you or me."

"That may be so, but let me tell you—"

The waitress appeared at James' side and handed him the bill.

Probably because he's the one in the fancy suit, Kristi thought with growing irritation, even if the waitress' assumption was right.

James pulled out his wallet. "As I was saying, once you've worked in the justice system as long as I have, you'll come to understand the truth about people."

"What 'truth' is that, James?" Kristi threw down her napkin and lurched to her feet, now outright angry.

He tossed several large bills on the table and stood up. "Love and money, honey. They can make people do terrible things."

5. At the Santa Barbara Public Library

Kristi was still fuming when she parted ways with James after lunch. Leaving the cool sanctuary of the restaurant, she headed out into the blazing afternoon and walked toward Anapamu Street and the public library to start her background research. She'd never suspected James of being a snob, but his comments about Brian and Rose, especially about Rose grated on her. Being poor wasn't a crime, though James did have a point that money was often a motive for evil. Kristi needed to meet Rose face-to-face and judge the woman for herself.

The heat was relentless, even when Kristi stepped into the tall shadow of Santa Barbara's big downtown public library. Maybe that's why the usual homeless people weren't out front. They were probably inside cooling off in the library's air-conditioning. Thinking about the homeless made her think again about money and what James had said.

She went to the pay phone on the wall beside the library entrance. Pushing up her sunglasses, she wiped the sweat from her face, dug a quarter from her purse, and called her answering machine, hoping Brian had called with a time for her to interview Rose. No messages from him or otherwise. She tried his office and got his answering machine. She found herself listening to the entire recording. There was something about the deep timbre of his voice, something compelling. Impatient with herself, she hung up and told herself to focus on the case.

A refreshing rush of cold air greeted her when she pulled open one of the library's heavy double doors. She loved the old library with its enormous reading room, huge walk-in fireplace, and large faded tapestries hanging on its two-story high walls. The place reminded her of times gone by, when people valued public spaces and were willing to pay the money and taxes needed to support them. Now the place had frayed around the edges and smelled tired.

Kristi headed past the checkout counter and card catalogs across the library's main floor to the Reference section, hoping someone there could help her. A young woman stood behind the counter at a computer, rapidly typing, a grin creasing her face. Kristi recognized the bright red hair tamed into a pair of long braids.

She whispered across the counter. "Rebecca?"

The red-haired woman looked up from the monitor and her grin broadened into a toothy smile. "Kristi McCormick! Long time no see."

"No kidding." Kristi gestured around the reference area. "Does this mean you finished library school?"

Rebecca nodded and her braids slid forward. She used both hands to toss them back over her shoulders. "Got my Masters in Library Science in June. I just started here last month."

"Cool." Kristi smiled. Having a friend at the library would be handy.

Rebecca was looking at her curiously. "What are you up to these days? Still working for your dad?"

Kristi shook her head. "I'm a private eye now." She took a business card out of her purse and slid it across the counter.

Rebecca picked it up. "'Eye Spy Private Eye.' I like it. Mysteries are my favorite genre."

"Mine, too," Kristi nodded. "I just wish real life were as easy as it seems in books."

When Rebecca made to hand back the card, Kristi waved it away. "Hold onto it. If anyone comes in here looking for a PI, can you pass it along? I need more clients."

"Sure thing." Rebecca opened a drawer beneath the counter and dropped the card inside. "So why are you here?"

"I need background on a case."

Rebecca's eyes sparked with interest. "What are you looking for?"

Kristi started to explain when an elderly man in a 70s-style powder blue leisure suit approached, pursing his lips in disapproval at them chatting together at the reference counter.

Rebecca whispered behind her hand to Kristi, "Hang on a second. He's a major donor and I've gotta help him." When she was done, she said to Kristi, "Last week's newspapers are over there in the periodical section, along with the microfiche. Bring me the call numbers if you need anything, and I can pull the microfilm for you." She started typing on the computer again.

Kristi watched her for a moment and then said hopefully, "Can't you just use that computer to look up stuff?"

"Like what?" The rapid tapping of Rebecca's typing didn't change tempo.

"I don't know. Like how much money ESL teachers make and how much does it cost to buy a low income condo in Santa Barbara?"

Rebecca looked up and laughed. "Hah! I wish it were that easy. Maybe someday, like in 2004 or something, but not now in 1994. You try one of those PI databases I've heard about?"

"I can't get access until I have a PI license—and enough money to pay for it." Kristi grimaced and stifled a yawn. "I've gotta confess, library work isn't really my thing." That's why she'd avoided college. She wasn't like her younger sisters, Tate and Izzy. Book stuff came easy to them.

"More legwork, less book work?"

Kristi nodded. "Yeah, but I'll try your suggestion and check out the newspapers."

Kristi had only ever hung out in the Fiction section of the library before, so she followed Reb's directions and found where Santa Barbara's two local papers were shelved. She took copies of everything since last Thursday to the periodical reading area and scanned them all, looking for anything that might be relevant to the case. There were only the two articles she'd already seen at home. The first was from last Friday, a short blurb about Catherine Cole being found dead. The second was an obituary in the Sunday edition. There was nothing else and no mention of Rose Schmidt.

Kristi reread the obituary with more attention. Most of it focused on Catherine's relatives. Her father had founded the extremely successful Cole Bank Worldwide, later run by her brother until he and his wife died in a car accident five years ago. Her only surviving relative was her brother's adult daughter, Anita Walker, who lived in Pacific Palisades. Kristi made a note to call the niece.

Her eyes went back to Catherine's head shot. It must've been taken decades ago, because Catherine looked about forty, with short, conservatively styled hair. She was smiling slightly, but her expression was remote. Her lips were closed over her teeth and her eyes looked somewhere off into the distance. With the prim-looking sweater set and single strand of pearls about her neck, she looked just like what Kristi imagined a banker's daughter would look like. Had someone killed her? Had Rose?

Kristi got up and went over to the periodicals card catalog. When she pulled open one of the drawers and saw the index cards packed tightly together inside, she groaned, remembering unpleasant high school research papers. Ugh. She hated the Dewey Decimal system. Running her fingertips over the tops of the index cards, her eyes glazed over and she started thinking again about Catherine, her wealth, and her family of bankers. Kristi had an idea.

She went back to the table where she'd left the newspapers. Flipping past the news section, she skimmed the business section. Nothing about Cole Bank. So much for that idea, she sighed.

Shifting her position in the uncomfortable, straight-backed wood library chair, Kristi turned idly to the Society page. Ah to be rich. There was a big photograph of a group of well-dressed older people posing with the governor. Beneath it was an article about a fundraiser held out in Santa Ynez. As she scanned the article, she frowned. The party had been held to raise money "in defense of marriage," those words her uncle Pete had told her were code for the political effort to repeal attempts to liberalize government policy toward homosexuals, such as the president's new "Don't Ask, Don't Tell" policy. It wasn't as if gay people could legally marry, so why did those people feel the need to defend marriage?

Curious to see who would host such a party, Kristi studied the smaller photograph, which featured the party hosts, a certain Beverly Carlyle, widow of the late businessman Mason Carlyle, and Ridley Niven, a horse breeder of fine Arabians. There was a caption mentioning that the couple announced their engagement at the fundraiser. How appropriate, Kristi thought, the hosts of a pro-marriage event announcing their own intention to marry. The woman looked glamorous, like Zaza Gabor, with white hair up in a fancy hairdo. The man beside her was tall and debonair with a thin mustache, but unlike the woman, who looked birdlike and delicate, he seemed quite fit for his age.

Kristi was about to put the society page aside when something caught her eye. The party happened last Thursday, the same night Catherine Cole died.

Interesting, she thought. Not all rich people were out partying that night.

She turned the page and found the Classifieds. After perusing the want ads, she learned that neither the fancy private language school in town nor the Adult Ed night classes at the public high school paid ESL teachers very much, certainly not enough to pay for a house in Santa Barbara.

This was further borne out by the Real Estate section of the paper, where Kristi found a small blurb about a new low income housing complex opening up across town. When Kristi saw the price tags, she grimaced. "Low income"? What a joke! No way could an ESL teacher afford those price tags. Neither could she.

Thinking about money again made her antsy to get out of there, but there was one more thing to check out. She headed back to her friend in the Reference section.

"You got anything on the law firm Byers and Martin and a guy named Brian Castillo?" she asked Rebecca.

"Fancy law firm. Who's the guy?"

"My client." She didn't bother to clarify that he was the lawyer representing her client.

Rebecca looked up from the computer screen. "Why are you researching your client?"

Kristi felt her cheeks flush and cursed her fair Irish skin.

"Oh, it's like that, huh?" Rebecca waggled an eyebrow at her.

Kristi scowled. "How's your love life?"

"Offense is the best defense, is that it?" Rebecca laughed. "Anyhoo, I'm waiting for Prince Charming. You know, one who loves books and red-headed nerds who still live at home."

"I still live at home, too."

"Tough on one's love life, isn't it?"

"You got that right." Kristi's dad was so old school she'd been afraid to bring home any of her dates, except maybe James, but their relationship hadn't gotten that far yet. She got the feeling that unless she was practically engaged, her dad would disapprove, and he didn't always keep his opinions to himself.

Rebecca looked thoughtful for a moment. "I'll be right back." She disappeared again into the stacks and then brought back a slim binder and a larger bound volume that Kristi recognized as a Santa Barbara High School yearbook. "Here you go."

"Thanks." Kristi took the material to one of the reference tables and sat down.

The binder contained a Byers and Martin media kit with glossy photos and press material featuring the two well-known and politically connected attorneys. Their law firm managed the estates of many of Santa Barbara's wealthiest residents. Inside the binder was also a list and brief bios of the firm's attorneys. She scanned down the list and found Brian's. Wow. He'd recently graduated summa cum laude with a law degree from Stanford. The guy was no wimp, despite what James had implied. No wonder he worked for a powerhouse like Byers and Martin. His student debt must be enormous.

Kristi put the binder aside and turned to the yearbook, smiling at the cover. This one had come out her Freshman year. She found Brian's photo in the Senior section. He looked young and slightly goofy, like pretty much everyone does in their school photos, but she didn't remember ever seeing him in high school. He looked so different now, so serious. She sighed. Growing up had a way of turning everything serious.

She glanced up at the large round clock on the wall and was surprised to see that it was almost 5 o'clock. Stretching, she went back to the Reference counter.

"Thanks, Reb. Good stuff." She pushed the material back across the counter to her friend. "Can I buy you a coffee sometime to pay you back for the help?"

"Sometime, anytime. I live for the stuff."

6. Carla Deville

The afternoon was still blazing hot when Kristi left the library. She was eager to get to the beach with Carla, but first she had to stop by her office to get her bathing suit and check her answering machine again. When she got there, her eyes went straight to the answering machine on her desk. The light was blinking. She pressed "Play" and her heart kicked up a beat. It was Brian.

"Kristi, I reached Rose. She can talk to you tonight, but she won't be done teaching until 9:30. Her class is in room 212 at Santa Barbara High. Please let me know if you can make it."

Kristi grinned. Her interview with Rose was on! She dialed Brian to confirm, but he didn't answer. She left a quick message and then collected her suit and towel from the hook on the back of the office door. Changing, she then pulled her street clothes back on over her suit, and grabbed her keys.

The sun had dipped below the roof line, when she stepped outside, but the dry air still felt like an oven. There was none of the moist marine breeze that usually blew in from the ocean in early evening. Instead, a hot wind blasted down from the Santa Ynez mountains. A similar sundowner a few years ago had torched over five hundred homes in the Painted Cave Fire. Kristi glanced up at the mountain range looming behind Santa Barbara and was relieved not to see smoke.

As she walked along the sidewalk, dry leaves in the sycamore trees above her rustled in a sudden gust of wind. State Street was bustling with rush hour traffic, most of it local. In the off season, there weren't many tourists mid-week. A couple of grizzled men sat on overturned milk crates, looking up at passersby and shaking collection cans at them. Kristi scrounged around in her purse and found a few coins to give the men. They were hurting for money more than she was.

When she reached Cota Street, she turned and headed into the old neighborhood where she and her younger sisters grew up, before her dad's insurance business took off and they moved uptown. They'd been friends with the two girls next door, Carla and Gwen Deville, and used to treat Cota Street like their front yard, playing hopscotch on the sidewalk or jacks on their front steps. Together, they had created the "Cota Club" and Cota Street was their stomping ground. As Kristi headed for the Magic Shop, she found herself missing the old days when they were all together.

A sign hung in the window next door to the Magic Shop. It was up for lease again. Rents were skyrocketing all over Santa Barbara. Carla and Gwen's mom, Madeline, had been smart to buy the Magic Shop building, years ago, back when the town's real estate wasn't so expensive.

Kristi sighed. Would she ever be able to afford to move out of her parents' house?

As she stepped inside the Magic Shop, the doorbell tinkled, and she was greeted with the familiar, distinctive smell of dust and sandalwood, mixed with other more exotic scents.

Carla sat on a stool behind a glass display case that housed an assortment of occult items and tourist trinkets. She looked up from the book she was reading and grinned. "Hey, Kristi!"

Carla was tall and lean with straight black hair, olive skin, and bright green eyes. As far as Kristi was concerned, she was the epitome of beauty, French and exotic, and nothing like Kristi and her own curly-haired sisters, with their freckles and pale skin that burned so easily.

"Sorry I'm not a customer," Kristi said. "You have any today?"

"A few. Not many in this heat. Man, I wish we had some air conditioning."

Carla secured the cash register, picked up her towel, and flipped over the "Closed" sign on the Magic Shop door before they left.

Kristi filled Carla in on her eventful day as they headed for the beach.

Carla burst out laughing when Kristi described her encounter with the building manager. "The guy's gotta outweigh you by more than fifty pounds."

"More like a hundred."

"But you were still able to boot him out of your office. Useful skill. Maybe I'll take some lessons from Izzy. It sounds like her martial arts training is really coming along."

"She's a star at Henry Yee's Green Dragon studio."

"No kidding. She always was a good student."

"More like Tate than me, that's for sure." Kristi didn't mean to sound bitter, but Tate, who was in her second year of college, was following the path her parents had wanted her to take.

"There's more to life than school," Carla said with emphasis, but then gave a sigh, looking uncharacteristically dejected.

Kristi knew that Carla fantasized about someday leaving the sleepy seaside town and living a life of adventure, maybe even being a spy. She reached out and gave Carla a sympathetic pat on the shoulder. "I know it's hard holding down the fort without your mom, but it's not forever. Gwen will graduate this year. Maybe she can take over running the Magic Shop. Besides, your mom may get better."

Carla scowled. "The docs at the mental hospital aren't optimistic."

"It's only been six months, right? Maybe the treatment just needs more time."

"Maybe."

"Enough about me. What's this about a new case?"

Kristi wasn't sure how much detail she could divulge and still maintain client confidentiality. She kept it vague as they headed down the newly completed underpass beneath the 101 freeway. "I've been hired by someone to prove that someone else is innocent of a crime."

"Sounds pretty straightforward to me."

"Except that I haven't met the other person yet, and I'm not even sure there's been a crime."

"Is it your client's husband or wife or something?"

"No." Kristi chuckled. "The woman's his client. He's a lawyer." She flash-backed to meeting Brian and how it felt when he shook her hand. She cleared her throat.

Carla grinned. "Hot, is he?"

"Yeah, but I work for him now."

Carla laughed. "Doesn't mean you can't look."

"It's not good to mix business and personal stuff." Kristi knew Carla thought she was a prude, but she believed in the maxim. She gave Carla a pointed look. "Besides, I'm seeing someone."

"Who, James? You just started seeing him. Not that I approve." Carla shook her head with emphasis. "The guy's a douche."

Kristi bristled. "How can you say that? You've only met him once." Carla could be way too sure of herself sometimes. "I think you're being too harsh. Besides, my parents like him."

"Of course, they do. He's rich and good-looking and part of the whole pattern."

Kristi put a hand on Carla's forearm and pulled her to a stop. "What do you mean?"

Carla shook off her hand. "Ever since your dad started getting bigger clients and you guys moved uptown, your folks have set their eyes on climbing up the social scene. You scoring James Roberts, Assistant DA and grandson of the famous Judge Roberts, that's huge. Especially if you get invited to some of those oolala parties. Could be great for your dad's business."

"My parents aren't such money grubbers. My dad works hard and is trying to make his business a success," Kristi said defensively, but a small part of her wondered. Was Carla right?

A tense silence descended between them as they crossed East Cabrillo Boulevard.

When they reached the grassy strip separating the road from the bike path and the beach, Carla tapped Kristi lightly on the shoulder. "Sorry. I was out of line. Rich boys are a sore subject with me."

At her friend's words, Kristi suddenly realized why James rubbed Carla the wrong way. He must remind Carla of Mark Lyons, the rich boy Carla dated in high school. Carla never explained their break up, and Kristi was still curious about what happened. She glanced over at her friend. "You ever see Mark anymore?"

Carla's green eyes sparked with anger. She stepped off the bike path and strode away onto the sand, leaving Kristi to hurry after her.

The sun had sunk behind the Mesa and the beach was in shadow. The mountains blazed purple-gold behind Santa Barbara, the sun still blazing on the high ridges. The sundowner blew offshore and flattened the waves, turning the ocean into a vast mirror that reflected the metallic blue of the slowly darkening sky.

"Race you!" Carla ditched her clothes and took off for the water, her long legs leaving Kristi in the dust.

Kristi followed as fast as she could, dove under a small breaker, and swam out into the Pacific. The cool water flowed over her body and washed away the heat and sweat of the day. Carla was faster on land, but this was Kristi's medium. She loved how powerful and strong she felt in the water. With sure strokes, she propelled herself smoothly through the ocean's undulating currents. She may be a newbie at the PI business, but she was a pro at swimming. She found her rhythm and pulled away from her friend as she swam out to the first of the offshore buoys.

Almost an hour later with night settling across the land and sea, Kristi hauled herself out of the water, feeling refreshed and invigorated. Carla was waiting for her, already dressed again in street clothes. Kristi picked up her towel and quickly dried off. As they started back along East Cabrillo toward State Street, the streetlights clicked on overhead.

"Whatcha doin' for dinner?" Kristi asked. Hanging out at the Magic Shop would be way more fun than going home and eating with her folks.

"Don't know, yet. Gwen's having dinner with Izzy at your house. I think they're studying for a Calculus test or something."

"I've got to go to the high school at 9:30 tonight for an interview."

"So late?"

Kristi shrugged. "It's the only time the woman's available."

"I've got cheese and tortillas in the fridge. Quesadillas?"

"Sure! Can we watch the news?" Maybe there'd be more coverage about the case.

7. Rose Schmidt

After dinner, Kristi drove over to the high school early so she could watch Rose teach and get a sense of the woman before formally meeting her. She still wasn't clear why Brian felt he had to be perform introductions, but she wasn't complaining. She wouldn't mind seeing him again.

Stifling a yawn, she locked her car and walked through the mostly vacant parking lot to the wide asphalt walkway that swept uphill. Unlike during busy normal school hours, she passed only a few people along the dimly lit path, adults who moved purposefully and without the casual saunter of high school students.

As she approached the main building, Kristi looked up at the two story Spanish-style structure, which was dramatically illuminated by exterior flood lights. Though she hadn't really enjoyed going to high school there, she'd always appreciated the building's beauty—its red-tiled roof, peach colored stucco, and ornately stylized facade.

She walked under one of three arched entryways and into the building, which was eerily quiet compared to a school day. None of the first floor classrooms were in use. Her footsteps echoed as she made her way up the stone stairwell to the second floor and headed to Room 212. She recognized it, remembering it was where she took History in eleventh grade. The class had been after lunch and so boring that she'd often dozed off.

Tonight, the door stood open and there was the murmur of voices. She stopped just outside and stayed out of view. A woman was speaking in a high-pitched, slightly breathy voice that also held a gentle authority as she instructed the class in an English lesson about the verb conjugations of "to be." It had to be Rose. A man with a thick Latin accent attempted to answer one of Rose's questions. The deferential tones of his voice conveyed the respect he had for her.

Curious, Kristi peeked around the door. About twenty people sat at individual desks facing Rose, who stood up front at the blackboard. Kristi's first impression of her client was that she was petite and quite thin, despite the fact she was wearing a long, baggy black tunic over a pair of black leggings. She wore glasses and her straight, dark brown hair hung in a simple ponytail down her back to her waist.

"You're early."

Kristi started at the deep voice behind her. She turned away from the door and found Brian. He still wore the same dark gray business suit as the morning, but he'd ditched the tie. The white shirt collar hung open and revealed a glimpse of smoothly muscled chest. She pulled her eyes upward, aware of how close he was standing.

She whispered, "I wanted to see Rose at work."

He dipped his head closer so his words wouldn't carry, his breath moving gently against her hair. "Did you catch the press conference tonight? It aired live on TV."

Kristi exhaled, long and slow, nodding. She'd watched the news conference with Carla on the small black and white TV in the kitchenette above the Magic Shop. The only new detail it revealed was that the coroner's report would be out tomorrow.

Brian continued. "If the coroner's report rules Miss Cole's death a homicide, the police will likely take Rose into custody tomorrow. This may be your only chance to talk to her freely." He stepped back from her at the sound of people getting up from their desks.

Students came out of the classroom, filing quietly by where they stood. All were of Latino origin but varied in age, from their twenties to a few with bent bodies and time-worn faces. Some glanced curiously at Kristi, and several exchanged open smiles with Brian. One woman paused and spoke with him in rapid-fire Spanish. Kristi's Spanish was OK, but she was by no means fluent. She gathered that the woman was thanking Brian for helping with something about her immigration status. He replied and made a dismissive gesture with his hands, something about paying him later. Uncle Pete was right. Brian was one of the good ones.

When the last student left, Kristi followed Brian into the classroom. Rose was wiping down the chalkboard, her all-black clothing accentuating her slim profile.

Brian announced their presence. "Hi Rose."

Rose turned around abruptly, a pendant dangling from a long silver chain around her neck glittered dully in the fluorescent lighting. The calm authority she'd displayed while teaching evaporated. Behind thick glasses, her dark eyes darted nervously from Brian to Kristi, and then back to Brian.

"This is Kristi McCormick, the private investigator I was telling you about." Brian added a reassuring tone to his voice. "Don't worry, as I told you, she's here to help."

Kristi remembered what he'd told her about Rose's fragile state of mind, so she gave Rose a friendly smile. "It's nice to meet you."

"You, too," Rose said, but she didn't quite look at Kristi. Her hand moved to clutch at the pendant spinning on its long silver chain.

"I'll give you two some time to talk." Brian looked at Rose. "You OK if I wait out in the hall?"

Rose nodded. As Brian strode out of the room, she offered Kristi a timid, perhaps worried smile, and then took a seat at one of the desks, her body stiff, her hands twisting together in her lap.

Kristi slid into the desk next to Rose and took her notepad and pencil from her purse. When she looked back at her client, the pendant caught her eye again as it spun slowly in motion. It was a beautiful, ornate piece, circular in shape and outlined in what appeared to be rhinestones. Or were they diamonds? A disturbing thought occurred to Kristi. How could an ESL teacher afford such an expensive-looking thing? "Nice necklace. Is it an antique?"

Rose's hand shot up and captured the pendant, hiding it in a closed fist. "I didn't steal it!"

Whoa, were did that come from? Kristi studied her client's face, wondering if Rose had stolen it from Catherine, though she couldn't imagine the timid woman being brazen enough to wear it in public. Indignant anger moved across Rose's features, but there was some other emotion there, too. Fear? Guilt? Kristi didn't know Rose well enough to decipher it. Calmly, she said, "I didn't mean to imply that you did. I simply wanted to say it's beautiful. Where did you get it?"

"It was a gift." Rose didn't elaborate. The thick lenses of her glasses acted like shields and obscured her eyes.

Was she telling the truth? Kristi leaned on her desk toward Rose. "I'm here to help you. That's why Brian hired me. Why do you think I'd accuse you of stealing it?"

Whatever Rose read in Kristi's face must have reassured her, because she unclasped her fist and the pendant fell free, spinning and sparkling against her black tunic. "That's what the police think, that I killed Catherine because she caught me stealing."

"But you didn't, right?"

"No!" Rose gave a short, sharp jerk of her head.

"Good. I'm here to help prove that. The easiest way to do it is to find out who really is guilty. What can you tell me about the intruder at Catherine's house the night she died?"

Rose frowned and she looked down at her hands, where she started picking at her flaking fingernail polish. "I'm sorry, but like I told Brian, I didn't get a good look at the man."

Kristi remembered Brian's notes. "You said he was big and dressed in dark clothes?"

"He had light-colored hair."

"Was he blond?"

"Maybe. Or gray, or white? I don't know. All I cared about was Catherine. She was lying there not moving, and I had to find out if she was still alive. As soon as the front door slammed and the man was gone, I ran to her. Poor, poor Catherine!"

Kristi wanted to ask Rose if she'd noticed anything else when she'd gone to check Catherine's pulse, but Rose's face suddenly crumpled. Shakily, Rose placed her glasses on the desk in front of her and buried her face in her hands. Sobs wracked her body. Kristi looked around the classroom and tried to figure out what to do to comfort the woman. There was a box of tissues on a bookshelf beside the teacher's desk. She hurried over and grabbed the box.

"Thanks." Rose clutched a handful of tissues and blew her nose. Her grief seemed sincere.

Kristi was at a loss for how to proceed. The woman was obviously distraught at remembering that night. Kristi tried a different angle. Gently, she said, "You knew Catherine well?"

Rose looked up and gave her a watery smile. Her words tumbled out in a breathy rush. "I only knew her for a year, but she was always so very nice to me, so polite, so considerate. Such a kind soul. Poor Catherine! I can't believe she's gone." Her tears started to flow again.

Time to steer the interview onto less emotional ground. "Why did Catherine need to hire you to house sit? Couldn't the groundskeeper take care of the cats?"

It seemed like a logical question to ask, but the instant the words were out of her mouth, a look of horror grew on Rose's tear-stained face.

"The police wouldn't let me go back to Catherine's house after—," she gulped, "after what happened. The poor kitties! Walnut and Balthazar must be traumatized without Catherine, and Balthazar is diabetic and needs special medicine. What will happen to them now?"

It was hard to believe someone who cared about cats could be a killer of old ladies. "You love cats, huh?"

"Catherine and I both did." Rose had such a look of exhausted anguish that Kristi didn't know what to say. Rose pressed the wad of tissues to her face and started to cry again. "I'm so sorry, but I don't think I can do this."

Kristi stared at her client blankly. How could she help Rose, if she didn't hear Rose's side of the story? She sat back in her chair and sighed. "It's been a long day, hasn't it?" She knew the comment sounded inane, but she was tired, too.

Rose blew her nose and wiped her eyes. "Talking to the police was the hardest part."

Kristi was afraid she might set Rose off crying again, but she risked asking, "Because you had to talk to them about that night?"

"I'm doing all I can not to remember that night. It was horrible. Horrible." Rose's face grew pale. "I'm sorry, it's just that I've already had to talk about it so many times."

"I can't even imagine how horrible it must've been," Kristi said. She really, really wanted Rose to tell her exactly what she saw that night and she wanted to ask about the groundskeeper, but it was obvious Rose wasn't up for it. Kristi glanced at the clock above the chalkboard. Time was ticking on the interview. "Why do you think Catherine came back early from her trip?"

Rose started picking again at the polish on her fingernails. "I don't know."

Kristi thought about the intruder angle again. He must've had a car, considering how expansive the grounds were.

"Let's go back to the beginning. When you first drove up to the house, did you see any other cars? Did you see Catherine's?"

"No, but she always parked in the garage behind the house."

"So you didn't know she was home when you drove up?"

Rose shook her head.

"Where did you park that night?"

"On the other side of the house by the kitchen door. It's where I always park."

"Where was the groundskeeper's car?"

"I don't know. I wasn't paying attention. It'd been a really long day and I was tired. I guess it was in his usual spot, over at the carriage house."

"What about the intruder's car, did you see it?"

Rose shook her head, still picking at her fingernail polish.

Kristi fought the urge to reach over and stop the nervous habit. She still had so many questions, but Rose was a mess and she didn't want to keep Brian waiting any longer. As she wrote down the questions she still had, Rose abruptly looked up, her meticulously plucked eyebrows arching in surprise.

"I just remembered something. When I went to unlock the kitchen door, only the bottom lock was on, not the deadbolt."

"Was that unusual?"

"I always lock both when I leave the house."

Kristi's heart rate ratcheted up. Was this a clue? "Didn't you think that was weird?"

"I guess." Rose looked off again into space, remembering. "I'm sorry, but I was just so tired and hungry that night. Thursdays are my longest teaching days. I hadn't had anything to eat since an energy bar for breakfast. I guess Tomas could've left it that way, or Catherine."

Kristi couldn't imagine going that long without food. She gnawed her lip, thinking. "So Tomas had a key to the house, too?"

"I don't know. I never did."

"Wait, but then how could you unlock the door?"

Rose picked up her glasses and slid them back into place. "Catherine hid a key outside the kitchen door. She said that way, none of us had to worry about losing it."

"'Us?' Who did she mean?"

Rose shrugged. "I don't know. Maybe Tomas. Maybe Eduardo."

Kristi jotted down a note. Either of the two groundskeepers could also have entered the house that night without breaking in. "Where did Catherine stash the key?"

"There are two little ceramic cats on the landing by the kitchen door. Catherine always kept the key under the left one."

"Do you know if it's still there?"

Rose shrugged again. "Probably." She looked up at the wall clock and gave a deep sigh. "It's been a really, really long day and I've got an early class tomorrow. Is anything I've said helpful?"

"I don't know, yet." Kristi flipped through her notes. "If you remember anything more about the intruder, please tell me. In the meantime, it sounds like Tomas and Eduardo are possible suspects.

"Not Eduardo. He never would've stolen from Catherine and never killed her."

"How can you be so sure?"

"He was my student. He's a good person."

"Can you think of anyone else who might've wanted to hurt Catherine?"

"No."

Hardly the response of a guilty person looking to shift suspicion onto someone else, Kristi thought, as she watched Rose go to the teacher's table at the front of the class and gather together a collection of binders, books, and sheets of paper. She put them into several large black canvas bags and then slung the bags over her shoulders.

Kristi followed her out of the classroom. "If I have more questions, can I call you?"

"Please do, but can you call before eight in the morning or after ten at night? Sorry, but my teaching schedule makes it so I don't have a lot of free time." Rose locked the door.

Brian stood in the hallway, leaning against one wall, his eyes closed. Had he been listening to their interview, Kristi wondered, or had he fallen asleep on his feet?

His eyes snapped open and connected with hers. She hastily looked away, uncomfortably aware of the sudden too fast kerthump of her heart. It was only then that she noticed that Rose had hurried past the two of them and was walking down the hall.

Brian pushed away from the wall and called after Rose. "You OK?"

"Yes, thanks. Sorry, but I need to get home." Rose gave a little wave over her shoulder before turning the corner and disappearing into the stairwell.

"How much of that did you hear?" Kristi gestured with her thumb toward the classroom door.

"Not much." Brian yawned. "What did you find out?"

Kristi found herself yawning, too. "Did you know that Catherine kept a hide-a-key?"

He looked at her blankly. "A hide-a-key?"

"You know, a key hidden outside the house. Catherine never gave Rose a house key. Turns out she always let herself in with a key hidden outside the kitchen door."

"Interesting."

"That means anyone who knew about the key could've easily gotten inside that night."

"Who else knew about the key?"

"Rose is unsure, but I bet Tomas did, and Rose thinks Eduardo may have known, too. I need to talk to them."

"Focus on Tomas. I don't know much about the guy. I seriously doubt Eduardo's a suspect, not with my dad vouching for him." Brian's hand came up to politely cover his mouth as he yawned again. "I don't know about you, but I'm beat."

As they walked together to the stairs, Kristi thought about the next steps of her investigation. "I'd like to see where Catherine lived and where she died. Maybe my uncle can help me get access."

Brian laughed, the sound reverberating in the stairwell as he trotted down the stairs ahead of her. "Already done."

"What?" She paused in mid-stride and then raced to catch up with him.

"I thought you might want to see the house. I do, too, all thing's considered. I talked to Pete about it this afternoon. He agreed. Reluctantly. He wants us in and out of there first thing tomorrow morning, and we aren't to touch anything. Can you meet me there at 7 am?"

"Definitely." Kristi scribbled Brian's directions to Catherine's house in her notepad. "Any chance I can talk to Tomas while we're over there?" she asked as she followed him out of the building. The night air had finally cooled and smelled slightly salty, moving in gently from the ocean.

"You can try, but from what Pete told me, Tomas hasn't been very cooperative."

"Sounds to me like he's more of a suspect than Rose, considering he just started working for Catherine a couple months ago."

"The police must have some reason for not targeting him, but let me know if you find anything."

"Of course."

The place was deserted as they walked down through the school grounds to the parking lot and the night wrapped around them in a kind of intimacy that made Kristi feel like they were the only two people in the world. Her thoughts and concerns about Rose and the case faded away in the darkness, replaced by an acute awareness of the man beside her.

When they reached her car, she dug out her keys and unlocked the door. Only a single dim streetlight illuminated the section of the parking lot where they stood, and there was no moon. Brian's face was all sharp angles and hollows under the dull orange glow. Kristi wanted to know what he was thinking, but his expression was shrouded in shadow. Silence stretched between them. Somewhere nearby, a lone cricket chirped.

Finally, he spoke. "Let me get that for you." He leaned forward, his long arm brushing hers as he opened the car door.

"Thanks." Her voice came out too breathy, her heart beating too fast as she climbed into the car.

"I'll see you tomorrow morning. Good night." He closed the door after her and gave a wave before striding away.

8. Family Tensions

Wednesday morning, Kristi went downstairs just as the sun came up. Her mom was seated at the kitchen table with the morning paper and a cup of coffee. "You sure were out late last night, and now here you are, dressed, and up at the crack of dawn. What's going on?"

Kristi opened the refrigerator and grabbed an apple. "I've got my first case."

"That's great, sweetie! What's it about?"

"The woman who died over in Montecito last week."

Her mom smoothed a hand across the paper. "One of the Coles. She was worth over fifty million dollars."

"Wow, I hadn't heard it was that much." Kristi took a bite of apple. It was cold, tart, and delicious. Nothing she'd seen in the library had hinted at the size of Catherine's estate. Compared to ESL teacher pay running under twenty thousand, fifty million put Catherine in the outer stratosphere. Motive for murder?

"Today's article is mainly about her dad and how he started Cole Bank. Says here he was friends with Judge Roberts. Isn't that James' grandfather?"

"Yup." Kristi went and stood beside her mom, crunching the apple, as she scanned the article. Nothing new.

Her mom pursed her lips in a small moue of distaste. "Heaven knows Santa Barbara feels small sometimes, I can only imagine how small Montecito must be."

Especially when you're talking about that social strata, Kristi thought, all too aware of the gulf that yawned like a chasm between people who lived in James' world and people like her and her own family.

Mary pushed the newspaper aside and looked up at her with that concerned motherly look she dreaded. "How are you and James, anyway? It's way past time you invite him over for dinner so we can really meet him."

"Mom." Kristi started to object, but then stopped. Her mom had a point. Except for pulling up to the curb and summoning her with a honk of his Beamer, James hadn't once set foot on their property. Part of it was that they'd just started seeing each other, but truth was, she'd been reluctant to invite him inside.

She glanced around at the avocado green kitchen cabinets and laminate countertops that her mom wanted to remodel someday when they had enough money. The 70s style was twenty years out of date, and Kristi cringed at the thought of James sitting at their dining room table while her mom labored in the kitchen. His mother never got her hands wet or dirty preparing food and washing dishes, because the Roberts family had a personal chef. Kristi only knew this from a passing comment James made, since she hadn't been invited to their estate in Montecito. So far, their dates had consisted mainly of going out to eat at his country club.

Tossing the finished apple core in the garbage, she said, "How about when things settle down. I'm pretty busy right now with my first case."

"What's this about a case?" Her dad came into the kitchen. He was already dressed for work, the dark business suit freshly pressed, his tie cinched tight, his thinning blond hair combed carefully straight. He headed for the coffee pot. "Who hired you?"

Kristi didn't want to get into it with him. He wouldn't admire Brian for doing work that didn't pay. She edged toward the kitchen door. "An attorney representing my client."

"That's vague. Who're you talking about? Give me some names." He poured himself a cup of coffee. "And what about this job, it doesn't involve anything illegal, does it?"

Her mom gave him a pointed look. "Hon, what's with the third degree?"

Her dad set the mug down on the counter with a clunk of emphasis. "You know how I feel about this whole detective stuff, Mary. I don't want Kristi getting mixed up with the wrong sort of people." He turned back to Kristi, his serious face even more serious than usual, his mouth compressed into a thin line. "You know how small this town is, Kristi. You've got to be careful—"

"—with whom I do business. You're a broken record, Dad."

And all you care about is your stupid company. He'd never understood her dream of becoming a PI. If he had his way, she'd be back safely ensconced and respectable at his company, dying of boredom and suffocating in the regulation nylons and skirts she'd had to wear when she worked for him.

There wasn't time to rehash their ongoing disagreement. Instead, she gave him a chipper smile she didn't feel. "It's nothing illegal and I'll be careful, Dad, but I've gotta go to work." As she walked past him, she noticed a piece of tissue stuck to the side of his neck where he'd nicked himself shaving. She couldn't resist a parting shot. "That tissue kind of ruins the proper look you're going for. Have a nice day!"

9. The Scene of the Crime

Kristi drove up Alamar Avenue and took Foothill Road to Montecito, still mad at her dad's comment about "the wrong sort of people." Brian helped people like Rose with inexpensive legal counsel, and Rose helped people learn English. A niggling voice reminded her that unlike James, who had gone to the same Ivy League college as his dad and grandfather and barely scraped by, Brian had graduated with top honors from Stanford.

She didn't like the turn of her thoughts, so she focused on the scenic view. The properties in Montecito were so huge that she could cruise along without having to deal with traffic lights and stop signs. The early morning sun flickered in and out of the eucalyptus trees, and the air blowing in through the open car window was still pleasant. Driving later wasn't going to be nearly so nice, not with her beater car's air conditioning on the fritz and Southern California locked in the fall heat wave.

Following Brian's directions, she took the next left onto a smaller road heading uphill, which led to an even smaller one. Everywhere she looked was green and lush, none of the homes visible from the road, and there were few security gates. It was as if the area lived in a world apart, remote and unafraid of the dangers other communities faced.

When she arrived at the front gate to Catherine's property, she looked around and confirmed Brian's observation that the place had no surveillance equipment. She took the long winding drive uphill, past lush vegetation, avocado trees, orange trees, and profusely blooming gardens flanking ponds with sparkling fountains. The heady fragrance of roses and citrus wafted in through the car windows and she inhaled deeply, savoring the perfumed air.

Everything was so incredibly beautiful, like something out of one of those glossy real estate mailers her folks were always getting, places they could never afford in a million years. Did James' place look like this? Wow. Money could buy a whole lot of beauty. No wonder Catherine had a full-time groundskeeper. It must cost a boatload to irrigate so much land, but to do it now, in the middle of a drought? The thought dampened her pleasure in looking at the gardens. Her parents were always arguing about getting rid of their small lawn, though personally, she'd do it in an instant, if it meant getting longer showers with a decent showerhead. She doubted Catherine and James and the other rich Montecito residents ever skimped on their showers.

The drive widened out in front of the house. Kristi parked beside a black pickup truck. It was empty. Brian's? More likely the groundskeeper's. It certainly looked well-used, its body dinged and dusty. Her old Toyota and the pickup looked totally out of place in front of the huge mansion, which was built in the classic Santa Barbara Spanish revival style, with a multi-level terracotta roof, wrought iron balconies, and a graceful archway framing the front door.

The corner of a small outbuilding was visible to the right beyond the main residence. Kristi figured it was the groundskeeper's quarters, based on what she'd read in Brian's notes. The garage where Rose said Catherine usually parked was out of sight behind the mansion.

As Kristi looked around, she tried to imagine what the place must have been like the night Catherine died. It sure would've been dark. She saw no flood lights or motion sensor lighting anywhere, and no lights on the drive up to the house. The only lighting were a few in-ground lights and an intricate wrought-iron lamp hanging under the arched entryway. Had Catherine liked star gazing? Maybe, but no question, the darkness would make it easy for an intruder to sneak around undetected.

Gravel crunched underfoot and Brian came around the right side of the house. Like yesterday, he was dressed in a dark business suit. His thick black hair was still damp from a morning shower and curled slightly above the sharp white line of his collar.

Kristi ignored how her heart skipped a beat. "Hi."

"Good morning." He held up a jangling cluster of keys. "Your uncle told me to check in with Tomas. Turns out he has a set."

"I wonder why Catherine didn't give Rose a house key. Did you see if the hide-a-key's still there?

"Not yet. Your uncle wants us out of here by eight o'clock, and I've got a breakfast meeting, which only gives us a half hour to check out the place."

Not nearly enough time, but it'd have to do. "I'd like to start with where the body was found."

"Sounds good." Brian led the way up the broad ,flagstone steps and unlocked the front door.

They entered an impressive, two-story foyer. A wrought-iron chandelier hung from the high, domed ceiling, and the floor was covered in a geometric pattern of large, diamond-shaped terracotta tiles. Dominating the space opposite where they stood was the grand staircase, its banister a study in ornate ironwork and its risers adorned with brightly colored, hand-painted tiles.

Kristi walked over to several yellow markers positioned at the bottom of the stairs. "This must be where Rose found Catherine's body."

Brian joined her. Crouching together, they examined the area inside the markers. There was no evidence that a woman had died there.

"I guess broken necks don't leave any blood, assuming that's how she died." Kristi rocked back on her heels and looked up the curving flight of stairs to the second floor landing. It was one heck of a long, steep staircase. Now that she'd seen it, she could easily imagine

Catherine falling down the stairs. Accident or murder? Had she stumbled over one of her cats? Come to think of it, where were the cats?

Kristi stood up and looked at Brian. "What happened to Catherine's cats?"

Brian braced his hands on his knees and pushed himself up to standing. "I have no idea. Someone must be caring for them."

"Were they with Tomas when you were over there?"

"Not that I saw."

Kristi made a note to follow up on the cat question as they climbed the stairs. A veritable gallery of paintings crowded the curving stucco wall up to the second floor, all distinctive and beautiful landscapes of the Santa Barbara countryside: oak-studded hills, the Santa Ynez Mountains, and the ocean. Kristi paused to appreciate their beauty. If a house tells a story about the person who lives there, Kristi thought, then it appeared that Catherine loved Santa Barbara nature as much as she did. They reached the second floor and walked along the corridor to the first door on the right.

"This should be Catherine's," Brian said

Inside was a large bedroom suite with dark, heavy furnishings in keeping with the mansion's Spanish revivalist style. A crucifix in wood and iron hung above the large, canopied bed, and several Medieval gold gilt icons of Mary and the baby Jesus hung on the walls. Kristi hadn't read anything about Catherine's religious beliefs. "Was Catherine Catholic?"

Brian gazed at the icons. "She was a parishioner at the Santa Barbara Mission years ago."

There was something in how he said it that made her ask, "How did you know that? Do you go there?"

"We stopped attending when my mom died." A flash of grief moved across his face.

"Wow, I'm sorry." Kristi didn't know what else to say.

Brian made a sweeping gesture with his hand. "Thanks. It was a long time ago."

How long ago? How old had he been? Kristi couldn't imagine her life without her own mom. She wanted to ask him more questions, but now wasn't the time. She spotted the safe across the room. It was in a wall above a row of built-in bookshelves and had been hidden behind a painting, which at the moment had been swung aside to reveal the safe.

Stepping around a pair of leather club chairs, peered inside the small, empty cavity. "How did the police know there was jewelry inside?"

Brian came up beside her and also took a look. "They must have obtained a copy of her insurance policy. She probably had a jewelry rider, which would've listed valuables. I'll make some inquiries. My firm represents her estate."

Small world, Kristi thought, her mom's words echoing in her head, but she supposed it made sense. Byers and Martin specialized in servicing the wealthy. Kristi looked at the empty safe. "Wouldn't she keep her really expensive jewelry and important stuff in a safe deposit box at her family's bank or something."

"Maybe. Her will may spell out those details."

"How long will it take before it's read?"

"Not long, especially if her death is ruled a homicide."

Kristi checked out the painting that hung over the safe's door. It was another gorgeous landscape and painted in the same distinctive style as the ones in the foyer.

Bending closer, she observed the artist's signature: "L. Bianchi." Had the artist known Catherine? The dead woman had liked Bianchi's work enough to have bought a great many of them. Kristi made a note of the name. Standing up again, she glanced at her watch. Twenty minutes left.

While Brian was looking at Catherine's bookshelves, Kristi went over to another door in the room and looked inside. Brilliant early morning sunshine streamed into a bathroom done in white marble and gold fixtures, with a claw foot tub under a large window. Envy twisted inside her. What she wouldn't give for her own bathroom! Maybe not something as fancy as this, but one she didn't have to share with the rest of her family.

Turning around, she then she went to the tall French doors that opened onto a second-floor balcony. No other houses were in sight, just the green foliage of bushes and trees that eventually faded away to the blue line of the ocean. On the distant horizon, Anacapa and Santa Cruz Islands seemed to float above the wide shimmering swath of the Santa Barbara Channel. A million dollar view, Kristi thought, again struck by Catherine's wealth. Enough to kill for?

Brian's voice cut into her thoughts. "This is a great book collection." He was still examining the books on the shelves beneath painting and rattled off a litany of authors she didn't recognize.

Kristi went over to the crowded bookshelves. "You like to read?"

"When I have the time. Do you?" He glanced at her.

Kristi doubted he meant reading popular mysteries like Sue Grafton's. Her eyes caught on a long row of paperbacks on a top shelf, all by the same author. "You read any Tabitha Tyson?"

"Never heard of her. You?"

Kristi shook her head. She wanted to pull down one of the books and read its back cover, but she remembered Pete's instructions not to touch anything. Instead, she pulled her notepad and pencil from the back pocket of her jeans.

Brian watched her jot down the author's name. "You think that's important?"

"I have no idea, but considering how little we know about Catherine, any detail might be." Kristi tucked away her notepad and pencil and went over to the large jewelry box sitting on the dresser.

It was black lacquer, inlaid with some kind of white bone, perhaps ivory, in delicate patterns of birds and vines. It was designed like a mini wardrobe with two doors. Both were open, and several of the small, interior drawers had been pulled partially out. They were empty. There were also several empty hooks inside the necklace compartment, which otherwise was carefully hung with an assortment of items, from simple pendants, to strands of beads, and a few heavy Navajo silver and turquoise antiques.

"Suspicious, huh?" Brian said.

"Yeah, I suppose." Kristi looked from the jewelry box to the safe. "I can maybe imagine Rose grabbing some of this jewelry, but safe-cracking?"

Brian shrugged. "Maybe she obtained the combination somehow."

Kristi took a closer look at the necklaces. She didn't know much about jewelry, but very little inside the box sparkled. "Something doesn't make sense."

"What are you thinking?"

"If the really valuable stuff was in the safe, why would the robber bother with this stuff? It doesn't look all that expensive, especially if there was a risk of getting caught."

"I don't know." Brian glanced at his watch. "We're almost out of time."

"Yup." Kristi took a quick look at the bed. A pristine white duvet covered the large, king-sized mattress, perfectly smooth and uncreased. No sign that Catherine had sat on the bed, let alone lain in it, the night she died. On the bedside table sat two framed photographs, both black and white formal family portraits taken years ago, judging by the haircuts and outfits. Kristi bent down and took a closer look. She recognized Richard Cole from the photos she'd seen in the paper, though here he was much younger. The woman at his side had to be the wife who'd divorced him and died shortly afterward. In front of the couple stood a young Catherine and her younger brother, posing with forced smiles. The second photograph showed the two children as young adults, standing on either side of their father, their faces somber and serious, nothing like Kristi's own family's silly photos, where everyone smiled and someone inevitably made a funny face.

Kristi started to look away, when something caught her eye. There was something odd about the sheen on the dark surface of the bedside table. Feeling like Sherlock Holmes, she pulled a small magnifying glass from the side pocket of her purse and peered at the area next to the photographs. Imprinted in the minute layer of dust were thin, peculiarly geometric lines.

Brian came over. "What have you found?"

"Take a look." She handed him the magnifying glass and pointed. "Do you see those lines in the dust?"

He bent over. "Interesting. What do you think made them?"

"Look at how those two frames are positioned on the table. My guess is that there was another frame standing there, too, but it was removed recently. Could the police have done that?"

He returned the magnifying glass to her. "Maybe."

Kristi remembered what her uncle had said about the room being wiped clean of fingerprints. "Maybe someone else took it, like the intruder Rose saw." She put the magnifying glass back in her purse. "But why, and what was it a photo of?"

Brian's face turned skeptical. "Or Catherine could've removed it. That's assuming, of course, there was another picture there. It's also possible that something else made those lines, like maybe her cats."

Kristi shook her head. "There'd be paw prints." If there had been a photograph there, where was it now? Maybe Brian was right, but she made a note to see if Catherine had a cleaning lady who might be able to solve the mystery of those lines.

Brian held up his forearm and checked the time again. "I'm sorry, but it's time."

On the way out, Kristi again admired the paintings on walls of the foyer and wondered about "L. Bianchi".

At the bottom of the stairs, Brian said, "I've gotta run the keys back to Tomas before I head out."

"Can I do it?" Maybe she could ask the groundskeeper a few questions while she was at it.

"Sure." As if reading her mind, Brian's eyes caught hers as he handed her the keys. "Just be careful how you talk to him. From what your uncle said, he's none too happy being questioned."

"Understood."

They were halfway across the foyer when the front door opened. A big man came in, carrying a camera and wearing a navy polo shirt and khakis. The moment he saw Kristi, his face broke into a wide grin, creasing his flushed, fleshy cheeks. "Kristi! Your uncle said you might still be here." The guy was one of the rookies who worked with Pete. He'd also once tried asking her out, but he was most definitely not her type.

"Hey, Dan." She smiled politely and introduced Brian. "This is Brian Castillo. He's representing my client, Rose Schmidt."

The two men acknowledged each other, then Brian turned to Kristi. "I'll catch up with you later."

She watched him walk out into the bright sunshine and down the flagstone steps to the pickup. Through the open front door came the sound of the pickup starting up.

"Aren't you, like, seeing that new assistant DA?" Dan said.

Kristi turned back to the big man with a small surge of irritation. She'd wanted to snoop around the house but not with him dogging her heels, and it was obvious from his expression that he still liked her. She softened what she was going to say. "I'm sorry, Dan, but my personal life isn't your business. See you." She started past him for the door.

"Is it true you're a PI now?"

His words made her pause on the threshold. Eager as she was to get out of there, she couldn't afford to pass up possible business. "That's right." She dug in her bag for a business card. "In case you hear of anyone needing a PI."

"'Eye Spy Private Eye.' I like it." Dan perused the card, then pulled out his billfold and tucked it carefully inside. When he looked at her again, his expression sharpened, becoming more cop-like. "You and your friend toured the crime scene. Didn't tamper with any evidence, did you?"

"Of course not." Kristi tried not to sound defensive, but the question was insulting. She was a professional! "Why are you here?"

He held up the camera. "More photos."

She took that as her cue to escape. "I'll let you get to it, then."

10. Thomas Silva

The sun was blazing in the crystal clear October morning sky when Kristi walked down the front steps of the mansion. It was slightly cooler in the shade of the large building as she took the gravel drive around its side to the kitchen door. Two blue and white ceramic cats stood like sentries on each side of it, just as Rose had described. Kristi took a tissue out of her purse. Glancing around to check that the coast was clear, she used the tissue to lift the cat on the left, making sure to leave no fingerprints. Beneath it, she saw the house key. Good to know, if she ever had to get into the house. She quickly put the cat back the way she found it and tucked the tissue back in her purse.

She took the gravel drive back to the outbuilding where the groundskeeper stayed. The first floor formed an open carport, and parked inside was a yellow sport scar with a vanity plate reading "TOMASUP." Strange kind of car for the groundskeeper of such a large estate. There were no other utility vehicles around. She didn't know much about high end cars, but no question Tomas' qualified. How could he afford to drive, much less maintain, such a thing?

A curtain flickered on the second floor. Someone had been watching her. She hurried up the exterior staircase to the second floor apartment. There was a black iron ring knocker on the door. She lifted and dropped it, the metal thudding heavily against oak, but there was no response. She stood for a minute and listened. Besides the distant cawing of crows and a closer mocking bird singing, she heard nothing from inside the apartment.

Leaning over the banister, she tried to peek inside the window. A curtain obscured most of her view, but through a crack, she glimpsed a poster on the wall above a white sofa. It depicted Rio de Janeiro, with the Christ the Redeemer statue prominently displayed, its arms outstretched protectively toward the city. Abruptly, the door swung open and Kristi lurched back.

A beefy guy glared at her. "Who are you?" He spoke with a thick accent, which she thought might be Portuguese, guessing from the poster she'd seen. He had very short black hair and wore a bright red tank top that showed off the bulging contours of his big biceps and immaculately hairless, heavily muscled chest. Obviously a body builder, the guy reminded her of Arnold Schwarzenegger.

Kristi tried to keep a straight face, despite having been caught peeping. "I'm Kristi McCormick. Brian Castillo sent me over to give you back the keys. Thanks for letting us borrow them."

Tomas held out a big hand with close-clipped, manicured nails. "Give to me."

She fumbled around in her purse, pretending to look for the keys. "Could I maybe ask you a few questions about Miss Cole?"

"Sem chance!"

"Excuse me?" She looked up at him, not understanding.

"In English, I think you say, 'No way!' I talk to police already." Tomas spoke impatiently and gestured expressively in the air, as if to push both her and the experience away from him.

"I understand, but I'm a private eye—" At the man's blank expression, Kristi tapped her chest. "I'm a detective. My job is to help find out what really happened last Thursday night."

"I no talk to you." Tomas' massively muscular frame crowded her backward onto the landing, a forbidding expression on his face. He held out his hand again. "Keys."

What was his problem? She took out the keys and tried one last time. "Did you see an intruder that night? Do you know where Catherine's cats are?"

His only response was to snatch the keys and slam the door in her face.

"Can't you at least tell me if Catherine had a cleaning lady? I need her number!" Kristi shouted through the closed door, but there was no response. Frustrated and annoyed, she stared at the door. Why wouldn't the guy answer a few simple questions? He obviously didn't speak English well. Did he simply dislike being questioned, or did he have something to hide? Just in case he had a change of heart, she slid one of her business cards under the door.

As Kristi drove back down through Catherine's property, she wondered about Tomas and about those marks she'd seen on the bedside table. When she reached the road, she was about to take a left back toward town but then noticed an older well-dressed woman walking a small white terrier on the path beside the road. She had an idea.

Pulling over, she hailed the woman. "Sorry to bother you, ma'am, but can I ask you something?"

The woman came over, a friendly smile on her face. "Yes, dear. How may I help you?"

"My name's Kristi McCormick. I'm a private investigator." She handed the woman her business card. "Were you a neighbor of Catherine Cole's?"

The woman nodded, her expression now concerned. "What's this about, Miss McCormick?"

"I'm looking into the events surrounding her death. Any chance you walked your dog past here that night?"

The woman picked up the dog and stroked its ears. "Of course. I walk Bessie twice a day, once in the morning and once at night."

"Do you remember exactly when you walked her that night?"

The woman thought, still stroking the dog's ears. "Let me see. I play bridge Thursday nights, so I didn't get back home until about 9. I guess I must have walked by here about 9:30 or so."

Kristi nodded. That was the right time frame if an intruder had left the property. Mentally crossing her fingers, Kristi asked, "Did you see anything unusual, like maybe a car you didn't recognize leaving Miss Cole's place?"

"I'm sorry, but I have no idea what would constitute an 'unusual car' with respect to Miss Cole's visitors. I never really knew her, not like her father. She never entertained and kept very much to herself."

Kristi's hope started to fade. "Did you see any cars at all?"

The woman put the dog down. When she straightened, she looked apologetic. "Deary, I'm getting on in years and it's hard enough to remember what I did yesterday, let alone something I saw four days ago."

"Thanks, anyway." Kristi was about to shift her car into gear when the woman called after her.

"I just remembered something, Miss McCormick. There was a car."

Kristi hit the brakes. "What make and model was it? Did you see the driver?"

The woman shook her head. "The car was traveling too quickly to see the driver, but it was some kind of sports car."

"What color?"

"Oh dear, I'm not sure. It was really dark. It could have been white or gray."

"Yellow?" Kristi asked, thinking again of the surly groundskeeper, but that didn't make sense. He was up at the house finding Rose and Catherine's body.

"I don't think so. Another thing, Miss McCormick, I only saw the car on the road. I didn't see if it actually came from Miss Cole's property."

Kristi thanked the woman and asked her to call if she remembered anything else. Heading back to Santa Barbara, Kristi puzzled over the car the woman had seen. Had it simply been a coincidence, or had it been the intruder making his getaway?

11. Lunch with Brian

Back at her office, there were several messages on her answering machine.

The first was from James. "Hey babe, where are you? Give me a call."

The cassette advanced and a heavily accented man's voice came on. She listened in surprise as Tomas spoke in halting English. He said Catherine's cats were at the vet and then tersely recited the phone number of Catherine's cleaning lady before hanging up.

James can wait, Kristi thought, picking up the phone and dialing the cleaning lady's number.

A woman answered. "Hola?"

"Maria Jose?"

"Si, quien es?"

"My name is Kristi McCormick. Do you speak English?"

"No hablo ingles. Por que mi llamando?" The woman sounded confused and possibly a little scared.

Uh oh. Kristi had no idea how to explain in Spanish why she was calling.

"Gracias." She hung up and kicked herself for not taking Spanish in high school. French had sounded so much more exotic and romantic, but now it meant she needed a translator to talk to the cleaning lady. Brian could do it.

She glanced at her watch. 9 o'clock. If his job was anything like James', he was probably already up to his eyeballs in meetings. Her hunch was right. Neither Brian nor James answered. Listening to their messages back to back, Kristi noticed how differently they spoke—James with smooth, casual self-assurance and Brian with a more formal intonation to his deep voice. She found both appealing.

Picking up the phone again, she called Rose, wanting to ask her if she knew anything about the photos on Catherine's bedside table, but again, she got an answering machine. Leaning back in her chair, her mind went back to the case and who else might be a potential suspect. Besides Rose, Tomas, and Eduardo, she only knew a few other people in Catherine's life: the vet and her niece, Anita Walker. Talk about a reclusive life! Kristi couldn't imagine living with so few friends, not to mention relatives. Kinsey Millhone and the detectives in her other favorite mysteries never seemed to have trouble lining up a list of potential suspects. This case was another story.

By 11 o'clock, the office had grown unbearably stuffy. Kristi went over and slid up the window. Heat flooded in, but so, too did the sound of traffic and the cheery chirping of sparrows nearby. A metallic rattling sound came up from the walkway that ran between her office building and the one next door. A homeless man was slowly shuffling along, pushing a shopping cart. He made her think again about money and all it signified: Catherine's extreme wealth and Rose's comparative poverty. Who would profit from Catherine's death? Who were Catherine's heirs?

Her stomach grumbled, the apple she'd eaten early in the morning a distant memory. Maybe she should use some of the money Brian had paid her to buy a decent lunch.

She was closing the window when the phone rang. She went over and picked up. "Eye Spy Private Eye."

As if conjured, Brian came on the line. "I got your message about needing my help as a translator. Is now a good time to come over?"

Her heart did a little flip. She squelched it. "That sounds great. Thanks."

A short while later, Brian entered her office, a grim expression on his face.

"What's wrong?"

Brian took a seat across the desk from her. "I just learned the police plan to call Rose and Tomas back in for further questioning this afternoon."

"Is there some new bit of evidence?"

The lines of Brian's face pulled down in a frown. "Looks like they have no plans to broaden their search for suspects."

"Well, I'd still like to pursue what Rose said about an intruder. On another topic, Tomas gave me the cleaning lady's number. Can you help me ask the cleaning lady if there was a third picture on Catherine's bedside table?"

Brian agreed, and when Maria Jose came on the line, Kristi only understood a few of the rapid-fire words he spoke.

As he conversed with the cleaning lady, Kristi watched him run a hand through his thick black hair. Is he seeing anyone? The question came out of left field. She squashed it down. She was with James.

"Adios." Brian handed Kristi the phone.

She took it, too aware when his hand brushed hers. "What did she say?"

"She only cleans Catherine's house once a month. The last time was three weeks ago."

That explained the dust. "What did she say about the pictures?"

"Only that there were a couple of them."

"Was there a third?"

"She doesn't remember."

Kristi looked at him in surprise. "How can she not remember?"

Brian shrugged. "Look at it from her point of view. She cleans a lot of houses, dusts a lot of photographs, pictures and knickknacks, and as you saw, Catherine's place is enormous. Maria Jose looks for dust when she cleans, not at what she's moving around. Besides, why would she pay any special attention to a couple of pictures among all the others?"

Kristi sighed, disappointed. "I guess you're right." Her stomach growled again so loudly that Brian heard it.

"Hungry?"

"Starved!"

"I am, too." He gave her a brief smile and looked at his watch. "I've got a little less than an hour. May I buy you lunch? We can discuss the case and call it a business meeting."

A short while later, they sat at a small sandwich shop a block off State Street. The place was humble and nothing like the restaurant James had taken her to the day before. An old air-conditioning unit rattled loudly, working overtime to cool the small space against the hot day. It was early, before the lunchtime rush, and the other two tables were empty. Brian sat across from her at the small Formica table, his knees almost touching hers.

Kristi picked up her paper cup, a welcome prop to hide her expression as she took a sip of water, telling herself he was just a client. It wasn't like this was a lunch date or something. And yet, when his gaze lingered on her, she felt too hot again. She was glad they were in a place James would never go. Not that she had anything to explain, but still.

"Thanks again for translating, and for lunch," she said, picking up her veggie sandwich.

"Too bad Maria Jose couldn't help us."

"Well, we learned one thing."

Brian looked up from his sandwich. "What's that?"

"It means someone else wiped down the room for fingerprints. I'm gonna ask Rose if she knows anything about a third photograph."

"You think it matters?"

"Something was taken off that table. Why?"

Brian nodded. "I can ask her this afternoon when I see her."

"Thanks."

The serious lines on his face relaxed and made him seem younger and more approachable. She smiled at him. "This hot weather is perfect for swimming."

"You like to swim?"

She nodded, her mouth full of sandwich.

He smiled, too. "I used to swim on the Stanford team, before Law School."

"Cool." She was impressed. "I never swam competitively. I mainly just swim in the ocean."

Brian looked thoughtful as he ate. "Ocean swimming is very different, the way the currents work. Do you have a favorite spot?"

"I like to swim the buoys off East Cabrillo," she said, remembering last night's swim with Carla.

When she looked up, he was studying her with an intensity that made her thoughts scatter. For a second, their eyes tangled, but then the bell over the door tinkled as another customer entered. The counter person came back into the room from the kitchen. The moment was gone.

Brian's face turned serious again. "Did Tomas tell you anything else, besides giving you Maria Jose's number?"

"No, he pretty much slammed the door in my face. I left my card." Kristi considered what she knew about the burly groundskeeper. "Do you know how Catherine came to hire him? I mean if she was so reclusive and all, how did she go about interviewing potential candidates to replace Eduardo?"

"I asked Rose about that. She thinks Catherine found Tomas through her vet."

"Interesting. I need to talk to the vet." Kristi thought again of her visit to Catherine's estate. "Tomas drives a pretty fancy sports car. Did you see that yellow one in the carport?"

Brian nodded. "A Ferrari."

"Shouldn't he drive a truck or something for his job?"

"Perhaps Catherine kept another vehicle for maintaining the estate."

Kristi thought about her own beater car and how much money it took to keep it running. It was way overdue for a checkup. "It must take a lot of money to keep up a Ferrari, right? And Tomas must have a gym membership somewhere with muscles like his. Where's all the money coming from? He can't make that much as a groundskeeper."

"Good question." Brian's eyes sparked with admiration.

Kristi felt a warm glow inside to know that he respected her thinking.

He glanced at his watch and then balled up his sandwich wrapper. "I'm off to the the police department. I want to be there when they question Rose and Eduardo."

"Can I come?"

He shook his head. "Sorry, not this time."

"Well, thanks for lunch."

"My pleasure." He rose and came around the table to pull the chair back for her, the gentlemanly gesture charming her.

12. The Coroner's Report

After a couple of hours fretting in her office about the police questioning Rose and the fact that Brian wasn't returning her calls, Kristi finally reached her uncle on the phone. Pete nixed the idea of her coming to the police station, but saying he needed a walk and some fresh air. They agreed to meet at the Courthouse gardens.

When he was late showing up, Kristi found a place to sit in the cool shadows of the Courthouse bell tower on the stone wall bordering the sunken garden. A young couple, the woman in a white sundress, had just gotten married, and they were mugging and hugging for a photographer on the broad sandstone steps below the Courthouse's iconic archway. Meanwhile, a large group of tourists came out of the Courthouse and meandered about snapping photos. The place really was beautiful.

Beauty and money, who had it, and who didn't. Until this morning, Kristi had never imagined a property as beautiful as Catherine's. At least this was a public garden and she could enjoy the view for free.

"Krissy!" Pete came across the grass from the direction of the Police Department. He was tall and slim, his shoulders broad from years of surfing off the Rincon and Hollister Ranch. He wore khaki slacks and a sky blue Polo shirt that Kristi knew mirrored his blue eyes, though they were shielded at the moment by a pair of Ray Bans.

Lines of tension creased his deeply tanned face. "The coroner's report in the Cole case was just released. Homicide.

Oh boy, Kristi thought, the stakes for her client had just shot way up.

They crossed Anapamu and walked up Santa Barbara Street toward Alameda Park.

Kristi looked over at Pete. "Does the report explain its conclusion?"

He nodded. "The velocity of the vic's fall, judged by the location of the body from the base of the stairs, was too great to have been due to simple gravity. The exam also found bruising on her wrists consistent with having been grabbed. We're considering there might've been a struggle before she was pushed down the stairs. Time of death put roughly at 9:30 pm, which matches Schmidt's claim for when she found the body."

Kristi remembered the staircase at the mansion. It was a horrible image, an old woman struggling at the top of that long staircase and then being shoved down them. Who would do such a thing? Rose? From what Kristi had seen of her client, it seemed unlikely. "Did you arrest Rose for Catherine's murder?"

"We had to let her go for now. Castillo's one hell of an attorney." Pete shook his head. "He's also thrown up a few roadblocks to delay our search warrant."

"Well, I'm glad you sent him to me," Kristi said, glad Brian had bought their client some more time.

They crossed East Sola and entered Alameda Park. It was a relief to get out of the sun and walk under the shade of the tall, stately trees in the park.

Kristi looked over again at her handsome uncle and had to ask the question that was still preying on her mind. "So, were you and he ever, you know, together?"

Pete laughed, the lines of his tanned face easing. "In my dreams, but he's straight. Why do you care?"

"Just curious." She grinned, relieved and suddenly happy.

They passed the recently completed Kids World playground. Little kids swarmed, screaming and laughing, all over the whimsical wooden castle and other climbing structures, attended by moms and nannies with babies in strollers. Kristi couldn't imagine being a mother, not for years and years, and certainly not before she succeeded at being a PI.

She turned to Pete. "Thanks for letting us check out Catherine's house this morning. There were two framed photographs on her bedside table, but it looked like a third had been removed. Did the police take it?"

"Photo?" Pete glanced at her. "There aren't any in evidence. What're you thinking?"

"Maybe nothing." Her theory that someone had removed a third photograph was starting to feel too far-fetched. "I talked to one of Catherine's neighbors. She saw a car speeding outside Catherine's place the night she died. What if it was the real killer, making a quick getaway? Rose could be innocent."

"Schmidt now claims she saw an intruder in the house that night but claims she can't ID him." Pete shook his head. "We're looking into it, but I'm sorry, Krissy. As the evidence stands, everything points to her."

"Come on, Pete. Rose had the opportunity and the means, but motive? Good jobs are hard enough to come by in this town, and with Catherine dead, she's lost a job and a reference for future house sitting gigs."

Pete's laugh sounded more like a cough. "You have no idea how much Miss Cole's jewelry's worth, do you?"

"How much?" Kristi didn't mind sounding naive with her uncle. She knew he was on her side.

"I don't have exact figures at this point, but let's just say that a single diamond ring could go anywhere from five to fifty grand."

"Fifty thousand dollars? Seriously?" One ring worth more than two years' work? "OK, maybe that's enough motive for murder, but if Rose is guilty, why now? Why wait a year into working for Catherine to rob her? And we still don't know why Catherine came back unexpectedly that night."

They turned onto East Figueroa Street and stopped when they reached the police department.

"I've got the same questions, Krissy. Something stinks about the whole thing. Definitely keep digging, but you should know I'm getting pressure from higher up to make a quick arrest and close out this case ASAP. Without another clear candidate, your client will remain our prime suspect."

Kristi nodded, feeling her tension rise. A block away, the Courthouse bell tolled out the 4 o'clock hour.

Pete gave her a smile. "I've gotta get back. Thanks for the walk. It was just what I needed."

She gave him a quick hug. "Me, too."

He was about to head up the steps into the police department, when he paused. "I forgot to tell you one thing the coroner found. On the palm of Catherine's right hand were trace amounts of ink and blue paper fibers reminiscent of an airmail letter. The fibers have been sent off to a lab in LA for further analysis."

Kristi frowned. She could understand ink running onto someone's hand, but not paper fibers. "How would paper fibers come off?"

"Considering the bruising on her wrists, maybe the paper was torn from her hand during the struggle with the killer."

"You didn't find any letters when you searched her house?"

"Nothing airmail and none relevant to the case." Pete hurried up the steps.

Heading back to her office, Kristi thought about what Pete had said. Maybe Rose could shed some light on the letter question. Once in her office, she sat at her desk and wrote out a time-line and her questions.

A year ago, Rose started house sitting for Catherine, based on a reference from Eduardo, Catherine's groundskeeper. Three months ago, Eduardo quit working to take care of his sick wife, and Catherine hired Tomas to take over the groundskeeper job. Last Thursday night, Catherine came home unexpectedly from a trip.

According to Rose, she surprised an intruder, who fled the house as she discovered Catherine's body. At that point, Tomas came in and found Rose over Catherine's body. Rose told Tomas she was checking for a pulse. Tomas called the police. About the same time, a neighbor saw a car speeding outside Catherine's property.

Had Rose really been checking for a pulse, or had she maybe taken a letter from Catherine's hand, stolen the jewelry, and made up the intruder story to cover her own guilt? Had she also removed a photograph from beside Catherine's bed? Why? And if she didn't, then what about Tomas? It sure seemed suspicious that he came into the house at that very moment. Could he have had an accomplice in the robbery and called the police to set Rose up?

13. Wednesday Night

As Kristi took State Street home after work, she again noticed how upper State didn't maintain the Spanish style of downtown. Turning off into a quiet suburban neighborhood of well-kept houses with carefully manicured lawns, she found herself missing Cota Street and the hubbub of her family's old downtown neighborhood. Here there was no sign of inhabitants, except for all the parked cars. She pulled up behind her mom's car.

Inside, the house felt even hotter and muggier than outside. She headed straight for the kitchen and a cold drink.

Her mom was there, putting away groceries. "Why aren't you at the beach?"

"I don't want to miss the 6 o'clock news. There might be something relevant to the case I'm working on." She poured a glass of lemonade over ice. "I saw Uncle Pete this afternoon."

Her mom glanced toward the den. "How is he?"

The sound of the TV explained why her mom lowered her voice. Kristi's dad was in the den.

Kristi took another sip of lemonade, wondering about her dad. Why was he so uptight? He didn't openly condemn his kid brother's "lifestyle," as he called it, but whenever the topic of Pete came up, her dad grew silent and tense. Her mom wouldn't talk about it, and Kristi had been afraid to ask, for fear of aggravating an already unpleasant situation.

Like her mom, she, too, lowered her voice. "He seems good to me, but he's really busy. He's one of the detectives working on the Cole case." The clock on the stove showed it was almost 6 o'clock. She headed with her mom into the den, where her dad sat on the couch sipping a gin and tonic.

He held up his drink in salute to them. "Two of my favorite ladies."

Kristi took a seat on the carpeted floor between her parents and leaned back against the couch as the news came on.

The anchor wore a grave expression. "Earlier today, the coroner's report was released in the death of Catherine Cole." He reiterated the same details Pete had shared with her and then said, "We will break now and go to live coverage of the press conference currently being held at the Santa Barbara Police Department."

The screen changed to show a crowded room with seated reporters and a panel of officers and officials, some in uniform and others in plainclothes. The Police Chief started by making a preliminary statement. When her uncle stepped up to the podium, Kristi felt her dad's leg shift beside her on the couch.

Izzy came into the den. "Hey, that's Uncle Pete."

"Shh." Mary gestured for Izzy to sit down.

Izzy sat with Kristi on the floor. Kristi listened with disappointment when Pete's statement revealed nothing new about the case. Rose was still a person of interest, as well as Tomas and Eduardo.

Izzy looked at Kristi, her blue eyes wide. "Any chance they might interview you?"

Kristi laughed. "We private eyes like to keep in the shadows. Hard to sleuth in the limelight." And she doubted any reporters would bother tracking her down.

"How's work going?" their dad asked.

Kristi lied. "Fantastic." Truth was, she hadn't accomplished anything useful yet, but if she told him that, he might crow and remind her that he was counting the days until her office lease was up and she'd have to come back to his insurance agency. She could just hear him say, "Where you belong."

Instead, he surprised her by simply saying, "That's nice."

After the news was over, he headed to the home office, and their mom returned to the kitchen. Kristi and Izzy stayed seated on the floor where the air was the coolest.

Izzy gave Kristi a pointed look. "How's your case really going?"

"You caught that, huh?" Kristi leaned back against the couch again and sighed. "Not as 'fantastic' as I told Dad, that's for sure. I need to find likely suspects other than my client. I've got appointments tomorrow to talk to Eduardo Garcia, one of the guys Uncle Pete mentioned on TV, and to the vet who took care of Catherine's cats."

Izzy shook her head. "No wonder we hardly ever see you around here anymore. With Tate off at college and you so busy, I'm starting to feel like an only child. I bet it won't be long before you move out, too."

Not soon enough, Kristi thought, but it was moments like this she'd miss.

Later that night after dinner, she was in her room doing the newspaper's daily crossword puzzle, when a knock sounded on the door.

"Come in," she called.

Her mom brought in the portable phone, which was pressed against her thigh. "It's James," she whispered, smiling, and held out the phone.

Kristi got off the bed and took the phone. She followed her mom to the door and closed it firmly, pausing before speaking to James. She doubted her mom would eavesdrop, but she wanted to make sure, given her mom's overly active interest in her love life.

When she heard her mom's footsteps fade away, she said, "Hi, James."

"I missed you today."

"Me, too." The moment the pat words were out of her mouth, she realized she hadn't missed him at all. Her eyes strayed back to the crossword puzzle. "You wouldn't happen to know the word for a 'billiard cushion,' would you?"

"It's called a 'bank.' Why?"

Of course he'd know that. She wouldn't be surprised if there was a billiard room somewhere in his family's mansion, but she didn't ask. "I'm doing a crossword."

James chuckled. "You need more help?"

"No thanks. What's new with you?"

He embarked on a lengthy monologue about life at the DA's office. She tuned him out and looked at the crossword puzzle again, until he mentioned her client.

She dropped her pencil onto the newspaper. "I'm sorry, what was that?"

"I said she's about as hard up for cash as they come. I went along with the cops today when they went to search her apartment."

"Wait, I thought there was a delay on the search warrant?"

"Hah. Castillo tried, but we got it overturned." Pride surged in James' voice.

Kristi wondered how the DA had done it, but before she could ask, he said, "God, you should see how that chick lives!" He paused dramatically. "She's got a six hundred square foot one bedroom condo, which she's subdivided so that she can rent out each room separately, and she sleeps on the floor of the kitchen's breakfast nook! There are five people living in there, not to mention the huge mutt that belongs to one of her subletters. And they all share one bathroom." He made a sound of distaste.

Kristi didn't know what to say. When her family lived on Cota Street, all five of them had shared the same bathroom, though their house had been twice as big as Rose's condo. She could only imagine how many bathrooms James' house must have, now that she'd seen Catherine's mansion.

"If we don't get her on the murder charge, she's in deep shit with the low income housing authority. They don't permit subleasing like that, not to mention the health and safety concerns of cramming so many people into such a small space."

Kristi felt a rising sense of injustice. Rose would end up in jail or out on the street, either way, she was going to pay for being poor. Kristi realized she'd probably lose her job, too. No one would hire her after all the negative publicity. Kristi vowed that, if Rose was innocent, she'd do all she could to help her at least avoid jail.

James broke into her thoughts. "There's this lawyer drinks thing on Friday night. You wanna be my date? You can meet my grandfather."

"Judge Roberts?" Kristi had never met such a prominent public figure. She felt a moment's trepidation.

"Don't worry, he'll like you," James said with unusual empathy. "So, what do you say?"

She recalled that the Judge had been close friends with Catherine's father. Maybe he could shed some light on who else knew Catherine and who might've had motive for killing her. Aloud, she said, "Sure."

"I can pick you up, say 4:30?"

"Thanks, but I'll drive myself. I may be coming from the beach."

He gave her the directions. "We still on for surfing Saturday?"

She yawned. "I'd love to, assuming nothing comes up with work."

She was deep in sleep when the phone jolted her awake. Scrabbling in the blankets, she found the portable and jabbed at it frantically in the darkness, trying to hit the 'On' button and stop it from ringing and waking up everyone else in the house.

"Hello?" she whispered, her eyes traveling to the digital clock glowing red on her dresser. 11:30 pm.

"Kristi? It's Rose." The breathy voice sounded even more tremulous than usual.

"What's wrong?"

"Someone broke into my car."

"What?"

"I can't talk now." Rose's voice faded to an almost inaudible whisper. "Can you come over, first thing tomorrow morning?"

"What time?"

"8 o'clock?"

"I'll be there."

14. Rose's Condo

Thursday morning, Kristi drove out to sprawling, unincorporated Goleta and a neighborhood tucked away between the 101 and Cathedral Oaks, her thoughts filled with concern. Rose had sounded so scared on the phone last night. Was it simply because someone had broken into her car, or was there more to it than that?

When she reached the low-income condo complex, she didn't see anything about the place that indicated poverty. There was no peeling paint or dying, untended gardens, as she'd expected from James' negative comments. Everything was bright and cheery, the buildings freshly painted in hues of gray and white. She found a parking spot assigned for guests in one of the carports.

Walking around the parking area, she looked for a car that had been vandalized, but found nothing more than a little broken glass in one spot on the asphalt. None of the cars looked broken into. Where was Rose's car?

Kristi left the parking area and walked along the sidewalk. Bougainvillea twined along the tops of the privacy fences, shielding small patios, and a motley assortment of potted succulents and cactus decorated the concrete stairway. She climbed up it and knocked on the door to Rose's condo. No answer. She tried again. Still nothing. She tried to listen through the door, but all she heard was a family in the condo behind her speaking and the sound of clattering dishes. Nothing came from Rose's apartment, not even a bark from the dog James had mentioned.

She looked at her watch. 8 o'clock on the dot. Where was Rose? Where were all her subletters? She knocked again, this time harder and louder, her eyes on the door's peephole, watching for movement on the other side. Nothing. What the heck was going on? Had something happened last night after Rose called, something worse than a car break in?

Kristi searched for another way into the condo. To the right of the landing was a window, but it hung two stories up, was sealed tight, and a pink drape hid the interior.

She stared at the door again as horrible visions of what might have happened to Rose and her renters ran through her mind. Home invasion? Maybe the intruder Rose was so afraid of had ID'd her and murdered her to cover his tracks? She should find a phone and call the police, but it sounded like the neighbors only spoke Spanish.

She looked over the railing downstairs and tried to spot a pay phone. No luck. The closest phone was probably at the service station she'd seen back at the freeway.

Her eyes fell on the doormat. Maybe Rose had a key stashed there. She bent and lifted the rubber mat. Bingo. The key was cool, hard steel in her hand. Did she dare break into Rose's apartment? Officially, it would be trespassing. She'd never outright broken the law. What if she got caught? But what if something really bad had happened?

Heart pounding, she slid the key into the lock and turned. It clicked. Holding her breath, she eased open the door and stepped inside. She exhaled with relief when she saw no sign of violence.

The apartment fit James' description to a T. It was tiny, cramped, and full of stuff; the small space subdivided into even smaller sub-sections.

To the left of where she stood, a wall had been added with a door in it. The door stood open, and through it, Kristi saw a room filled with two twins, a narrow walkway between them, and a dog bed shoved in the far corner on one side of the room. At the far end, a slider opened onto a tiny covered balcony, filled with potted plants, Buddha figurines, wind chimes, and an assortment of pillows and a sleeping bag on the floor.

To her right was a dining nook and kitchen area. The dining nook was separated off the small galley kitchen by a tall wooden screen. The kitchen was neat and tidy and showed no sign of any recent meals, though the aroma of recently brewed coffee lingered. A dog's food bowl and water dish sat on the floor beside the refrigerator.

Kristi peeked around the wooden screen. A red sleeping bag lay on the carpeted floor, and a jumble of dark-colored clothes lay piled along the wall by the window, which was covered by the pink curtain she'd seen from the landing. A plastic milk crate sat in the corner. On it were several pink candles and a long stick of incense placed vertically in a glass bowl, which was filled with white sand. Kristi recognized the earthy scent of sandalwood incense. Where was Rose?

She stepped carefully over the sleeping bag and lifted the pink curtain. A portion of the parking area was visible. Had Rose seen who broke into her car? Had the person seen her?

Kristi moved back to the entry area, when the other door in the unit swung open. A model-gorgeous guy dressed only in a fluffy white towel came out, rubbing his hand through a golden mane of wet hair. He looked like Fabio, but young and better-looking.

He grinned. "Who are you?"

"Uh—" She gulped, momentarily at a loss for words, her eyes staring blindly at his deeply tanned abs, her mind still stuck in danger mode.

A young woman appeared behind the guy and slid her arms around his lean waist. She looked curiously over his muscular shoulder at Kristi with big blue eyes. "What's going on?"

Kristi mentally shook herself. Obviously, no one was in danger and these had to be some of the subletters. "Hi, I'm Kristi McCormick. I was supposed to meet Rose here this morning. Do you know where she is? Is she OK?"

"Beats me." The Greek god shrugged casually and edged past her, the towel riding low on his narrow hips. "I'm starved. Want a smoothie?" He glanced at Kristi and then at his girlfriend.

Kristi shook her head, but the willowy woman towering beside her nodded.

"Thanks, Kyle. I'm Tara," she said to Kristi, pushing her long blond hair back from her face with fingernails painted shiny pink. She wore a lacy pink tank top and white short shorts that emphasized her impossibly long, perfectly tanned legs. "Rose is fine. I heard her leave earlier this morning."

"Where'd she go?"

Tara shrugged, her long blond hair bouncing. "Teaching, is my guess. She probably picked up an early class."

Kristi frowned. Why hadn't Rose called to cancel their meeting? Maybe these two subletters could help shed some light on Rose's character. "I'm a private investigator working for Rose. You know she's a suspect in a murder case, right?"

"Murder?" Tara's mouth dropped open.

Kyle looked up from adding things to a blender on the kitchen counter. "Steve told me the cops were here yesterday, but he didn't say anything about murder."

Kristi looked at him in confusion. "Who's Steve?"

Tara gestured with her thumb over her shoulder toward the room with the two twin beds. "One of the guys staying in there."

"The cops should've searched her car rather than waste their time coming through here and messing up our place. Rose keeps most of her stuff in her car, anyway," Kyle said, before blasting the blender and concocting something in an unappealing shade of light green.

Kristi was surprised the police hadn't been more thorough. When the blender stopped, she said, "They didn't search her car?"

"God, I hope they didn't, not while she was at work." Tara's plump lips tightened, and she shuddered. "Can you imagine how that'd look, cops all over? My boss would fire me on the spot."

"So you don't know if they searched Rose's car?"

They both shook their heads as Kyle handed Tara a glass of the green drink.

Kristi ran a hand through her hair and made a note to ask Pete. "What about Rose's car being broken into, you know anything about that?"

They both shook their heads again, but then Kyle laughed. "Who'd bother doing that? Her car's a rolling disaster, and it's just got her teaching stuff and clothes in it. None of it's worth a damn."

Kristi thought about Rose's call. "Were either of you here last night around 11:30?"

"I was, but I went to bed around 10 o'clock." Kyle turned to his girlfriend. "You got back from bartending around 11:30, right?"

"Yeah." A puzzled look crinkled Tara's eyebrows, marring her otherwise flawless face. "It's probably nothing, but I saw some kind of sports car pull out when I was driving into our unit's driveway."

A thrill traveled up Kristi's spine. "What color was it?"

"Silver, maybe? I'm sorry, but it was it was dark and I wasn't really paying attention."

Kristi chewed her lip. Was it the same car Catherine's neighbor had seen, or was it simply a coincidence? "Did you see Rose when you came inside?"

"No, but I heard her in there." Tara pointed to the wooden screen separating off the dining nook. "She was on the phone. I didn't talk to her, just went straight to bed."

Kristi looked through the open apartment door. "Are there a lot of car break-ins around here?"

Kyle stopped chugging his smoothie long enough to say, "Nah. We all look out for each other, mostly."

"Honey, what about when someone stole Steve's Walkman out of his car?" Tara turned to Kristi. "It does happen sometimes."

The break-in could've been a random act, but Kristi wouldn't know for sure until she talked to Rose. Time to switch gears. She looked at Tara. "How long have you known Rose?"

Tara tossed her long blond hair back with an air of impatience. "It's not a question of how long we knew her. With Rose, you just know. You know what I'm saying?"

Kristi nodded but had no idea what she meant.

"We moved in six months ago, if that's what you're asking," Kyle said.

Tara looked at Kristi. "Rose is an old soul. She puts other people before herself, not like most people—"

"More like self-sacrificing, if you ask me," Kyle interrupted.

"Come on, baby. You have to admit she wouldn't harm a fly. The material world doesn't matter to her."

"It should." Kyle set his empty smoothie glass down on the counter with a clink. "Can't eat fairy dust, if you ask me."

Kristi tried to get them back on topic. "Have Rose's financial circumstances changed recently?"

"She hasn't won the lottery, if that's what you mean." Kyle took his glass to the sink. Over his shoulder, he said, "But she's got a little more money right now."

"Really?" Kristi spoke up over the running water. "Why's that?"

"Well, she has a house sitting gig that pays pretty good, and she's got a friend visiting from Costa Rica who's sleeping on the deck. Not sure how long he'll be here, but I think he's paying some rent. Doesn't speak any English."

Kristi looked toward the room with the two twins. "Who else besides Steve sleeps in there?"

"Some dude. He's hardly ever here. I think he's some kind of science grad student at UCSB, maybe Chinese." Kyle looked at Tara. "You know?

Tara shook her head. "No, but he seems nice. He likes green tea."

Kristi took in the crowded living arrangement. It looked like James had miscounted. "Six people are living here?"

Kyle nodded. "It's pretty tight, right now."

"Doesn't the lack of privacy bother you?" It used to drive her nuts, sharing a room with her two younger sisters, back when they lived in their small house on Cota Street.

Tara shrugged. "We're all so busy, the only time there's any real overlap is at night."

"And it's cheap, but its definitely not a permanent arrangement, at least not for us." Kyle grinned at his girlfriend.

Kristi didn't have the heart to tell them that they might have to move out sooner than expected. Rose would likely lose her condo, now that her illegal subletting operation had been revealed to the police.

"I'm sorry, but my day job starts at 9, and I've still gotta shower." Tara gave a little wave of her pink fingernails before sashaying past them and disappearing through the door into their part of the apartment.

"Thanks for your time," Kristi said to Kyle. "One last thing. Do know if Rose has a boyfriend or anything like that?"

"Hah!" Kyle laughed and shook his head. "I don't know how she'd fit it in with her work schedule. She's barely got time enough to eat and sleep. If you ask me, the hours they make her teach are criminal, and even then, she doesn't make enough to cover this place. That's why I'm studying to go to med school. I'm gonna make some real money."

15. Eduardo Garcia

Kristi needed to follow up with Rose about what was stolen from her car, but she couldn't reach her client by phone. She decided before her 10 o'clock interview with Catherine's former groundskeeper to take a detour by the English language school where Rose taught during the day.

The school parking lot was crowded with BMWs, Mercedes, and a few Porsches, not at all the kind of cars Kristi expected students to drive. She was also surprised to see that none of the many arriving students were Latino, quite unlike the ESL class she observed at the public high school. Almost all were Asian and young, most younger than herself, and it was clear from how they dressed and carried themselves that they came from money.

As Kristi followed the flow of students into the school, it struck her as sad that Rose spent her days teaching at a place that catered to such wealthy people but paid its teachers so poorly they could barely afford living in Santa Barbara. She came to a large open lobby area with a semi-circular counter in the center. A middle-aged woman with her hair in a big bun on top of her head stood behind the counter.

She greeted Kristi with a friendly smile. "May I help you?"

Kristi widened her eyes and tried to look as young as possible, hoping she could maybe pass as a student. "I need a conference with Miss Schmidt. Does she have time today?" No point revealing she was a PI. She didn't want to bring any more scandal to Rose than necessary, considering Rose's name had been mentioned on TV last night in connection with a murder.

"Let's see." The woman flipped through a three ring binder on the counter.

Kristi leaned over and tried to read Rose's schedule upside down.

The woman didn't seem to mind. "She's got 15 minutes free at 10:30. Would you like to wait over there?" She pointed to a carpeted area with couches and beanbags off to one side of the large lobby.

Kristi's appointment with Eduardo was set for 10. An idea popped into her mind. Putting on her most ingratiating smile, she said, "I'm sorry, but I've got another class then. I know her schedule's pretty packed. Is there any chance I could have a copy of her schedule to see when she's free?

The receptionist shook her head. "I'm sorry, but we're not supposed to give out teacher schedules."

"Maybe you could write down a list of when she isn't teaching, so I know when to catch her?"

The woman looked down at the schedule. "She's only got 15 minute breaks throughout the day. Her next is at 12:30. There's another at 2:30. If that doesn't work for you, she's done with classes at 5:30."

"Every day?" Kristi failed to mask her surprise. Rose didn't even get a decent lunch break!

"All but Saturday and Sunday, of course. Her schedule's more open on Saturdays, depending on if we have testing going on, and if she has to proctor."

"OK, thanks."

Kristi left the language school and drove to the east side of town, feeling a niggle of worry. Could James and her uncle be right about Rose? She worked like a dog all day long, and that didn't even include her night classes at the high school. Kristi could imagine the poor woman might've gotten desperate enough to steal. Heck, even she'd be tempted to, if she had to work like that.

Eduardo Garcia lived in an area of town now chopped into a series of dead end streets because of the newly finished 101 Freeway. His narrow street was crowded with parked cars. Kristi finally found a spot at the dead end where the freeway roared overhead. Walking back up the block, she looked around at the tightly packed houses, painted in a rainbow of bright colors. The warm morning air smelled rich with the savory aroma of frying corn tortillas. An elderly man with a dark, wizened face under a straw cowboy hat sat on a low stucco wall, watching her approach. As she passed, she said, 'Hola.' He tipped his brim at her.

Eduardo's house was painted bright pink with white trim, and the tiny front garden was a colorful explosion of roses, their sweet perfume filling the air as she stepped up to the front stoop. Knocking on the door, she dug out a business card from her purse. A middle-aged Latino man with salt and pepper hair and a friendly face opened the door. He was trim, only slightly taller than she, and dressed in a white T-shirt and jeans, both of which were well-worn but clean. His arms and hands were roped with muscle and deeply tanned, probably from years of working outside in the sun.

"Mr. Garcia?" she asked, handing him the card.

"Senorita McCormick, please, come in." He stepped back and gestured for her to enter the living room.

Blinking, she had to let her eyes adapt after having been outside in the bright sunlight. The small living room was dark and cool, and filled to capacity with furniture—chairs, recliners, end tables, bookshelves, a couch, and framed photographs of people covering the walls. Eduardo indicated a seat for her on the well-worn couch by the window.

"Would you like a coffee or tea?" he asked politely, his English impeccable, despite the heavy accent.

"No, thanks." She was eager to get down to business. "As I mentioned on the phone yesterday, Brian Castillo hired me to find evidence that will prove Rose didn't murder Catherine Cole."

Eduardo eased himself into the velour recliner beside her, conflicting emotions of sadness and outrage moving across his face.

89

"I still cannot believe Senora Catherine was killed. It is crazy. La Profesora did not kill her, and she would never steal."

"Why do you think that?"

"La Profesora is a kind person who cares about everybody. She treats everybody with love and respect. She works hard to help us learn English so we can get better jobs and make more money for our families." He tapped his chest. "She has helped me so much. When I heard she might be in trouble, I wanted to help her."

Rose had a staunch ally in Eduardo. "How did you hear she was in trouble?"

"My daughter read in the newspaper about La Senora dying and that La Profesora found the body. I knew la policia would suspect her."

"Why?"

Eduardo shook his head. "La policia cannot be trusted."

Kristi stifled the urge to defend Pete and the SBPD. It was obvious this man's experience as an immigrant in the United States had colored his feelings about law enforcement. "So you went to Brian. How do you know him?"

"His father and me. We're friends."

Kristi nodded. That jibed with what Brian had told her. Time to move on. "You first met Rose when you took a class with her, right?"

"Yes."

"Did you ever see her outside class?"

"Sometimes at the house of La Senora when I used to work there."

"Why did you introduce Rose to Catherine?"

"It was a while ago. Let me think." He looked off into space for a moment, and then said, "La Profesora sometimes had us practice conversation in class. I talked about working for La Senora and when she bought two cats. La Profesora said how much she loved cats." He pushed out of the recliner and went to a chest of drawers. He pulled open the top drawer, sorted through it, and pulled out a card. He handed it to her. "La Profesora gave me this and said, if La Senora ever traveled, she could house-sit and take care of La Senora's cats."

Kristi looked at the card as he sat back down. It wasn't much, just Rose's name, her house-sitting business 'Guardian Angel,' and her phone number. Kristi made a mental note to follow up with Rose. Maybe if Rose had house-sat for other rich people without trouble, they could provide character references for her.

Kristi handed the card back to Eduardo. "Had Catherine ever had a house sitter before?"

He shook his head. "Not while I worked for her."

"How long was that?"

"My uncle used to be her gardener, but he was getting too old, so when I came from Mexico, I used to help him. He died five years ago and that's when La Senora hired me full-time." Eduardo's eyes suddenly welled up with tears.

Kristi had no idea why the man had grown sad, but it wasn't her place to ask. Instead, she said, "How often did Catherine go away?"

"Every two or three months.

"Did Rose ever visit with her at other times?"

Eduardo shrugged. "Maybe. I worked in the gardens, often far from the house and maybe not see."

A firm knock sounded on the front door and a man shouted, "Police. Open up."

Eduardo launched himself to his feet and rushed to the door, his face tight with fear. He opened the door and a uniformed officer pushed in, followed by her uncle Pete, who looked at her in surprise.

"Eduardo Garcia, you are under arrest on suspicion of robbery and the murder of Catherine Cole." The uniformed officer proceeded to read Eduardo his rights and cuff him.

Kristi jumped up and went to her uncle. "I thought Rose was your prime suspect?"

Pete frowned. "This is a police matter, Krissy. Make yourself scarce. Now." He pointed to the open front door.

She grabbed him by the arm. "I don't understand!"

Pete pried her hand off his arm. "Look, you don't have all the facts." He took a deep breath and then blew it out sharply as he watched the officer take Eduardo outside. In a tired voice, he said, "We just got confirmation that Garcia's alibi is full of shit. Turns out Miss Cole fired him three months ago. Yesterday, he tried to pawn a pair of diamond earrings that belonged to her. They appraised at more than twenty thousand bucks."

"Who said he was fired?"

"Silva." Pete strode out the door as Kristi's brain scrambled to make sense of what he'd just told her.

"Wait!" She ran after him out of the house. "What does this mean for Rose?"

He was headed for the police cruiser parked in the middle of the road, its lights flashing. Over his shoulder, he said. "Off the hook for now, Krissy. We'll talk later."

Kristi ran to the back of the cruiser and shouted through the closed window to Eduardo. "Why didn't you tell me about the earrings?"

"I didn't steal them!" Eduardo shouted back. "La Senora gave them to me to help me with my wife. I swear. Talk to my daughter, Sofia. She works at the Cha Cha. She can explain."

Kristi drove back to her office in a state of shock, her mind reeling. Was Rose off the hook? Was her job over?

Back at her office, she called Brian and launched into her concerns about the case.

He interrupted, sounding harried. "Hang on a second, Kristi. I'm on my way to the police department right now to help Eduardo. No matter what Pete told you, Eduardo hasn't yet been formally charged, which means the case is still wide open. Go ahead and continue with your investigation. I'll reimburse you for any work you do on Eduardo's behalf."

After they hung up, sat at her desk and looked at her notes. The coroner's report had found ink and distinctive paper fibers on Catherine's hand. Did they factor into the case, and if so, how? Meanwhile, all three suspects had motive, means, and opportunity. No question both Rose and Eduardo could benefit from extra money, and Tomas seemed to have some pretty expensive habits. She got up and paced the small confines of her office, her mind buzzing with questions.

Why did everything happen last Thursday night? Eduardo could've robbed Catherine years ago, before she had cats and a house sitter. Tomas could've robbed her at any time while she was away on her trip. If Rose was guilty, why did she choose last Thursday night right after work to commit the crime, and without any kind of alibi? Or was her claim of the intruder an attempt at an alibi?

Kristi's thoughts turned back to Tomas. He could easily have committed the robbery and then waited to come in and find Rose over the body, thereby pointing suspicion at her, and now, he'd pointed suspicion at Eduardo, by telling the police Catherine had fired Eduardo.

Maybe her interview with Catherine's vet might help her learn more about Tomas.

16. The Veterinarian

At 1:30 pm, Kristi left her office and walked to her car in the blazing heat. When she got in, she cranked the air conditioning. Nothing but hot air blew across her sweaty face. Cursing, she realized the darned thing was on the fritz again. Driving down State Street with her arm out the window to capture the breeze, she vowed that as soon as she had enough money, she'd give the car a much-needed tuneup.

The air cooled near the beach. Kristi hung a left on East Cabrillo and drove along the waterfront toward Montecito. East Beach's sand sparkled white in the sun, and she glanced longingly at the glistening blue ocean beyond. Maybe later she'd get in a swim.

The Montecito Pet Hospital was located in a quaint but pricey shopping district on the inland side of the 101. A blast of arctic air instantly dried the sweat off Kristi's skin when she entered the clinic. Except for a receptionist at the counter, the place was empty.

She approached the woman. "Hi, I'm Kristi McCormick. I have a 2 o'clock appointment with Dr. Lange."

"I'll let him know you're here." The receptionist picked up the phone.

While she waited, Kristi walked around the waiting area and looked at the pictures on the wall. Besides the usual posters reminding people to clean their pets' teeth and advertisements for pet products, there were several cutouts from the local paper and framed head shots of the three vets who ran the practice. Kristi located Catherine's vet and leaned in for a closer look. Josh Lange appeared to be in his thirties, maybe early forties, with brown hair and a close-clipped beard. Unlike the other two vets, who mugged with big smiles for the camera, Josh's mouth was closed in a firm, straight line.

Maybe he's camera shy, Kristi thought, when the receptionist announced, "He's ready for you."

Kristi followed the receptionist's directions down a short hallway to an office done in cool shades of blue and green. Several large potted plants sat on the floor by the window, their exotically broad leaves shiny with good health.

She stepped inside. "Dr. Lange?"

"Come in, Miss McCormick."

The vet sat at a desk that was completely bare, except for the single open folder he was writing in, a large blue glass paperweight, and a framed photograph of a pure white Persian cat. The word that came to Kristi's mind was meticulous. Nothing was out of place. Unfortunately, his expression looked almost identical to the one she'd seen in his head shot. In person, he seemed even less approachable.

Uh oh. She tried to ignore the sinking sensation that told her the interview was going to be a tough one.

"It's not often I'm called by a private investigator." The vet's eyes traveled over her, coldly assessing, and one brow arched. "You wanted to talk to me about Miss Cole?"

"I do." Kristi squared her shoulders and took a seat in the leather chair in front of his desk. Adjusting the timbre of her voice, she tried to sound as mature and professional as possible. "I represent a former employee of hers, who was house sitting and caring for her cats at the time of her death."

The vet closed the folder and placed the fountain pen on top of it. "I thought you were here about Miss Cole?"

"I am." Kristi felt like the Titanic heading for the proverbial iceberg. "It's my understanding that you recommended Tomas Silva to her old groundskeeper—"

Surprise and something else moved behind the vet's remote brown eyes before his face froze with anger. He crossed his hands over his chest, his eyes now glacial. "That is irrelevant."

Kristi cleared her throat and tried to smile, willing him to cooperate. "Well, I'm wondering what you can tell me about Tomas."

He rose to his feet. "The police are after your client, Miss McCormick, not Tomas. Now, you must excuse me, but I have another appointment." He ushered her out the door.

Minutes later, Kristi pulled out of the parking lot and headed west along Coast Village Road, puzzling over the interview. No question, the vet was a cold fish, but why would Catherine want to work with a guy like him and not one of the cheerful vets she'd seen smiling in those head shots on the clinic wall? More importantly, why was he so unwilling to talk about Tomas? She got the sense he was hiding something, but what? Was he Tomas' accomplice? It suddenly occurred to her that they might be lovers.

Distracted by her thoughts, she only partially registered the luxury convertible approaching her from the opposite direction. It wasn't until the car passed by that she realized it was James' BMW and that he had a passenger. Glancing over her shoulder, she got a glimpse of long blond hair blowing in the breeze. Who was that?

17. The Beach

Kristi spent the rest of the afternoon stewing in her horribly hot office, her mind a mess with the case and questions about the long blond-haired woman in James' car. Client? Friend? Someone else...? Probably a client, she told herself, but by the time she closed up shop and headed for the beach to meet Carla, she was desperate for a swim and her friend's clearheaded perspective.

Another ferocious sundowner gusted down the slopes of the Santa Ynez Mountains and across Santa Barbara to the ocean, making the air even hotter, as Kristi and Carla jogged across the sand. Swim first, talk later, Kristi thought, as she ditched her work clothes and raced with Carla for the surf.

After a half hour cooling off in the shore pounders, they got out and lay on the warm sand. Kristi looked over at her tall friend stretched out beside her and wondered how best to raise the subject of James.

Carla beat her to the punch. "What's bugging you?"

"It's probably nothing."

"Yeah, right. Out with it."

Kristi sat up and ran a hand through her short wet hair. "I know you're no fan of James, but I need you to be objective about something."

Carla sat up, too, her green eyes narrowed. "What is it? Did he do something?"

"Geez, Carla, so much for being objective."

"OK, OK. Get to the point."

"It's probably nothing. It's just that while I was over in Montecito this afternoon, I saw him drive by with a woman in his car."

"Was she hot?"

"I don't know. She had long blond hair. She was probably a client."

"Did you ask him?"

"He hasn't returned my calls."

"Did you try the receptionist at his office?

Kristi shot Carla a look. "I'm a PI, remember?"

"So?"

"So, she said he was out, but she didn't know the details, except that he had several meetings."

"You worried he might be seeing someone else?"

Kristi rolled over onto her towel and stretched out, the hot breeze blowing over her body. "I don't know." 'Worried' wasn't the word she'd use to describe the emotions tightening her chest. It was more like conflicted.

Carla changed the subject. "Tate called me today."

Kristi was relieved to let the subject of James drop. "I haven't talked to her in ages. She always seems to call home when I'm out. How's she doing?"

"Good. It's snowing back there."

"Wow, I can't imagine what that must be like." Tate had chosen a college on the East Coast because she'd wanted to try something different than sunny SoCal.

Carla continued. "The big news is that she's decided on a major."

"Yeah?"

"Criminal justice. She says she wants to work for the FBI, or maybe the CIA."

"Cool," Kristi said, but she was thinking about her parents and how her dad would react to the news. They'd been so proud when Tate got into that prestigious university, but if her dad disliked her being a PI, she could only imagine what he'd think of Tate wanting to be a spy.

"I've always dreamed of becoming a spy someday and traveling to exotic places and doing exciting things." Desire and longing glowed in Carla's eyes.

Kristi nudged her playfully on the arm. "Go for it! The moment Gwen turns eighteen, follow your passion and do what you love."

"So says the rookie PI, who's still trying to solve her first case. How's it going, anyway?"

"I don't know." Kristi sat up again and hugged her knees to her chest. "The police arrested the guy I was interviewing this morning for Catherine Cole's murder."

"That's good for your client, right?"

"Maybe." Kristi sighed. "But neither my client nor the guy they arrested seem like the types to kill people. You think I'm being naive?"

Carla pushed her long wet black hair back over her tanned shoulders. "You've got good instincts, Kristi. I say trust them. Go with your gut."

"That sounds great in theory, but the problem is the murder victim was a recluse. It's not like I've got a list of other suspects I can easily check out." Kristi thought again about Tomas and the strange interview with Catherine's vet. "Well, there is this one guy. He had the means and opportunity, since he lives right there on the estate, and money could've been his motive. He has a fancy sports car and he's gotta have a gym membership with a body like his. The guy's so buff, he's built like a tank."

"Good-looking?"

Kristi laughed. "If you're into that kind of thing." Bodybuilders were so not her type. She preferred them long and lean, like James. Like Brian. She was hot again. "You wanna swim some more?"

"No thanks. I'm gonna relax." Carla lay back on her towel and closed her eyes.

Kristi got up and headed for the water. It being October and almost sunset, she was the only one venturing out for a late swim. The sundowner's strong offshore wind was pushing the waves out to sea, affecting the current, and as Kristi sighted her swim line between the buoys, she knew she'd have to adjust her course to compensate. She set out at a crawl for the first buoy, periodically lifting her head to maintain course.

On the return trip, she spotted an approaching swimmer. The dark-haired man looked up, his eyes masked by a pair of goggles, and waved.

He swam to her side. "Hey, it's me, Brian."

She stopped swimming and treaded water. "What are you doing here?"

"Going for a swim." His black hair lay seal-flat against his head, and his gray eyes, framed by the clear goggles, mirrored the color of the ocean.

She wiped saltwater from her own eyes. "How'd you know I was out here?"

He pointed toward shore. Carla stood watching them with her towel bundled under arm and her street clothes on. She returned Kristi's wave, but then turned and walked back up the beach toward East Cabrillo.

What the heck? Kristi's heart lurched in her chest. Carla was leaving her alone with Brian?

"Can I swim with you?" He was treading water beside her, watching her.

"I'm almost done."

"Me, too."

They set out for shore. His long body slid smoothly through the water beside her. He had to be slowing his pace. The thought made her push harder. He adjusted his cadence, so she swam even faster. Soon they were racing.

Spluttering and laughing, Kristi hauled herself out and found Brian standing beside her, his goggles dangling from one hand and a wide grin on his face. Their eyes tangled. The laughter died in her throat, and she was suddenly too aware of how the water dripped down his lean, deeply tanned body.

He was still smiling. "I think it was a tie."

"You let me win," she said, feeling naked in her bikini, as she turned and led the way back up the beach. When she saw how he'd lain a towel beside hers, all kinds of scandalous thoughts zinged through her head. Grabbing her towel, she shook it out and wrapped it protectively around her body.

He picked up his towel. "You're much stronger than I expected. Probably all the ocean swimming, right?"

"Probably." She gazed out at the water. The wind had died, and thankfully, the temperature was finally dropping, now that the sun had set. A few pearly clouds hovering above the Channel Islands lit up in a soft pink glow. She couldn't imagine trading so much dynamic natural beauty to swim in a boring, chlorinated pool. "I love the ocean."

"I do, too." There was something about the way he said it that made her turn.

He was watching her in a way that made her forget what were talking about. The moment stretched as she stared up into his eyes. Finally, he broke the contact and lifted a section of his towel to more thoroughly dry his face.

She exhaled long and low and told herself to get a grip and focus on her job. "What did you find out when you met with Eduardo this afternoon?"

When Brian looked at her again, the lawyer was back, despite the lack of suit and tie. "He still maintains that he quit working for Catherine three months ago. He says it was so he could care for his sick wife and that Catherine gave him the earrings to cover his wife's medical bills. I asked my dad about it. My dad says Eduardo always told him he quit, not that he was fired, but Eduardo never told him anything about the earrings"

Kristi thoughts went to Tomas. "Why would Tomas say Eduardo was fired?"

Brian frowned. "I don't know. I followed up with your uncle, but he was clear that Tomas said Eduardo was fired."

Who was lying, Eduardo or Tomas? Why hadn't Eduardo mentioned the earrings to Brian's dad? Another thing occurred to her. "If Eduardo needed money, why didn't Catherine give him cash? And why did he try to pawn the earrings now?"

"Good questions." The admiration in Brian's eyes made her feel warm again. "He said Catherine didn't have cash to give him and that the health insurance his wife had from her old job ran out and that he needed more money to cover the funeral expenses. His wife died last week."

"Wow, what a tough time for him." Kristi shook her head, now understanding why Eduardo had become emotional during their interview. "I thought Catherine was super rich. Why couldn't give him cash?"

Brian rubbed his jaw. "Can you follow up on that? And I want to know what Eduardo was really doing the night she died."

Kristi remembered what Pete had said. "What's wrong with his alibi?"

"Turns out he wasn't with his daughter, as he originally claimed." Brian's face darkened. "I'm not happy with the discrepancies in Eduardo's statements."

Kristi nodded. "I'm gonna see his daughter tonight. Maybe she can help clear things up."

"Good."

The beach grew darker as twilight descended. Kristi's mind spun with the other unanswered question she had about the case. "Did my uncle tell you his theory about why Catherine had ink and paper fibers on her hand when she died?"

"You're talking about the finding in the coroner's report?"

Kristi nodded. "Could she have been holding a letter when she died?"

"It's possible, but—" Brian draped his towel around his neck and shrugged "—there could be myriad other reasons why. Without evidence of an actual letter, it's merely conjecture. I also don't see how Eduardo might be connected."

Kristi didn't see how, either. She also couldn't imagine why Eduardo would take a photograph from Catherine's bedside table, assuming her hunch was right and one had been taken.

Brian turned to her, his expression still all business. "You should know that Catherine's funeral will be held at 10 am on Saturday at the Mission."

"Sounds like it might be useful if I go." She'd read enough murder mysteries to know that anyone attending the victim's funeral could be a suspect, though it was hard to imagine who might be there, considering Catherine was so reclusive. "Who made the arrangements?"

"The Cole family estate attorney, as per her estate plan. You might also want to attend the vigil tomorrow night."

"'Vigil'?"

"It's a Catholic thing, when close family and friends view the deceased and say their goodbyes."

View the deceased? Kristi swallowed. She'd never seen a dead body, let alone attended a funeral.

He must have noticed her reaction, because he said, "Don't worry, it's not as bad as it sounds. I've been to a few over the years."

She still wasn't convinced. The whole thing sounded too intimate. "Will it be OK if I'm there? I don't want to intrude."

He smiled. "I think you'll be sensitive."

"Will you be there?" she asked, hopefully.

"No. I've got something else going on." He pulled a white T-shirt over his head, the fabric looking stark against his dark skin. "I've gotta get going."

The unhappy thought occurred to her that he might have a dinner date with a girlfriend or something. It was none of her business. He was just her employer. Still, she asked, "Where to?"

"My dad and I have dinner together every Thursday night. It's kind of a thing." He tucked his towel under his arm.

"Hang on a sec. I'm leaving, too." Kristi hastily pulled on her street clothes over her damp bikini and grabbed her towel.

The clouds over the Channel Islands had lost their glow and night was closing in, as they walked up the beach to the street. The dusty black pickup she remembered from the morning at Catherine's estate was parked behind her sedan. It didn't match the kind of car she imagined Brian driving, something more sporty and less utilitarian.

"Your truck?" she asked.

"My dad's. He's letting me borrow it until I have enough money saved up to buy my own."

She nodded, remembering his Stanford education. He was probably still paying off huge student loans.

As she dug her car keys from the pocket of her jeans, another question came to her mind. "I meant to ask you earlier, how did you know I was going to be here at this particular beach tonight?"

His mouth crooked upwards in an almost smile. "Would you believe coincidence?"

She shook her head emphatically. "No way."

He chuckled. "I remember you telling me yesterday at lunch about swimming the buoys down here. It was so hot today, I wanted a swim, and I had a feeling you'd want one, too." He moved a little closer and pushed a loose strand of her curly hair back from her face. "I'm glad I came."

"Me, too," she managed to croak, but he'd already turned away and was walking to the truck. It was only then that she realized she hadn't thought once about James.

18. Sofia Garcia at the Cha Cha

After dinner, Kristi tracked down Eduardo Garcia's daughter at a Mexican dive bar a half block off Milpas, where she worked as a bartender. In her late twenties, Sofia Garcia wore her long black hair pulled back in a tight ponytail, and her makeup accentuated the size and shape of her large, dark eyes. Her white tank top displayed a Mexican beer brand and her generous cleavage.

When Kristi explained she was there on behalf of Sofia's father, Sofia pushed a margarita across the counter to her. "On the house."

"Thanks." Kristi sampled the cocktail. It was full of salt and lime and liquor and so delicious she wanted to smack her lips.

Sofia moved down the bar to take payment from another customer. While Kristi waited, she sipped the drink and munched tortilla chips from a yellow plastic bowl on the counter. The place was dimly lit, with small red lights in the shape of chili peppers strung up around the ceiling, and bright neon Mexican beer signs on the wall behind the bar. A TV hung on one wall and aired a soccer game, its volume on low. A couple of men sat at the bar, and a few people sat at the tables clustered about the room.

When Sofia returned, Kristi kept her voice down. "Why are the police saying your dad lied about his alibi?"

Sofia shook her head. "I fucked up."

"What do you mean?"

"I lied when I gave Pa his alibi. It came back to bite us both on the butt. I mean, I didn't know where the hell he was that night, and when the cops came asking, I guess I panicked." She gave Kristi an assessing look and then leaned forward over the bar, dropping her voice even lower. "My pa's undocumented." She shook her head, her mouth turning down in a frown. "Man, I sure hope he doesn't get deported. First his wife gets sick and dies, now this."

"His wife wasn't your mom?"

"My mom died before we left Mexico, when I was just a kid."

Kristi nodded. "What exactly did you tell the police?"

"I told 'em that me and Pa were at home the whole night. I thought it'd work, 'cause I was the only customer washing clothes at the laundromat, but Senora Velasquez must've blabbed to the cops. She's the lady who runs the laundromat. She must've seen me. I don't know. I never saw her. But shit, now the cops have my pa in lockup and talking to me about 'obstruction of justice.'"

"They think he killed Catherine Cole while stealing a pair of her diamond earrings."

"Hell no!" Sofia slapped the bar with her hand, her dark eyes sparking fire. "No way my pa's a thief, and he's not a goddamn murderer, either. He's a good man. Decent. Hardworking."

"Do you know how he got Catherine's earrings?"

"Look, I don't know nothing about no earrings. Pa never told me about 'em. But here's the thing, he quit working for that lady to take care of his wife when she was dying of cancer. That was three months ago. He took it hard when she got sick, but shit, then she died just a week ago...and now this—" Sofia broke off, a grim, sad look on her face. She picked up a cocktail napkin and blotted at her mascara.

As Kristi watched the bartender, she wondered what Eduardo had meant when he'd said Sofia could explain about the earrings. Maybe he hadn't meant about the earrings but about his wife's dying. Kristi moved on to her next question. "Your dad said he quit working for Catherine, but I heard he was fired."

"Fired?" Sofia shook her head. "No, he quit."

Kristi took another sip of the margarita and then set it down on the counter. "I don't know how to help keep your dad from being deported, but I do know he can beat the murder rap if he has a real alibi, one that can be backed up by witnesses. Do you have any idea where he actually was last Thursday night?"

"Man, I wish I did, but I don't. He could've been at home by himself, or at his wife's graveside, but either way, no one could back 'im up." Sofia took a glass from behind the counter and began polishing it with a towel, her eyes narrowed in thought. Finally, she stopped rubbing the glass and said, "There's only one place I can think of where he might've been seen. Try that corner store, La Paloma's. They got card games there in the back sometimes, and I know he goes and plays. He thinks I don't know, but hey, I'm a bartender. I hear things. Man, I hope that's where he was."

"But if he was there, why didn't he tell the police?"

"He wouldn't want to get his those guys in trouble." Sofia shot Kristi a critical look. "My pa wouldn't blab to the cops like Senora Velasquez, no way."

"Blab about what? I don't get it."

"The games. They gamble for money. It's not exactly legal. Neither are most of the players. Pa wouldn't risk getting anyone deported. Excuse me." Sofia stepped down the bar to where another customer was signaling for her.

Kristi finished the margarita and crunched on an ice cube, thinking. Why had Eduardo told her to talk to his daughter if Sofia knew nothing about the earrings? Or, had Sofia lied about not knowing about them? But why would she lie? That didn't make sense.

In reflecting on what Sofia had told her, Kristi realized that Eduardo probably couldn't have a bank account or credit cards and probably had to conduct transactions in cash, considering he was undocumented. Undoubtedly, he had huge medical bills due to his wife's illness and possible gambling debts, too, all of which brought her back to Catherine and those diamond earrings. Why hadn't Catherine just paid him in cash?

19. La Paloma Corner Store

By the time Kristi reached the corner store Sofia Garcia had mentioned, the margarita had worn off and she was tired. Glancing at her watch, she was surprised to see that it was only 9 pm. It felt later.

Entering La Paloma, she was reminded of the place where she and the Cota Club used to go in her old neighborhood. It was small and tightly packed with the usual stuff: aisle of junk food, one side featuring sweet, the other salty, and another aisle of canned goods and assorted household items. A refrigerated unit stood along the side wall with dairy and beer. There was a closed door at the rear of the store. It didn't have a restroom sign. Was that where the card games happened?

She approached the counter, which was manned by a swarthy dude with a bald head. The edge of a snake tattoo reared up from the neckline of his black T-shirt, two eyes and a forked tongue, just visible above the man's left clavicle. He was surrounded by candies, packets of gum, newspapers—some in English, some Spanish—and behind him was an an array of cigarette boxes on the wall shelves, where Kristi also noticed a video camera.

The man watched her with black expressionless eyes. Snake eyes, she thought as she pulled out one of her business cards and gave the man a polite smile.

"Hi, my name's Kristi McCormick."

The man's cold eyes slithered slowly from her hair down to her T-shirt, where they stared rudely at her breasts, before sliding down to her jeans and then back up to the card she was holding. She stood and waited, arm outstretched with the card, and resisted the urge to either cross her arms over her chest or tell the guy to mind his bleeping manners.

Finally, he took the card but barely glanced at it before dropping it on the counter like it wasn't worth his time. "What do you want?"

What a jerk. She dropped the smile. "Sofia Garcia from the Cha Cha on East Haley sent me."

"Why?"

"I'm trying to help her dad, Eduardo. You know him?"

No response.

Kristi pressed on. "He's been arrested for murder. The only way to get him off the hook is to get him a solid alibi for last Thursday night.

The man said nothing, his face a dark, inscrutable mask. She was tired and impatient, and he was really starting to piss her off.

"Look, I heard about the card games that go on back there." She pointed toward the closed door at the back. "Was there a game last Thursday night?"

"I don't know nothing about no card game." The man shook open the newspaper he'd been reading and pointedly ignored her.

She stared at him, gritting her teeth. Was he protecting Eduardo and the other gamblers? Or maybe he just didn't want to answer questions from some young gringa. Whatever the reason, he didn't have to be so darned rude.

Fighting the urge to raise her voice, she made her voice extra polite. "Excuse me, sir, but can you please call Sofia? She'll explain why I'm here."

The man glanced up at her, gave one terse dismissive shake of his head, and resumed reading.

She couldn't stop the anger then. Putting both hands on the counter, she leaned toward him. "I need to talk to your boss. You have his number?"

Still no response. Furious, she made a grab for the newspaper. The man twitched it away and gave her a ferocious glare. He muttered something under his breath that sounded like "puta."

Kristi knew enough Spanish to understand the slur. Putting her hands on her hips, she glared back. If he thought her a self-entitled gringa, so be it. "I'm not leaving until you give me your boss' number. Got that?" She was aware of the video camera trained on her and realized he might call the police, but she was too mad to care.

They scowled at each other for a long moment, and then the man backed down. Swearing a string of oaths under his breath, he picked up one of the pens for sale on the counter and scribbled a number on the back of her business card. He tossed the card at her.

She wanted to rub her victory in his face, so in mocking deference, she bobbed her head with dramatic flair and said, "Thank-you!"

She headed outside to the pay phone, realizing the man had probably simply been trying to protect his friends. Still, he didn't have to be such a jerk about it.

As she called the number he'd written down, she wondered if his boss even know about the card games.

"Hello?"

"Is this the owner of La Paloma corner store?"

"Kristi?"

The deep male voice sounded weirdly familiar. Her heart flipped as she placed it. "Brian?"

"Hi."

Surprised and confused, Kristi said, "You own La Paloma?"

"My dad does. This is his home number. How did you get it?"

"The man working at La Paloma."

"What were you doing there?"

She explained. "But he wouldn't tell me anything. He gave me this number."

"I see." Brian was silent for a moment.

What he was thinking? Was he, like her, replaying their time together at the beach? She still couldn't believe that he of all people had answered the phone. She pressed the receiver closer against her ear and felt his quiet presence on the other end of the line.

Finally, he said, "I've never heard about card games at my dad's store. I could ask him, but he's already gone to bed, and I'm not sure I'll see him tomorrow morning, because I've got a really early start." She heard him shift the receiver to his other ear. "I'll leave him a note that you want to talk to him. Would 10 am work for you?"

"Sure."

The door of the corner store swung open and two men came out, one carrying a six pack of cola cans and the other a paper bag. Kristi watched them turn down Laguna Street. "You know this is great news."

"What is?"

"If Eduardo was playing cards, he couldn't have killed Catherine. He'd have a real alibi."

Brian yawned. "True, assuming someone can corroborate it. Keep digging and see what you can find." He yawned again, but there was a smile in his voice. "I have faith in you, Kristi."

The compliment caused her such a thrill she barely registered him saying "Goodnight."

She hung up the pay phone and headed for her car, walking on air.

20. More Family Tensions

Friday morning, Kristi awoke with a smile, Brian's words still ringing in her ears. When she felt a twinge of guilt about James, she told herself Brian's compliment had been purely professional. Downstairs, her mom was in the kitchen scrambling eggs, and Izzy cutting oranges.

Her mom smiled. "We're talking about having a barbecue tonight. The hot weather's perfect for it. Why don't you invite James to join us?"

Kristi still wasn't ready yet to bring James home, especially not now with them working against each other on the case. She was glad she had a valid excuse for turning her mom down. "Thanks for the offer, Mom, but James invited me to a party tonight."

A few minutes later, Mary said, "What about tomorrow night, then?"

Izzy laughed. "Geez, Mom, way to not be pushy."

Mary dished out the breakfast with a frown. "I don't think it's too much to ask for us all to get together. We've barely met the man."

Izzy gave Kristi a pointed look. "Maybe Kristi wants it that way."

"It's not like that." Kristi was starting to feel distinctly uncomfortable.

"Then what way is it?" Mary was starting to look offended.

It was times like these that Kristi really, really wished she lived on her own and didn't have to be answerable to anyone but herself. The joy of Brian's compliment fizzled. "I've told you. James works such long hours that I barely see him. In fact, we've only gone out to dinner once so far. It's nothing personal, Mom."

The moment she spoke the words, she realized their irony, maybe not about James, but certainly about her own life. Her love life was personal. It was her business, and she didn't feel like she should have to explain it to her family, or to anyone.

Izzy spoke up. "The important thing is, do you like him, Sis?"

"Of course." The words were glib, but inside, she wondered. No question he was good-looking, polite, and took her out to fancy places to eat, but did she actually like him?

Memories of her night at the beach with Brian welled up, the touch of his hand on her hair, and then later, his quiet, serious voice coming over the telephone line, telling her he had faith in her. Who was she trying to kid? What she was feeling for Brian wasn't just professional. She felt another twinge of guilt.

Unaware of her inner turmoil, Izzy started for the kitchen door. "Well, I'm off to school. TGIF! I'll see you later."

Kristi's mom collected the breakfast plates, the china clattering, and she had a stubborn look on her face. "Seems to me that if James has enough time to take you to cocktail parties, then he's got enough time to come over for dinner."

Kristi brought the coffee mugs to the sink. "The party's a work thing. It's a bunch of lawyers or something, and he asked me to go as his date. It's not some random party."

"I'm sorry, but actions speak louder than words. If he really cared about you, he'd want to get to know your family."

"Mom, give him a break. We've only been seeing each other a month." Kristi remembered the one time she'd met James' mother at the country club. It had been in passing, but his mother had been no more than coldly polite. Kristi had never met James' father. She had assumed that would change as her relationship with James grew.

Her mom paused in her dishwashing and turned from the sink, her clear blue eyes catching Kristi's. "You know, I'm starting to think he's not good enough for you."

Kristi couldn't believe her ears. Her parents had made it sound like they thought James was the perfect catch, but regardless, it was way past time she told her mom to mind her own business. She just didn't know how to do it without hurting her feelings.

Going over, she kissed her mom on the cheek. "I appreciate that you care, and I know you love me, but I need to live my own life, OK? I've gotta go to work now."

21. Brian's Dad

At 10 o'clock sharp, Kristi parked on Laguna Street at the address Brian had given here. The house was a modest, single story craftsman bungalow, similar to the other houses on the street. She looked around, curious to see where he lived, and wondered, he grown up there? The front yard wasn't much, just two patches of dried lawn with a tall palm tree rising from one side and a lemon tree from the other, bisected by a concrete walkway that led to a covered front porch. She headed up the steps and knocked on the front door.

An older man with sun-wizened, dark skin and a thatch of thick gray hair greeted her with a polite smile. "Good morning, you must be Kristi McCormick. I'm Brian's father."

"Nice to meet you, Mr. Castillo." Unlike Brian, his eyes were jet black, and he was much shorter than his son.

"Please, come in. I was just about to have a coffee. Would you like one?" He stepped aside for her to enter.

"Thanks, but I've already had my morning cup. I'll take a glass of water, though."

"I'll be right back." He disappeared down the call.

As she waited, she looked at the framed photographs on the walls. Most were family photos, some from ancient days in black and white, others more recent. She scanned each, looking for Brian. There were several of him at swim meets and a couple of graduation photos.

One photograph caught her eye. Unlike the others, where everyone had black hair and dark faces, this photograph included a striking young woman with a pale complexion, blue eyes, and curly red hair, standing beside a much younger Mr. Castillo. They were flanked by two girls and a boy, who Kristi guessed was a young Brian.

Brian's dad came back and noticed what she was looking at. "That's my wife, Vanessa. Wasn't she beautiful?"

"Very." Kristi looked over at him. "I'm sorry, but did she pass away?"

He nodded, still gazing at the photograph.

She looked at the young Brian, his face uncolored by sorrow. Now she knew where his eyes got their distinctive color. "How old was Brian?"

"Just five."

Kristi wanted to know more about Brian's mom, a young woman who looked like she'd come from a very different background than Brian's dad, but Kristi didn't want to come across as too intrusive. Instead, she said, "You never remarried?"

"Never." A private expression of grief and love moved across his face before he turned away. "It's still nice outside and not too hot. Let's sit on the porch."

Kristi followed him outside, where he eased himself down onto the rocker, and she took a seat on one of the wrought-iron chairs. "Did Brian tell you why I'm here?"

"He left me a note. Said you wanted to talk to me about Eduardo Garcia?"

Brian hadn't known about the illegal card games at the corner store. Did his dad? If he knew Eduardo had an alibi, wouldn't he have told Brian to help Eduardo's case? Kristi took a sip of ice water. "Do you know about the card games at La Paloma?"

Mr. Castillo didn't immediately respond, but she caught a glint of comprehension in his eyes. He did know.

She pressed him. "Was Eduardo there last Thursday night?"

Tension tightened the creases of Mr. Castillo's face and his gray brows furrowed. He rocked in the chair slowly for a long moment, indecision in his eyes.

Kristi took a guess at his reticence. "It's OK, Mr. Castillo. I realize that Brian doesn't know about the games. If you do, we can keep this conversation between ourselves, OK?"

His expression didn't lighten. "I will not compromise my son's integrity."

"Of course." Kristi nodded. "I respect your desire to protect your son."

Mr. Castillo put his coffee cup down and rubbed his hands together in a worried gesture. His eyes shifted to hers. "Promise me you'll say nothing to my son?"

Kristi promised, but she'd talk to Brian if necessary. He was the one who'd hired her.

Mr. Castillo continued. "I realize Eduardo needs an alibi, but I don't know what to do. My friends and I like to play cards, but the games sometimes involve gambling." He looked at her apologetically, as if he was worried she'd think the worse of him. "Illegal, I know, and many of the players and Eduardo are undocumented. I don't see how I can give him an alibi without exposing the other players. Or myself. I can't risk losing my store."

"I see the dilemma," Kristi said, but she was frustrated. Here was the evidence she needed to free Eduardo, but she couldn't use it. She tried another angle. "Eduardo's daughter told me his wife had been sick?"

Mr. Castillo nodded with a sad expression. "Poor Amelia. Her cancer was so terrible, Eduardo had to quit his job to take care of her at the end. It was almost a relief when she did pass away."

"He wasn't fired, right?"

Brian's dad looked confused by the question. "Fired? He couldn't work and take care of her at the same time. She was too ill."

Kristi nodded. So Tomas had lied to the police.

Mr. Castillo continued. "He told me there was some money from when Amelia was working, before she got sick. But it couldn't have been enough, not nearly enough."

"Did Miss Cole give him any money?"

"I don't know."

"Did he tell you about the diamond earrings, which the police say he stole from Miss Cole?"

Mr. Castillo shook his head. "I never heard about them until I watched the news last night." He looked as frustrated as she felt. "I don't believe what they're saying about him. Eduardo was a good man. There's got to be some way to help him."

Kristi thought over what he'd said. The money and earrings were still a problem, but none of that would matter, if they could establish Eduardo's alibi the night Catherine was killed. She had an idea. "You play the card games in the back room of La Paloma, right?"

He nodded.

"Does the room have a back door out of the store?"

"No."

Kristi realized there might be a solution to their problem. "That means that, if someone goes into that room, there's no other way out of the store but the front door, right?"

He looked puzzled. "Why does that matter?"

"The security camera by the front door would capture anyone entering or leaving the store."

Mr. Castillo's dark face eased into a smile. "I like your thinking."

"Is there any chance you have footage from last week? If we're in luck, it should have a time stamp of when Eduardo came and left."

He nodded. "The security video does provide a time stamp, though it resets every week. I'll go down to the store right away and check it."

He was about to push himself out of the rocker, when he abruptly sank back down again, the optimism draining from his face. "If the footage is still there, it will show the other players, too. It will show me. Won't the police want to question all of us?"

Kristi considered the possible scenarios, aware that she didn't know enough yet about the intricacies of evidence and witness testimony, but she did believe Brian was a good attorney.

She leaned forward and put a reassuring hand on his forearm. "Trust your son, Mr. Castillo. If the footage is good, give it to Brian. He'll be sensitive to your concerns, and he'll know how to handle the police."

He still looked torn. "I don't want him to know about the gambling."

Kristi leaned back, the wrought iron back of her chair rigid against her shoulder blades. "The videocamera footage won't show you gambling. Who's to say what was going on in that room? Maybe you were all just hanging out talking or something. Maybe having a few beers. Right?"

She could tell Brian's dad wasn't happy about the proposition of either lying to his son or the police, but it was the only option she could think of. Privately, she didn't think Brian would be as upset by the truth as his father feared. She finished by saying, "If you decide to use the videotape for Eduardo's alibi, make sure to talk to the other players and get your stories straight, just in case."

22. Following up with Pete

After her interview with Brian's dad, Kristi drove to the Santa Barbara Police Department. She'd thought about calling her uncle, but if Pete was busy, he'd let his calls go through to his answering machine. If she showed up in person, she maybe could grab a few moments of his time and find out how the police handle videotapes and alibis.

At the police station, the desk clerk checked her photo ID, buzzed her uncle, and pointed to a bench along the wall. "Please wait over there, Miss McCormick."

Kristi took a seat between a man wearing dark glasses, a lot of leather, and multiple earrings, and a woman with a baby asleep on her lap. The day outside was heating up to be another scorcher, and whenever anyone went through the outside door, a gust of hot air swept into the room. Kristi sat sweating until the clerk called her name.

Passing through the metal detector and into the squad room, she found the place buzzing with activity. The rookie officer Dan gave her a friendly wave from across the room. She waved back and then went down the hallway to the station offices, where her uncle shared a room with another detective in the Crimes Unit. Pete was alone at his desk, running his hands through his hair, as he pored over a pile of papers and open folders spread in front of him.

When he looked up, his face eased into a smile. "Krissy, what's up?"

She closed the door. "I know you're super busy, but I need to talk to you about Eduardo Garcia."

"I thought Rose Schmidt was your client." The smile faded and he was back to hard-boiled police detective.

Kristi took a seat across the desk from him. "They both are now."

"Glad to hear you're keeping out of trouble." He picked up a pencil from the desk and twined it expertly through his fingers. "What's up?"

"I just talked to a friend of Eduardo's, who confirms Eduardo's claim that he quit working for Catherine to take care of his sick wife. He wasn't fired like Tomas said."

Pete shook his head, impatiently. "Tomas wasn't lying. Turns out his English is pretty bad. He used the wrong word when he meant to say 'quit.'"

Kristi remembered her encounter with the burly groundskeeper. His English was terrible. "So if Eduardo was telling the truth, couldn't he also be telling the truth about the earrings and that Catherine gave them to him to help pay for his wife's medical expenses?"

"We haven't located anyone can corroborate his claim." Pete's sharp blue eyes caught hers. "Think about it, Krissy. If he needed the money, why would a rich lady give her gardener a pair of pricey earrings instead of cash? And why would he wait until now to pawn them? You have to admit the timing's a coincidence, and not in a good way. I'm sorry, Krissy, but his story doesn't add up."

Her uncle was right. She needed to track down Catherine's money person, but she wasn't about to back down about Eduardo not now that she knew he had a reliable alibi. "Who's to say what Catherine's motivations were for giving him the earrings? The woman's a mystery." She got back to her real reason for being there. "Hypothetically speaking, what if there was a videotape that showed Eduardo somewhere other than the murder scene at the time of Catherine's death—would that be enough to clear him of her murder?"

"Is there one?"

"Hypothetically speaking—"

"Where is it?"

Darn, she was no good at lying to him. She felt an uncomfortable heat creep up her neck.

"Are you withholding evidence from me?" His blue eyes felt like two laser beams cutting into her.

"No." Besides, maybe the security tape had reset. Maybe the footage of Eduardo no longer existed.

But Sofia's words, 'obstruction of justice,' rang in her ears, and Kristi realized she couldn't risk saying anything more about hypothetical videotapes to him. He was her uncle, but he was a police officer, first and foremost.

Time to change the subject. "Have you turned up anything on the intruder Rose saw the night Catherine was killed?"

Pete's eyes were still sharp. "You mean the alleged intruder? I'm sorry, Krissy but we've found nothing to substantiate Schmidt's claim."

Darn. So much for things being easy. "Did you hear Rose's car was broken into late Wednesday night?"

"No police report was filed. Anything stolen?"

Kristi shrugged. "I don't know. I haven't talked to Rose yet. Are you going to Catherine's funeral or her vigil?"

"No. I've got the weekend off." Pete's eyes drifted to the pile of paper in front of him.

She knew he needed to get back to work, but she wasn't ready to give up on Eduardo. "Uncle Pete, what if you arrested the wrong guy?"

He looked up. "Who else is there?"

"What about Tomas?"

He shook his head. "Not a suspect."

"Why not? Tomas had just as much means and opportunity to kill Catherine. He could easily have gone into the house whenever he wanted and fiddled with the safe, or looked through Catherine's stuff to find the combo. I mean, why did he choose at that very moment to come into the house and find Rose over Catherine's body? He could be setting Rose up."

Pete gave an impatient shake of his head. "You're barking up the wrong tree."

"Why?"

The intercom on Pete's desk buzzed and he glanced at his watch in surprise. "Sorry, Krissy, but I'm late for my 12 o'clock." He came around the desk and escorted her from the office. "Tell me if you come across any videotapes, OK?" He pivoted and headed down the hall.

As Kristi left the police department, she wondered how he could be so certain about Tomas. She also realized she'd forgotten to ask him what the police had found out about Tomas' connection to Catherine's vet, Josh Lange.

23. Judge Roberts

Kristi headed out Friday evening to meet James at the cocktail party in a bad mood. Brian's dad had called and told her the security footage had been reset, which meant there was no solid proof of Eduardo's alibi, and she hadn't been able to reach Brian to debrief him. On top of that, she'd failed to reach Rose to ask about the car break-in, as well as the possible photograph on Catherine's bedside table and the coroner's finding of ink and blue fibers on Catherine's hand. Rose hadn't returned her calls, and when Kristi'd gone by the school to track her client down, she discovered that Rose was on an all-day field trip with her class.

A short while later, Kristi found herself standing beside James in a large conference room filled to capacity with a well-dressed crowd. She sipped the gin and tonic James bought her and tried to ignore her cramped toes, which were jammed into a pair of blue high heel shoes that matched the color of her silky cocktail dress. He'd gallantly told her the dress mirrored her eyes, but little did he know, she'd scored it on a recent thrift shop hunt.

The room was so loud that James had to tilt his head down to speak into her ear. "My grandfather's over there. I'd like to meet him."

Kristi nodded. James had said his grandfather was friends with the Coles. Maybe he could shed some light on Catherine.

James finished his second G and T and placed it on a passing waiter's tray. Slipping his arm around her waist, he escorted her through the crowd to the far end of the room, where Judge Roberts was holding court.

"Grandfather, I'd like to introduce you to my date this evening." James urged her forward. "This is Kristi McCormick. She's a private eye."

The Judge was tall and broad with a full head of white hair and dressed in a tuxedo. He was a formidable-looking man, despite his advanced years, his manner every bit as self-assured and entitled as his grandson's.

"The prettiest little PI I've had the pleasure to meet." The big man thrust out a hand, his blue eyes twinkling. He probably meant the condescending comment as a compliment.

Nonetheless, Kristi put extra power into her grip, just to show him she wasn't some helpless young thing. "Nice to meet you, sir."

"Excuse me, but I'm going to buy another round of drinks." James left her side and disappeared into the sea of people.

The Judge was still grinning at her, his teeth too white for someone his age. Had they been bleached, or were they dentures? "So, tell me, Miss McCormick, what kind of things do you investigate?"

Growing sick of his patronizing tone, she wanted to say something snarky, but she remembered what her mom had said about Santa Barbara being a small town. She couldn't afford to alienate people, especially powerful ones, and she needed his help. "I'm trying to find out who killed Catherine Cole. You knew her, right?"

"Ah, poor Catherine. I knew her father." The Judge frowned and took a sip of his highball. "James told me the police have made an arrest."

"They've got the wrong guy." She knew irritation colored her voice, but she didn't care. She believed Brian's dad and that Eduardo didn't kill Catherine.

"Do you know that for a fact?" The Judge was studying her closely.

"I do." She returned his scrutiny and suddenly had an idea. Batting her eyelashes at him, she gave him a wide smile, knowing she was laying it on pretty thick, but if he thought she was a helpless damsel in distress, maybe his sense of chivalry would kick in and he'd try to help her. "But I'm having such trouble proving it. Maybe with all your years of experience, you give me some insight?"

"How so?"

When she saw him look intrigued, she knew she'd hooked him. "The problem is tracking down who knew Catherine and who might really have had motive to kill her. I'm sure you've read how the papers describe her as 'The Recluse of Montecito.'"

"A ridiculous appellation." The Judge shook his head and took another sip of his cocktail. "She may have become that in her later years, but back in the day, she was a wild one."

"'A wild one?'" Kristi looked at him in surprise. Nothing she'd heard about Catherine fit that description.

"Oh, yes. Years back, she used to run around with some artist or other. Gave her father no end of grief. She did settle down over the years, though." His bushy white eyebrows suddenly beetled. "Good Lord. The last time I saw Catherine was last week at a fundraiser. That was the same night she died."

"Wait, Catherine was at a party?" Kristi stared at him in confusion. Why would Catherine go to a party?

He nodded. "It was an early evening drinks thing, over at the Carlyle estate in Santa Ynez. Ridley Niven and Belinda Carlyle hosted."

The names sounded familiar, and then Kristi remembered. They were the hosts of the "in defense of marriage" fundraiser she'd read about at the library.

Why had Catherine gone to such a party? Why had the Judge? When Kristi thought of his role in upholding the morays of conservative Santa Barbara, her surprise faded to dismay. Did James share similar homophobic sentiments?

She looked at the Judge. "Did you tell the police about Catherine being there?"

"Why no. I only just now remembered. You have to understand, I only glimpsed her from afar, and it was only that once. I suppose that's why it slipped my mind. The affair was quite well-attended and my attention was directed elsewhere."

"What time did you see her?"

"Let's see." The Judge rubbed his chin with a thickly veined hand. "It must have been early on. She was out on the terrace, and the sun hadn't yet set. It would have been about 5:30 or so."

"Was she with anyone?"

"I don't think so. As I said, I only caught a glimpse of her." A group of people surged up, all vying for the Judge's attention. He gave Kristi a polite smile. "If you'll please excuse me, Miss McCormick?"

As the entourage engulfed the him, Kristi's mind spun with questions. What had the Judge meant by "wild one"? Like "recluse," the label could mean a lot of different things. The fact that Catherine had been at that party, especially one "in defense of marriage", flew in the face of everything she knew about the woman. Not only that, but Catherine was at a party the very night she was murdered. Why? More importantly, why did she leave the party and show up at home unexpectedly in Montecito? This had to be a lead, Kristi could feel it, but what?

Kristi looked around the crowd and tried to locate James. Had he been at that party, too? Despite her heels, she was surrounded by big men and towering women, who were made even taller by their own high heels.

The sea of people parted, and she spotted James across the room by the bar. He was talking to a beautiful woman with long blond hair. The same woman from the car? Maybe, but at least half the women in the room had blond hair of varying lengths, including herself.

Kristi started to push forward through the crowd, when her heel caught against someone's shoe. She stumbled forward and fell against the back of a tall, black-haired man.

He turned and caught her in his arms. "Kristi?"

It was Brian.

Ugh, how embarrassing! Her face was pressed unceremoniously into the knot of his tie, her hands against the smooth fabric of his suit coat. He gripped her elbows and helped her upright.

"I'm sorry." She felt her face heat with embarrassment. They were standing so close she could smell his aftershave and his hands were warm on the bare skin of her arms. "What are you doing here?"

He shrugged with a self-deprecating smile and released her elbows. "What all the other lawyers are doing, I suppose."

She wasn't sure what he meant, but she wasn't thinking about that as she looked up at him. His thick black hair curled slightly along the tanned column of his neck.

"Hey babe." James' voice made her step hastily back from him. James came up beside her. "I thought you'd like a refresher on your G & T."

She pulled her eyes from Brian and turned to James. He was shorter and seemed pale in comparison. Guilty at the thought, she gave him a smile and accepted the drink. "Thanks."

James shot out a hand to Brian. "Castillo, I haven't thanked you yet for giving my girlfriend a job."

Girlfriend? Kristi stared at James in surprise. When had she been promoted? Or was he simply staking out his turf?

The two men shook hands.

Brian's gaze drifted to hers. "I'm glad she's helping me out."

Kristi took a sip of the cold, tart drink, feeling self-conscious but also frustrated. She needed to tell Brian what she'd learned from the Judge, but she didn't want James to overhear.

James was looking at Brian. "How's the pro bono work going?"

The tension between the two men felt tangible, one man a scion of Santa Barbara society, the other a righteous crusader. As they traded polite comments that simmered with constrained contempt for each other, Kristi glanced at her watch, relieved to see that it was time for her to go.

"Please don't let me interrupt, but I need to leave for Catherine's vigil." She put the unfinished drink down and turned to James. "Sorry again for bailing on the surf trip tomorrow."

"Another time." James leaned over and made a show of kissing her on the mouth.

She barely registered how cold his lips felt with their hint of icy gin and tonic, because she was too aware of Brian standing beside them, watching.

When James released her, she turned to Brian."I'll talk to you later, OK?"

"Of course." An impassive mask had closed over his face, making him look as distant and remote as the first time they'd met.

It wasn't until she left the crowded cocktail party and stepped out into the cool, quiet evening that she could think freely. With a jolt of dismay, she realized Brian hadn't known that James and she were a thing, maybe not girlfriend/boyfriend as James had said, but that they were seeing each other. She couldn't get Brian's expression out of her mind. Had he been disappointed?

24. The Vigil

No sooner had Kristi set out for Catherine's vigil than she realized her blue cocktail dress and heels were completely the wrong thing for such an affair. Cursing her shortsightedness, she took a hasty detour by her house and raided her closet for something black, but there was nothing. She hated black and had nothing in the color except a hoodie she kept in her office. She ran down the hall to her sister's room and pawed through Tate's old outfits. Fortunately, her sister hadn't cleaned out her closet before going off to college a month ago. Kristi found a sleeveless black dress that would work, though because Tate was taller, the hemline was too long and the straps kept sliding off her shoulders. She found a black sweater to help compensate and grabbed the one pair of black shoes she owned, before rushing back to her car.

The end result was that by the time she pulled into the parking lot of the chapel, it was 7:30 pm and half way through the scheduled service. There were only a handful of cars. Not surprising, considering Catherine had been a recluse, at least in recent years. Kristi scanned the cars, nondescript sedans of various sizes. None stood out as luxurious or high end, the kind she would've expected a wealthy woman's circle of friends to drive.

A dented older model Volvo with the glass missing in one of its back windows pulled into the parking lot. Kristi recognized Rose behind the wheel and was surprised. Brian had said vigils were for close family and friends. Why had Catherine's house sitter, an employee, been invited?

Kristi waited for Rose to get out of her car, eager to talk to her and finally get some answers.

Rose was dressed in all black, an outfit mirroring what she'd worn the night Kristi interviewed her, except she wasn't wearing the pendant necklace. She looked tired but gave Kristi a smile. "Hi Kristi, what are you doing here?"

Kristi smiled back. "I could say the same."

"Someone called me from Catherine's law firm and invited me, but I was on a class field trip. I hope I'm not too late." Rose started to move toward the chapel.

Kristi hurried after her. "Rose, wait. You know I've been trying to reach you, right?"

"I know, I'm sorry. I've been so busy. I should've called to cancel the other day, but I had a pickup class and didn't get the chance. I'm sorry I wasted your time." She gave Kristi an anxious look.

"It's OK." Her trip to Rose's hadn't been a complete waste, since she'd had the chance to case out Rose's living situation and meet a few of her subletters. "Was anything stolen from your car?"

"I don't think so, but I haven't had time to check."

"Why do you think someone broke into it? I mean you're car doesn't have anything valuable in it, right?"

"No." Rose gave a slight shrug of her thin shoulders. "I don't know. Sometimes bad things just happen."

Kristi thought about what the subletter had told her. "Did you see a silver sports car around your condo complex that night?"

Rose's dark eyes shifted behind her thick glasses, glancing at Kristi before darting away. Her soft breathy voice came out in a rush. "I'm sorry I called you that night. It was so late and I was so tired that I think I just overreacted." She started moving away again.

Kristi stared after her. Overreaction? No way, she'd sounded terrified. Why? Had she seen the same sports car her subletter had? Kristi suddenly remembered what Catherine's neighbor had said about a light-colored sports car the night of the murder. What if they were the same car? The night of the car break-in, had Rose seen the intruder? Was that why she'd been so scared? Why deny it now? If it had been the intruder, why would he break into her car? Why would anyone, considering the thing was more of a dump than her own car?

Kristi remembered her other questions and hurried after Rose, who was climbing the chapel steps. "There's something else I need to ask you."

Rose glanced back. "Can we talk later? I don't want to miss the service."

Frustrated, Kristi followed Rose into the chapel. She still hadn't gotten answers from Rose about the possibility of letter in Catherine's hand when she died and of a third photograph on Catherine's bedside table.

The chapel was smaller than Kristi expected, having seats for maybe thirty people, but she only counted ten sprinkled about the rows, including herself and the priest. From her vantage point, she couldn't see their faces, only that there were two men and the rest women, most with gray or white hair. Her eyes shot past the stained glass and Catholic statuary to the casket, which stood prominently at the front on an elevated platform, tall white candles on floor candlesticks burning at each end. The priest stood at a podium to one side, delivering a prayer service.

Kristi slid into the back row beside Rose. As she watched the proceedings, she considered herself lucky that she'd never been to a funeral. Her grandparents were still alive and well, living in Nebraska, and though they still retained their Irish Catholic faith, her dad had married a non-believer and stopped practicing. Kristi didn't know much about Catholic liturgy, so she took her cue from Rose about when to kneel.

After the prayer service, the priest invited the attendees to come forward and speak about their feelings and memories of the deceased. A dark-haired woman walked forward with tight, sharp steps, her black heels rapping out staccato notes on the terracotta tile floor. She paused for a brief moment at the casket and then went to the podium.

"It's a tragedy and an outrage that my aunt's life was taken from her too soon." The woman had a strong, distinctive voice.

That must be Anita Walker, Catherine's niece, Kristi realized, remembering what she'd read in Catherine's obituary. As Catherine's sole surviving blood relative, Anita was most likely heir to Catherine's wealth. Kristi definitely needed to talk to her.

Anita's posture shifted and her voice softened. "Aunt Catherine was a true lady. I remember coming out from New York to visit her at the Cole House when I was little and my parents were still alive. She always served a wonderful tea in her lovely garden. It was so special. She made me feel like a princess." Anita gave a small sigh, caught and amplified by the microphone. "I wish I'd visited her more often. So many years have passed. Too many. I can't believe my aunt's life had to end like this. It isn't right." Shaking her head, she went back to her seat.

There was a lengthy pause. Kristi got the sense that everyone was waiting for someone else to speak. Finally, one of three white-haired ladies sitting together in the front row stood and went to the podium. The elderly woman had short, permed hair and clothes that made the phrase "church lady" pop into Kristi's mind.

The woman spoke on behalf of the women's auxiliary, praising the charitable work Catherine had once done, especially with an organization in Africa. She expressed sadness that Catherine had stopped attending church. As Kristi listened, she remembered the coroner's theory that the blue paper fibers on Catherine's hand had come from an airmail letter. From Africa? Had Catherine been holding a letter from Africa when she died? Why? And when had Catherine stopped participating in church activities? Kristi needed to talk to the woman after the service.

The next person to come forward was an older man with a full head of gray hair and wearing a black velvet dress coat over a black silk shirt and jeans. The dramatic way the light and shadow played over the strong bones of his face told Kristi he'd once been quite handsome. He paused for a long moment beside the head of the casket and genuflected. He brought his hand up to his mouth as if kissing it and then touched something inside the casket. Yuck. Had he touched the corpse? Tamping down her morbid thoughts, she focused on the relevant question: who had this man been to Catherine?

The man spoke in a heavy accent. "Catherine was a phenomenal woman, a lover of beauty, of the world, of the arts. Una bella donna—" He pulled a white handkerchief from his coat pocket, dabbed at his face, and blew his nose, the sound echoing through the chapel. Was he Italian? Kristi hadn't heard much Italian before. She remembered the paintings at Catherine's. "L. Bianchi" sounded Italian. Was this the artist that the Judge had mentioned Catherine was once involved with? Kristi definitely needed to follow up with him.

The next woman to speak was a tall woman in a shapeless long-sleeved black dress. Like the man, she, too, was older with gray hair, but it was cut short, and unlike him, she purposefully avoided approaching the casket or looking at it in any way. She walked directly to the podium and spoke in a voice that held no inflection of emotion whatsoever. "Catherine loved books. She was generous and kindhearted. I am thankful for that."

There was something about the woman's expression, like her voice, that seemed intentional in its blankness, as if it were a lid covering a seething cauldron of emotion. Or am I reading too much into it, Kristi wondered.

As the woman left the podium, Kristi looked around at the rest of the people. There was a woman in the third row, but all she could see of the woman was long, flowing white hair and a bright purple scarf around the woman's shoulders. Further along that same row was a dark-haired man. As if feeling her eyes on him, the man turned and looked over his shoulder. His eyes narrowed when they met hers. Josh Lange? Why was Catherine's vet at the vigil?

A stifled sob made Kristi turn to Rose. Tears were streaming down her client's face. She leaned over and whispered, "You want to go up and say something?"

Rose shook her head violently and took off her glasses so she could scrub at her eyes with the palms of her hands.

When it was clear that no one else was going to speak, the priest welcomed anyone who wished to view the recently departed to come forward. The room reverberated with the sound of people rising from their chairs.

Rose whispered to Kristi. "I need to see Catherine. Will you come with me?"

People were beginning to leave. The Italian man and the vet were coming down the aisle toward them.

"I've gotta talk to those guys." Kristi started to scoot along the row to intercept the two men, but Rose reached out and clutched her forearm.

"I can't go alone."

Kristi looked away from the departing men and found Rose's face wracked with grief. Her fingers were cold and bony on Kristi's arm.

"Please?" Rose's voice hitched.

"OK." She'd have to track down those men later.

Rose's black clogs clunked loudly as they walked together up the aisle. The casket was a polished light brown color with gold handles along its sides and sat on a platform that brought it to waist level. Rose went to the head of the casket and looked down, her shoulders shaking with emotion.

Kristi approached more slowly, feeling a moment's trepidation at seeing a dead body. She took a calming breath and then looked down. Catherine didn't much look like the photograph in her obituary. This was an old woman with short gray hair, who lay in repose, cushioned by white satiny pillows sewn into the casket lining. At first glance, she looked asleep, until Kristi studied her face more closely. Something was off—the colors and texture of the powdered makeup didn't look quite right, and there was a strange, absolute stillness of the body. There was also an unpleasant chemical smell. Revulsion lurched through Kristi and her stomach heaved, but then simultaneously, tears welled up to think that someone had killed her. Poor woman.

Rose still stood crying silently beside her. None of the other attendees exhibited such strong emotion. A disturbing thought occurred to Kristi. Was Rose's grief out of proportion? Was there something more there...like remorse? Guilt?

As the priest came over and offered Rose a tissue, Kristi noticed Catherine's niece heading toward the exit.

She hurried after Anita and caught her just outside the chapel. "Excuse me, Anita?"

The woman's plucked eyebrows shot upward. "Do I know you?"

"I'm Kristi McCormick. I'm a private investigator—" She whipped out one of her business cards and held it toward the woman.

Anita's dark eyes raked her from head to toe, her lip curling in disgust. "Do you really think this is the appropriate time or place? "

"I'm sorry, but I'm trying to find out who killed your aunt."

"The police have arrested the murderer. Now, leave me alone." Giving a violent wave of her perfectly manicured hand, Anita slapped the card from Kristi's hand and hurried off to a large black Cadillac that had pulled up to the curb at the bottom of the chapel steps.

The woman was entitled to her feelings, but what a bitch, Kristi thought, kneeling to retrieve her card. As she stood up, she noticed the dark parking lot was almost empty. Darn. No sign of the Italian or the vet, and the church ladies were getting into their respective cars. She considered going after them to ask about Catherine, when the growl of a powerful engine caught her attention. Out at the street, a sports car vroomed to life.

Squinting in the darkness, she saw that it was light colored, but was it yellow or white, or maybe silver?. She raced across the parking lot toward the street, hoping to better ID it, but it shot off in a glow of red taillights. Who had it been? Tomas? Why would he be there? Because of Catherine's vet? Or had it been that other mysterious sports car, the silver one?

Kristi headed back across the parking lot and into the chapel. Rose had disappeared, and Kristi realized she must have slipped out while Kristi was talking to Anita. The only person left was the priest. He was coming up the aisle, the casket still stood open behind him with the tall candles burning at each end.

"Would you like to pay any final respects?" He was quite a young man, not much older than she.

"No thanks. May I ask you a couple of questions?"

"Sure, but I need to close up."

She accompanied him to the door, where he switched off the lights. The chapel fell into silent gloom, lit only by the two candles flickering in the big dark space. There was something creepy but also sad about the body lying there, alone and unattended.

A shiver whispered down Kristi's spine and she turned away, thankful to leave the place of death and step out again into the night. "I'm a private investigator looking into Catherine's murder. Did you know her at all?"

He shook his head. "Only by reputation. It's my understanding that the Cole family were church members in high standing for many decades, something like fifty years, I think, or whenever it was her parents moved to Montecito. Our parish continues to thrive thanks in part to the extremely generous bequest they made."

"Do you know why Catherine stopped attending church?"

"I'm sorry, but that was before my time." He locked the door to the chapel and pocketed the keys in his robes. "Gossip does get around, though. For what it's worth, I heard she stopped receiving confession many years ago."

"Any idea how long ago?"

The priest shrugged. "Maybe something like a decade or so. I'm sorry, but I need to go."

"I understand. Thanks for your help."

Kristi headed to her car and thought about the dead woman. In her past, Catherine had been much more than a simple recluse. She'd been a "wild one," a patron of the arts, a philanthropist, a churchgoer. Something happened to change her. What? And did it have anything to do with why she'd been killed?

25. The Funeral

Saturday morning broke sunny and warm. Kristi awoke before the rest of her family, so she grabbed an energy bar and headed out, eager for a swim. On the drive to the beach, she thought about the case. There were so many hanging threads. There was Rose's claim about encountering an intruder the night Catherine was murdered, but like the police, Kristi had found nothing concrete to back up the claim. She still didn't understand Rose's contradictory statements about the car break-in, and Rose still hadn't answered her other questions. Her client wasn't making it easy. Last night, she'd disappeared after the vigil, and she wasn't returning Kristi's calls. The thought occurred to Kristi that Rose might be avoiding her, but when Kristi considered Rose's crowded living situation and her crazy teaching schedule, she thought it more likely that the poor woman just didn't have the time or the privacy to call and talk.

Then there was the question of Catherine's earrings and Eduardo. Kristi still didn't understand why Catherine hadn't given him money, though she knew he didn't kill her. What of Tomas? Despite what her uncle said, she couldn't rule him out. Why had he gone into the house at the very moment Rose found Catherine's body? And from what she now knew of Rose's work schedule, Tomas had more means and opportunity than Rose to kill Catherine.

There was also what the Judge had said, that Catherine had not always been so reclusive and that she'd been at that fundraiser. At the vigil, Kristi also learned that in the past Catherine had a few strong and caring relationships. Did that extend to her employees as well? Given the small number of people at the vigil, the fact that Catherine's vet and house sitter were invited seemed important. Had Eduardo been invited but couldn't attend because he was in jail? What about Tomas?

Once at the beach, Kristi swam out into the calm morning water and began her usual lap between the buoys, but the ocean did little to calm the thoughts swirling in her head. There was the lingering question of Catherine's estate and who would inherit. Would Anita Walker get everything? Had she maybe wanted the money sooner and expedited her aunt's demise? What about other potential suspects? There was that old Italian guy at the vigil. Could he have been the lover the Judge mentioned? If so, that was years ago. Why kill her now? Kristi finished her swim even more confused. She had no idea which of the hanging threads to pull on to untangle the mystery.

By the time she got home, she was running late for the funeral. She said a quick hello to her parents before dashing off to shower and put on the same black dress she'd worn to the vigil. When she got to the Mission, the place was a zoo. It being a Saturday, the parking lot was full and a tourist bus was parked illegally in a red zone, idling a cloud of exhaust. Clusters of gawking tourists clicking photos milled around the area as well as some people dressed in black. Kristi finally found a parking spot down by the rose garden. As she hurried up the sloping lawn, the heady scent of late season roses floated on the hot sunny air and the Mission bells clanged the 10 o'clock hour. She crossed the street and passed a news van parked by the Mission's old lavanderia.

A trickle of people flowed up the Mission's broad stone steps. She spotted the Italian man from the vigil. Rushing forward, she hoped to catch him before he disappeared inside the Mission, but her way was blocked by a big white-haired man and a couple of other people.

"Excuse me." She tried to move around them.

The white-haired man turned and she looked up into the patrician face of James' grandfather. "Miss McCormick?"

"Good morning," she said politely, but she leaned to the side and tried to see past him to the Mission door. Unfortunately, the Judge blocked her view.

"I had the pleasure of meeting Miss McCormick last night," the Judge said to the couple beside him.

Bringing her attention back, Kristi realized the woman was James' mother. There was no sign of James.

To Kristi, the Judge said, "This is my son, Weston, and my daughter-in-law, Joyce."

James' father held out a polite hand to Kristi. "How do you do?"

"Nice to meet you." Kristi shook his hand and studied him with curiosity.

The family resemblance between the Judge and Weston was striking, and James' father looked exactly as she imagined James would in twenty years, the same light coloring and blue eyes, the same air of supreme self-confidence. It was obvious by his distant manner that he had no idea she was seeing his son.

James' mother was enclosed in a black silk sheath that emphasized her extremely slim body and reminded Kristi of a saying she'd once heard, something about how a woman could never be "too rich or too thin." Joyce's over-sized dark glasses shielded her eyes, but the curl of her perfectly colored lips spoke volumes.

She turned her back on Kristi and took her husband by the arm. "Let's go in."

So that's what it's like to get snubbed, Kristi thought. She'd read about people being snubbed in books but had never experienced it first hand. Another less polite saying popped into her head as she watched Joyce go into the Mission. Rich bitch. With a mom like that, no wonder James preferred to go surfing than attend a funeral with her.

Kristi scanned the few remaining people going into the Mission but didn't recognize anyone, so she stepped through the Mission's large oak doors. Inside was cool and dark. The funeral mass had already begun, so she quietly took a seat toward the back. The place was by no means filled, but there were still many more people than she expected. After what the priest had told her last night, she wondered if many were simply there to pay their respects to the last of the Cole family. The woman in the row ahead of her was busy taking notes, and Kristi wondered if she was the reporter who'd been covering the Cole murder story in the local newspaper.

The congregants rose to take communion. A burly guy caught Kristi's attention. Tomas. She watched him accept a wafer from the priest and hoped she could catch him afterward to ask why he'd gone into Catherine's house that night. When the service ended and the closed casket was carried ceremoniously up the aisle and out the front door, Kristi waited in her row, watching as people filed out and planning to catch Tomas as he passed, but then she noticed the Italian man from the vigil approaching. She'd catch Tomas in a moment. Sidling along her aisle, she reached the man just outside the Mission door. The sun blasted down with heat and blinding light.

Squinting in the glare, she tapped the man on the shoulder. "Excuse me, sir?"

"Yes?" The man turned. In his sixties, he had a strongly cleft chin and an expressive mouth. She couldn't see his eyes behind the dark sunglasses.

"My name's Kristi McCormick. I'm sorry to bother you, but I'm a private investigator looking into Catherine Cole's death. I saw you at her vigil last night. May I ask you about her?"

The man's mouth turned down, whether in sadness or displeasure at her approaching him, she couldn't tell.

She hurried on. "I realize that now isn't the best time, but maybe we could talk later when it's convenient for you?" She pulled out one of her business cards and handed it to him.

He took the card, studied it for a moment, and then tucked it into the breast pocket of his black linen suit coat. "Certo. Of course." He held out his hand. "I am Lorenzo Bianchi."

"Nice to meet you." Kristi smile, shaking his hand. He had to be the artist, "L. Bianchi". "Is there a good number for me to call?" She took her pencil and notebook from her purse.

He gave it to her, adding, "Call me on Monday. I'll be back home then."

He disappeared into the sea of people outside the Mission, not just people from the funeral, but a large tour group snapping photos and listening to a guide talking about Mission history, as well as a television reporter interviewing someone with a TV new screw in tow.

Kristi felt like she was swimming through a strong tide as she weaved her way among the people, looking for Tomas.

She spotted his big frame and short hair. She called out, "Tomas!"

The groundskeeper stopped and turned. He wore a black blazer stretched over his broad chest, the sleeves tight over his big biceps. Mirrored sunglasses covered his eyes. When she looked at his face, all she could see was a double image of herself. It was very distracting.

"What you want?" He scowled at her, but she took heart that he didn't simply tell her to leave him alone.

"I need to ask you something about the night Catherine died."

"Por que? Why?"

"Why did you go into the house that night?"

"Catherine," he pronounced it 'cat-a-reen,'"she ring bell, so I go."

"What bell?"

"In apartment is bell. She rings when she needs me."

"A bell," Kristi repeated, nodding. Of course! Catherine needed a way to signal the groundskeeper if she wanted something.

"So that night she rang the bell?"

"Sim. Yes." The groundskeeper moved away.

"Wait," Kristi called out, but then she noticed that the hearse and funeral procession were pulling out of the parking lot. She didn't want to miss the interment and who might be there.

Hurrying down through the rose garden to her car, she wondered how long the delay had been between Catherine pressing the bell and the groundskeeper responding. Sometime between those two moments, assuming Tomas was telling the truth, Catherine had been pushed down the stairs to her death.

Kristi eventually caught up with the funeral procession when it reached the cemetery, which was located on a hill overlooking the ocean in Montecito. She'd never been there before and was surprised by how scenic the place was. Much of it was lawn with the requisite headstones, but there were also stately trees scattered about, as well as stone statues, obelisks, and mausoleums.

She followed the hearse and handful of cars as they wound their way up a long curving drive and stopped at the top of the hill. She parked behind the last of the cars, underneath the shade of a towering eucalyptus.

A refreshing breeze blew off the ocean and through the open windows of her car as she watched the casket be unloaded from the hearse and the people get out of their cars. The Judge climbed out of a black BMW with James' parents. Anita Walker and a man who was probably her husband climbed out of the black Cadillac Kristi recognized from the vigil. A tall, thin white-haired man got out of a gold Mercedes and hurried around to the passenger side to open the door for a tiny white-haired woman.

The distinctive couple seemed strangely familiar. As Kristi watched them, she remembered where she'd seen them: in the photographs at the library. They were Ridley Niven and Beverly Carlyle, the hosts of the "pro marriage" fundraiser the Judge and Catherine had attended. They walked over to join the Roberts' clan.

The door of the beige Honda in front of Kristi's opened. The woman who climbed out was them same older woman who'd spoken at the vigil about Catherine's love of books. Kristi hurried from her car, hoping to ask the woman about Catherine, but then she noticed the tears streaming down the woman's face. Maybe now wasn't the best time.

Instead, she went to stand in the shade of a large magnolia tree and watch the people follow the coffin, as it was carried up the lawn to a mausoleum at the crest of the hill. Marble columns bordered each side of the door, and the name "COLE" was engraved across the top of the Grecian-style pitched roof.

"There goes the last of the Coles," said a woman who'd come up beside her. It was the reporter she'd seen taking notes at the funeral.

Kristi took a guess. "Grace Teller?"

Grace nodded and grinned. "You must be Kristi McCormick, the aspiring new private eye I've heard about."

"How did you know?" Kristi couldn't help returning the woman's friendly, infectious smile.

"A good reporter never reveals her sources." Grace laughed. "But seriously, I found out there was a PI looking into things when I was down at the police station. Hard to keep secrets in that place."

Had Pete told the reporter about her? Kristi doubted it. He wasn't the type to blab, not like that rookie, Dan. Kristi pointed to the open door of the Cole mausoleum, where the people had gone inside. "Is this the end of your news story?"

"You tell me. If Eduardo Garcia's guilty and the mystery's solved, why are you here?"

Kristi knew enough from the murder mysteries she'd read not to trust reporters, despite how friendly and approachable Grace seemed. She gave a casual shrug. "Closure, I guess. What do your sources say about Eduardo? Do you think he killed Catherine?"

Grace was grinning again. She had braces-perfect teeth and a wide smile. "I don't get paid to make conjectures. I'm here to report about the funeral."

Two could play the quizzing game. "Does that mean you know who everyone in there is?" Kristi pointed again to the mausoleum.

Grace held up a hand and started ticking off fingers. "Well, there's Judge Roberts, Weston and Joyce Roberts, Anita and Richard Walker, Beverly Carlyle, and Ridley Niven—"

"Wait." Kristi had an idea for how to pump Grace for information. She certainly wasn't about to show her own hand. "Didn't I read something in the paper about Ms. Carlyle and Mr. Niven hosting a big party last week?"

Grace nodded. "I covered the story. It was a political fundraiser attended by a lot of Santa Barbara big wigs. Even the governor was there. Ms. Carlyle and Mr. Niven announced their engagement at the event. Strange coincidence that it was the same night Catherine was murdered, huh?"

"Wow." Kristi pretended to act surprised. She glanced at Grace, whose eyes were still trained on the mausoleum. It was clear the reporter didn't know Catherine had been at the party. Kristi still wondered why Catherine would attend a pro-marriage fundraiser, when she herself had never married.

People filtered out of the mausoleum, and Grace moved toward them. Kristi tagged along, hoping to catch a moment with Beverly and Ridley. They came out with the Judge and James' parents.

Grace said, "Judge Roberts, would you like to offer any comments to the Herald?"

James' grandfather adjusted his tie, cleared his throat, and started speaking in an officious tone, sounding like a well-rehearsed press release.

As Grace started scribbling his words into a notebook, Beverly and Ridley moved off across the lawn. Grace's head shot up and she called out, "Ms. Carlyle, Mr. Niven, anything you'd like to add for my piece in the Herald?"

"No comment." Ridley took Beverly's elbow and steered her toward the gold Mercedes.

Kristi followed along.

Beverly looked up at Ridley. "Shouldn't we say something?"

"My dearest, you know how the press twists things. Come along, my darling."

Kristi caught up with them at the street. "Excuse me. May I talk to you?"

She got the sense that Ridley was very protective of Beverly. His arm went around the tiny woman's narrow shoulders. They looked just like the photo in the paper Kristi had seen in the library. Beverly wore her white hair swept up like Zsa Zsa Gabor, and the jewels at her ears and neck sparkled in the sunlight like diamonds, which they probably were. Ridley, despite his graying hair and white pencil mustache, was tall and athletic-looking. Kristi guessed Ridley was in his sixties and Beverly was perhaps ten years older, though with all the cosmetic work and makeup, it was hard to tell.

Kristi held out her business card. "My name's Kristi McCormick. I'm a private investigator."

Ridley took it, his eyes narrowing as he perused it. "What's this about?"

"I'd like to ask you about the fundraiser you hosted last week."

Ridley frowned. "You are being impertinent, young lady. This is a place of mourning, not a time to ask questions about parties." He pushed open the car door and ushered Beverly inside.

As he went around to the driver side of the Mercedes, Kristi called out. "I'm sorry, Mr. Niven. I didn't mean to be insensitive, but I really need to talk to you about the party. Please call me when it's convenient. Thanks."

"Why are you interested in that fundraiser?" Grace had come over.

At the same moment, Kristi noticed the woman from the vigil getting into her Honda. Darn, she'd hoped to talk to the woman, but not when the reporter was watching her with eagle eyes.

She jerked her own eyes away from the Honda and the Mercedes as the two cars took off and told herself to come up with a lie, quick. "I was using the party as an excuse to ask Ms. Carlyle and Mr. Niven about Catherine. I'm having trouble finding out much about her. You should know how hard that is, considering you were the one who coined the catchy phrase, 'Recluse of Montecito.' Right?"

Grace grinned. "Good one, huh?" The compliment did the trick and distracted the reporter.

"It sure fits. What else can you tell me about her?"

Grace's attention had moved to the remaining cars. "Excuse me, but I need a quote from Ms. Cole's next of kin. I'll catch up with you later."

Not if I can help it, Kristi thought as she watched the reporter hurry off in pursuit of Anita Walker and her husband.

26. One Suspect Cleared

Late Saturday afternoon, Kristi and Carla headed for cocktail hour at Pete's place. Later, they planned to go dancing with the rest of the Cota Club at the Wildcat Lounge, a new bar and dance place off State Street that had opened over the summer. Ladies danced free and the age limit was eighteen, so Izzy and Gwen could dance, too.

"You weren't kidding about Brian Castillo," Carla said to Kristi as they drove through the cross-town traffic on East Cota, which was jammed with both locals and the usual LA weekend tourists.

Kristi took her eyes from the car in front of her and glanced over at her friend. "What do you mean?"

"The guy's totally hot!"

"You interested?" She felt a dropping sensation in her stomach. Carla was gorgeous, irresistible, and available. How could Brian, or any man, resist her?

Carla shook her head. "Not my type. Besides, I think his interest lies elsewhere. How'd it go with him at the beach the other night?"

Kristi's relief at Carla's response gave way to suspicion. "Is that why you took off?"

Carla grinned. "You dump James, yet?"

"None of your beeswax. Wait, what do you mean, Brian's 'interest lies elsewhere'?"

"You, silly."

Kristi frowned. "I work for the guy."

"So?"

"So, I don't think someone like him mixes business and pleasure." She added a guilty beat too late, "Neither do I." The electric moment when he'd stood beside her, close, and brushed the hair from her face still burned bright inside.

"Yeah, right." Carla laughed. "If you ask me, Castillo's the perfect guy for you—upstanding, hard working, and hot to boot." She turned her gaze out the window. "Anyway, thanks for driving tonight. It'll be good to see your uncle. It's been a while."

Kristi was relieved to get off the subject of her love life. "I've been seeing Pete a lot lately, what with the Cole case."

"You solve it for him, yet?"

"I wish." Kristi sighed. "Let's just say we don't see eye to eye about who killed Catherine."

"I put my vote on you."

"Thanks." Kristi appreciated her friend's vote of confidence, but considering how many questions still remained unanswered, she wasn't so sure. The only thing she knew for certain was the police had arrested the wrong person.

Her uncle lived in a rental at the back of a larger property on the Santa Barbara Riviera. He'd lived there for as long as Kristi could remember. The apartment was small but picturesque. Bougainvillea twined out front with a tiny patio that had an even tinier ocean view between the roof line of the main house and several eucalyptus trees down the hill.

"Hey there, two of my favorite gals," Pete said, when they reached his patio. He wore the usual Polo shirt, but he'd ditched the khaki slacks in favor of a pair of shorts and flip flops. The hard cop face he wore when working was gone, at least for now, and though he didn't look exactly carefree, the lines and creases of his tanned face had smoothed a bit. "The hot weather's put me in the mood for a summery drink. How do Cosmos sound?" He stood up from the small wrought iron table and the makeshift bar he'd assembled to give them each a peck on the cheek.

"You're a god." Carla dropped into one of the seats and immediately kicked off her strappy heels.

Kristi took the third seat. "Thanks for having us over."

He did the honors, mixing the drinks and shaking them thoroughly with ice before pouring them into the cocktail glasses, which were garnished with thin lime slices.

The sun had set behind the building next door and the hot October day had finally started to cool. No sundowner blew, and unlike the past few days, the air was still and calm and smelled of eucalyptus.

Pete looked at Carla. "I don't think I've seen you since..." He gave her a sympathetic smile.

"Since my mom got put in the loony bin?" Carla tossed back her long black hair. "No need to pussyfoot around the subject. I'm OK with it."

Pete nodded. "How's life treating you these days?"

"Meh." Carla took a long sip of her cosmo. "To tell you the truth, it's boring as hell. I spend my days working at the Magic Shop and taking care of Gwen, but now that she's eighteen and almost an adult, she doesn't need much taking care of." Her green eyes moved to Kristi. "I live vicariously through Kristi. A PI's life is way more interesting than mine."

Kristi took that as her cue. "Mind if I talk a little shop with Pete?"

Carla grinned. "Go for it."

Pete put down his empty glass and gave Kristi a wry smile. "I think I'd better have another drink. Anyone?"

Carla drained her glass and handed it over. "Sure."

"I'm good," Kristi said. She was Carla's designated driver and she wasn't a big fan of sweet vodka drinks. Once Pete was done pouring fresh drinks, she said, "You know the reporter, Grace Teller?"

"Yeah."

"She says someone at the police department told her I'm investigating the Cole case."

"Who?"

"She wouldn't say, but she did tell me the place can't keep secrets." Kristi gave her uncle a worried look. He'd managed to keep being gay hidden from the public eye for the last umpteen years, but it didn't mean at some point he might not be outed. Things were bad enough with her dad and him, she didn't want to think about how some of his coworkers might act if they found out.

Pete's blue eyes met hers over the rim of his cosmo glass. "Don't worry, Krissy, my secret's safe."

"This town is too damned small," Carla said angrily. "It's nobody's business, bunch of nosy parkers."

Kristi detected Carla's bitter feelings about Mark Lyons in her words. Kristi didn't know the specifics of how their relationship blew up, except that it had something to do with his wealthy and prominent family not approving of Carla. Prejudice came in all types.

Pete spoke into the silence. "You said you wanted to talk shop?"

"Yes." Kristi turned her thoughts back to Catherine's murder and her questions. "Did the coroner get the lab results back about the blue paper fibers found on Catherine's hand?"

Pete nodded. "His theory was right. They were fibers from an airmail letter."

"Where's the letter?"

"None's turned up, but may be unrelated to the murder, in any case."

Kristi frowned, thinking. "Maybe not, but then how did she get the fibers on her hand? And wouldn't the letter have to be somewhere in the house, unless someone took it, like the intruder?"

Before answering, Pete took another sip of his cosmo. He regarded her for a long moment, his blue eyes thoughtful. "You've got a point about the letter, but unless it surfaces, we have no way of knowing if or how it's relevant to the case."

Kristi sighed. She had no idea how to locate the letter. She thought of the other question she had. "Did you ever find out if a third photo was taken from Catherine's bedside table?"

Pete shook his head. "I haven't had the time. To be honest, Krissy, I'm not sure why you think it matters."

She wasn't sure it did, either. Taking a sip of her drink, she moved on. "I found out Catherine went to a party in Santa Ynez the same day she died."

Pete grimaced. "A right wing fundraiser opposed to gay rights."

"Don't you think it's weird that the 'Recluse of Montecito' went to a party and then suddenly and unexpectedly returned home? Maybe something happened at the party that made her change her plans. Seems suspicious to me, considering she was murdered only hours later."

"Yeah, the coincidence does seem strange, but—" Pete shrugged. "We've talked to the party hosts and many of the attendees. There's nothing to suggest it was anything other than a coincidence. Besides, we've arrested the perp."

Kristi wanted to defend Eduardo, but they'd already been over that before. She finished her cosmo and put the glass on the table. "I still don't understand why you don't consider Tomas Silva a suspect."

Pete frowned. "He's not."

"Why? In fact—" Maybe it was the cosmo she'd drunk, but she decided to go out on a limb and air a theory she'd started to formulate "—what about him and that vet, Josh Lange, the guy who took care of Catherine's cats?"

"What do you mean?" The lines on Pete's face hardened and the police detective was back.

"I don't know." She didn't want to sound like an idiot. "I've got a hunch there's something there worth investigating."

Pete put down his drink. "Explain."

"Well, first of all, think about how Tomas and," she made brackets with her fingers, "'the Recluse of Montecito' met? The vet knew Catherine was a wealthy woman, and when Eduardo left, he suggested his friend Tomas replace him."

"What's your point?"

Kristi hurried on. "Think about it. What if Josh and Tomas were in together on the murder? Maybe they were biding their time, waiting for the perfect moment to rob Catherine, and then Rose comes along, a teacher barely getting by with her little house sitting gig on the side. What better patsy for them to set up to take the fall?"

"Wow, that'd be pretty evil," Carla piped up.

Pete shook his head. "Good try, kiddo, but you've got it all wrong."

"Why?"

"Just believe me, OK?"

"I'm sorry, Uncle Pete, but I'm a PI. I don't operate on belief. I need evidence."

Pete stood up and circled the small patio, pausing to deadhead a spent geranium from one of the potted plants on the low stucco wall forming one side of the patio. When he turned back, he gave both Kristi and Carla a serious look. "I trust your discretion, but I need both of you to promise me that you'll keep what I'm about to tell you a secret."

They nodded.

He returned to his seat and said in a low voice, "Josh and Tomas are lovers."

"No way!" Two cosmos made Carla even more dramatic than usual.

Kristi was surprised but also confused. "I knew something was going on with them, but why does that discount my theory?"

Pete took another sip of his drink before answering. "The night Catherine was killed, Josh was with Tomas in his apartment. They weren't expecting her and didn't hear the service bell. Let's just say it took a while before Tomas noticed the call light was on and that Catherine needed him. When he went to check in on Catherine at the main house, Josh left and went home."

"Does Josh drive a light-colored sports car?"

"It's a silver BMW."

"So it was Josh's car that Catherine's neighbor saw that night?"

Pete shrugged. "Seems likely."

Had Josh been the intruder Rose saw? That didn't make sense, because Josh had dark, not light-colored hair as Rose had described. "Still, I don't see why my theory's wrong. If anything, it's stronger. I mean as lovers Tomas and Josh had even more reason to cover for each other."

"I'm sorry, Krissy, but you're wrong on two counts. The first is that you're assigning a motive to them that doesn't make sense. Josh makes good money at his job. Why would he need to rob Catherine? Secondly," Pete finished the dregs of his drink, his expression wry, "it may be 1994, but society has a long way to go toward accepting people who aren't straight, especially here in Santa Barbara. Josh risked a whole lot when he backed up Tomas' alibi. If their relationship became public, he could lose a lot of clients. No way would he have come forward if it wasn't true."

"Why wasn't any of this in the police report?"

Pete frowned and ran a hand through his short, sun-bleached hair as his eyes traveled between Kristi and Carla. "Look, Josh and I have history. I cut a deal with him to keep their relationship off the books unless it became absolutely relevant to the investigation."

Pete and Josh? Kristi looked at her uncle in astonishment. She'd never met any of his lovers, but Josh? The guy had acted so cold and unfriendly to her. With a pang, she wondered if he merely hadn't liked her, or was he close-minded in his own way and had stereotyped her? She'd certainly dealt with enough people discounting her for being young and blonde. Regardless, it was clear that Pete believed Josh and Tomas were innocent, and she had to admit that from what he'd told her it sounded likely. She sighed. So much for her theory, though her hunch that Tomas and Josh were a couple had been right.

"Like I said before, this town is too damned small!" Carla tossed back her drink and slammed the empty glass down on the tabletop. "Don't people have bigger things to worry about than who's sleeping with whom?"

"People are people. They love gossip." Pete's lips twisted. "We all have to survive the best we can."

His words made Kristi think about Rose and how hard it was to survive financially in Santa Barbara. Had Rose's financial needs been desperate enough to drive her to rob and kill Catherine?

Aloud, she said, "Have you found out anything about the intruder Rose says was in the house the night Catherine was killed? Did either Tomas or Josh see him?"

"No. I don't know why she said what she did about an intruder." Pete rubbed his jaw. "Sometimes people make things up when they panic."

Kristi didn't buy it. "What about the other people at her vigil and the funeral. Isn't it possible that one of them killed Catherine for a motive we don't yet know about?" She knew it sounded like she was grasping at straws, but if Rose, Eduardo, and Tomas weren't guilty, then who was?

Pete frowned. "Krissy, I'm a police detective. I've got to work with what I've got and go where the evidence takes me. Right now, that means Eduardo's the perp, unless you've got evidence otherwise?" He shot her a pointed look.

"Nope." That was true, now that there wasn't any security footage from La Paloma.

"Well," Carla slipped on her shoes and lunged to her feet, her statuesque form towering over them. "The evidence of this dress and these shoes and a couple of comos means I've gotta go dancing! You wanna come with us, Pete?"

He pushed back from his chair and stood up. "Thanks for the offer, but it's like what you said, Carla."

"Yeah?"

"Santa Barbara's too small a place sometimes. I've got plans in LA later tonight."

Kristi got up and gave him a hug. "I love you, Uncle Pete."

When they stepped back from each other, he raised his hand and tipped her an imaginary salute. "You're a good PI, Krissy. Your instincts were right about Tomas and Josh, just not in the way you suspected. Trust your instincts and follow them. If you turn up another suspect, let me know. Police procedure and politics dictate what I can do, but I definitely don't want innocent people to be wrongfully punished."

27. Sunday at the Beach

Kristi slept in late Sunday morning. When she awoke, she lay in bed and studied the pebbly-looking surface of her bedroom's popcorn ceiling and reconsidered the facts about the night Catherine died. James' grandfather had seen Catherine alive and well about 5:30 pm at the party hosted by Beverly and Ridley in Santa Ynez. About 9:30 pm the same night, someone pushed Catherine down the stairs to her death at her home in Montecito. The coroner's report found traces of ink and paper fibers from an airmail letter on her right hand and bruising on Catherine's wrist. Rose found the body, and then Tomas came in, saw Rose, and called the police shortly after that. The safe in Catherine's room was found open and empty, her jewelry box partially emptied, and her bedroom wiped free of fingerprints. There were also the mysterious markings in the dust on Catherine's bedside table.

Beyond those facts, the rest was conjecture. Like who broke into the safe and wiped her room clean, and why? Had a photograph been taken from her bedside table? By whom and why? Did the bruises on her wrist mean she'd struggled with someone right before she died? Why? And did the ink and fibers on her hand mean she'd been holding a letter shortly before she died? If so, where was it? And why had she gone to that party in Santa Ynez? And why had she left the party and gone home to Montecito, days earlier than planned?

Kristi remembered the Italian man she'd met at the funeral and thought of the beautiful landscape paintings on the walls in Catherine's house. Lorenzo Bianchi spoken with such passion about Catherine at the vigil, and James' grandfather had mentioned she'd once had an affair with an artist. Kristi's instincts told her he'd been Catherine's lover, but her PI brain said, so what? Even if that were true, it didn't mean he killed her.

She rolled over and glanced at the clock on her bedside table. Half past eleven. The sheer curtains in her room did little to keep out the heat. Outside had to be hotter than Hades and a perfect day for the beach. She picked up the phone and dialed James. She hadn't been able to go surfing with him yesterday, but maybe today he could go swimming with her.

His answering machine clicked on, and she sighed. He hadn't called her back after the message she left him yesterday after the funeral. She didn't want to seem too clingy, so she hung up without leaving another message.

As she put the cordless phone back down on the bedside table, her eyes fell on her business card and Brian's home number. She'd written it there the night she'd talked to the jerk at La Paloma. Should she call him? She needed to update him on the case, so it'd be business and not a date or anything.

Maybe he won't even be home, she thought as she picked up the phone and dialed. "Brian?"

"Kristi." He said it without pause.

The way her heart flipped in her chest had nothing to do with business. She ignored it. "I'm going to the beach. You want to come?"

"Sure."

A short time later, Carla and Izzy drove to the beach. Her sister didn't have a car, and Kristi hadn't been able to deny Izzy's request to join her, not on such a hot day. When Izzy had then suggested inviting Carla and Gwen, Kristi figured, why not? Maybe it was safer if the Cota Club had her back, especially after what Carla had said about Brian liking her, plus her own muddled feelings.

The ocean off East Beach sparkled like a million sapphire blue gems under the hot October sun. Kristi and her sister stepped off the grassy berm and onto the sand.

"Gwen and Carla are over there." Izzy pointed to where their two friends lay on towels waving to them.

"Hooray for the Cota Club!" Gwen cheered when they arrived. "All we need is Tate to make it the full five. The magic number."

"Enough with the magic stuff, G." Carla held up her hand in a stop gesture toward her younger sister. "It's bad enough having to work at a magic shop six days a week. I don't need more of it on my one day off."

Izzy laughed. "Ever the rationalist, aren't you, Carla?"

"It's too hot for this conversation." Carla got to her feet. "Who wants to go swimming?"

"Brian's planning to meet me here. I'll wait, so he knows where to find me." Kristi watched everyone else dash off. She tried to ignore how intensely the sun beat down on her head and shoulders, and looked longingly at the others in the cold water.

"Hey there." Brian's familiar deep voice made her spin around. He wore only faded red swim trunks, a blue beach towel around his neck, and a pair of dark sunglasses. He was dark and tan, and when he smiled at her, he looked good. Too good.

She swallowed. "Perfect day for a swim, huh?"

"Sure is. Thanks for the invite." He gestured at the three towels lying beside hers. "Who else is here?"

"My sister and a couple of friends. Remember Carla from the other night?"

"Of course." He slid the towel from his shoulders and flipped it out beside hers. They stood together and looked out at the ocean and her friends romping in the water.

"Back when we lived on West Cota, Carla and her little sister Gwen were our neighbors."

"You used to live on Cota?"

"You sound surprised?"

He shrugged lean muscled shoulders, his eyes hidden behind the dark sunglasses. "No reason."

No reason, hah! She wasn't about to let his unspoken assumption go. Despite appearances, suburbia was so not her. "Look, my dad and mom wanted to move uptown, not me. I don't know about Izzy, but I miss living near our friends and the downtown vibe."

"I understand." He cleared his throat. "While we have a moment alone, I'd like to talk to you about something."

The serious tone of his voice made her look over at him. "What?"

His eyes were hidden behind the sunglasses, but his mouth twisted in a rueful shape. "Maybe it's not for me to say."

"What's going on?" Concern suddenly whooshed through her. "Is it about Rose?"

"Nothing like that. Forget it. It's none of my business. Let's go swim." He tossed his sunglasses on his towel and started toward the water.

She caught up with him and put a hand on his arm. No way was she going to let it drop, not when it was clear something was bothering him. "What's got you so worked up?"

"I'm not worked up. Like I said, it's none of my business."

"You've made it mine by starting this conversation, so come on, Brian, talk to me."

His eyes, normally so direct, didn't quite meet hers. "It's about the cocktail party the other night."

"What about it?" She had no idea what he was getting at.

"I'm probably reading more into it than I should."

Frustrated by his reticence, she put her hands on her hips and glared at him. "Out with it. What's bothering you?"

"After you left the party, James spent the rest of the evening with another woman. They left together."

"I see." Had it been that woman she'd seen in the car with James?

Brian looked out at the ocean. "I know it's none of my business, but if you don't mind my asking, how long has he been your boyfriend?"

"He's not my boyfriend." The words shot out of her mouth before she remembered that Brian hadn't known about her and James. Her heart did another little flip. Did his concern mean what she thought it did? "James and I only started seeing each other a month ago."

Brian's eyes drifted back to hers, but his face didn't give away what he was feeling. "You're not hurt about what I said?"

She shrugged. "You're probably reading too much into it." She didn't want to think about James and that woman. "What about you?" Taking a deep breath, she braved the question that had lurked in the back of her mind since meeting him. "You have a girlfriend?"

His lean, muscular shoulders lifted in a casual shrug. "It's been a while."

She couldn't stop the grin spreading across her face. Despite a twinge of guilt about James, knowing Brian was a free agent made her happy. "Let's go swimming!"

They ran down to the water and dove into the shorebreak. Swimming past the Cota Club, they set off at a fast pace toward the buoys, Brian adjusting his longer stroke to match hers. Kristi reveled in the sensual pleasure of propelling herself forward with powerful strokes, adjusting the cadence of her breath to match the force of her exertion, the cool water sliding along the length of her body. The whole experience felt magnified with Brian beside her.

When they paused at the turnaround point and treaded water to catch their breaths, Kristi looked back at the white strip of beach, the palm trees lining the grassy park by the road, and the high backdrop of the Santa Ynez Mountains, dark with chaparral. Smoke billowed up behind the eastern end of the range, its growing black plume marring an otherwise perfect, cerulean blue sky.

"It looks like there's a wildfire in the back country," Brian said.

Kristi thought of the Painted Cave Fire that had caused such devastation a couple of years ago. "I hope it stays back there."

"I don't think we have to worry. It looks pretty far away."

A pod of dolphins suddenly surfaced nearby, the sound of their breaths filling the air. Kristi and Brian watched silently together as the slick gray bodies slid smoothly upward and then back down into the sea. The pod swam by and continued eastward toward the beaches in Montecito.

Kristi smiled. "Aren't they awesome?"

"There's a Chumash story about dolphins that my dad learned from his grandpa. He used to tell it to me when I was little," Brian said.

Kristi pulled her eyes away from the dolphins. "Yeah?"

"It's about a rainbow bridge that once stretched all the way across the Santa Barbara Channel from Santa Cruz Island to the mainland. According to the legend, the Chumash used to be able to travel across the bridge. Every now and then, sometimes people fell off into the channel while crossing. Those people turned into dolphins, but they never forgot their family. And we never forgot them. That's why the Chumash have a tradition of calling the dolphins brothers."

Kristi watched the pod disappear and appreciated how rich and connected Brian's cultural heritage was to the world around him. "Thanks for sharing such a beautiful story with me."

"My pleasure." His eyes met hers.

He was treading water so close to her that she could see how the water beaded on his shoulders and made his hair seal-slick. She didn't want the moment to end, but she'd seen the others back on shore and knew they were probably wondering what she and Brian were doing, hanging out at the far buoy. "Race you back?"

Brian grinned. "Remember, I used to race swim team in college, so I'll give you a head start. Let's go!"

The rest of the afternoon passed for Kristi in a blur of delight. Everyone peppered Brian with questions, and he laughed and responded with a good-natured, carefree attitude she'd never seen before.

By the time they headed up from the beach, sun-dazed and salty, Kristi felt like they were all friends who'd known each other for years. Carla and Gwen left on foot to walk back to the Magic Shop, while Izzy climbed into Kristi's car and rolled down the windows to cool off the interior.

Kristi looked up at Brian. "Thanks for coming today. I had a great time."

He smiled back. "I did, too."

"We didn't get around to talking about my investigation." She hadn't wanted to ruin the perfect afternoon by bringing up work.

He shrugged. "We can do that tomorrow."

"Kristi!" Izzy shouted from the car, the sound of pop music pumping from the stereo. "What's taking you so long?"

Brian started to leave. Wanting, needing physical contact with him, Kristi reached out and grabbed his hand. He paused and looked down at her, his eyes masked by the dark sunglasses. She gave his hand a squeeze.

"Bye." She smiled self-consciously, embarrassed by her impulsive gesture.

Before she could pull her hand back, Brian captured it and lifted it to his mouth. When he pressed a kiss to the back of it, the warm contact of his lips sparked her all the way down to her toes.

"Come on!" Izzy shouted.

He released her hand and strode away to his dad's truck. Kristi stood watching him, tingling all over, until Izzy stuck her head out of the car and yelled again. Curling her fingers closed, she tried to hold on to the fading electricity. In that moment, she realized James had never made her feel like that.

28. The Money Man

Monday morning, Kristi walked into her office at the usual hour of 8 am. Unusually, the light was blinking on the answering machine. Maybe, just maybe, a potential new client had called. Rose's case wasn't going to last forever, and without more clients, Eye Spy Private Eye wasn't going to survive without a new infusion of money.

Thinking hopeful thoughts, Kristi pressed the "Play" button.

"Kristi, it's Brian. Please call me when you get a chance. I've got news."

At the sound of his voice, bright sunlit memories of the beach shimmered through her. It had been a wonderful afternoon, but it was past time they talked shop. She picked up the phone. "Good morning. Kristi here. What's up?"

"Hang on a sec." She heard a thump and guessed he must have put the phone down. Papers rustled and she heard him talking to someone, then a door closed. "Sorry about that. Anyway, I just spoke with my colleague handling Catherine's estate this morning. The distribution of assets will be made today."

"Can I be there when the will's read?" Maybe that would reveal someone with a real motive for killing Catherine.

Brian chuckled. "It's not like the movies where everyone gathers in one place for a series of dramatic revelations, at least not in this case. The recipients will be individually notified."

Kristi swallowed her embarrassment at sounding naive. "Did you find out who they are?"

"Got something to write with?"

She pulled the pad on her desk over and grabbed a pencil. "Shoot."

"The recipients include Catherine's niece Anita Walker, Rose Schmidt, Tabitha Tyson, Lorenzo Bianchi, and Sara Grice. The will also specifies the Montecito Pet Hospital and a relief organization in Africa."

Africa again? Kristi remembered what the church lady said. "Why did Catherine support an organization in Africa?"

"I have no idea. Is it relevant?"

"I don't know, but Pete told me the coroner's determined the paper fibers on Catherine's hand did come from an airmail letter. The letter must've been from Africa, considering there's no evidence Catherine had any other international connections."

"Does that matter?"

Kristi shrugged. "I don't know, but it's weird that the police didn't turn up any airmail letters when they searched her house. If she'd been holding one shortly before she died, where is it? The fact it's missing seems suspicious, like someone took it or something."

"You think Rose did?"

"Maybe, but the intruder could've, too."

"It does seem odd, but—" Brian exhaled, "how does it help prove Eduardo innocent?"

"It doesn't, not unless I can find the letter." It was Kristi's turn to sigh. "I found out Catherine was at a political fundraiser in Santa Ynez last Thursday."

"Really?"

"I know. Surprising for a 'recluse' to be out partying, especially on the night she was murdered. I'm going to talk to the party hosts and see if I can find out more about who Catherine was with at the party. I think we need to widen our net of suspects."

"Maybe."

Kristi wished Brian sounded more enthusiastic and less noncommittal, but it was true she was a long way from finding anything tangible to help Eduardo. She looked down at the names she'd written down. "You know anything about Tabitha Tyson or Sara Grice?"

"Nothing more than that Tabitha Tyson's a novelist. Remember the collection of her books in Catherine's bedroom?"

"Yeah." She needed to ask her librarian friend Rebecca if she'd read any of Tabitha's mysteries. Looking again at the list of names she'd written down, Kristi noticed something. "Don't you think it strange that Catherine singled out Rose but none of her other employees in her will?"

"She gave Eduardo those earrings."

"We don't have any proof of that, unless—" Kristi remembered that she still needed to talk to Catherine's money person.

"Yes?"

"Maybe there's a written record of her gifting the earrings to Eduardo. Do you think Catherine's money person has records of her financial transactions?"

"It's possible, but I'm not sure how her finances are handled. You should start by talking to her estate attorney, Julian Montclair. He's here at Byers and Martin on the second floor, but don't get your hopes up. The issue of confidentiality may keep him from sharing much." There came a knock on his end of the line and he said, "Sorry, but I've gotta go."

Kristi lucked out when she reached the estate attorney. He had a fifteen minute slot open at 9:45 am. When she left her office for the appointment, heat was already rising from the sidewalk as the sun beat down. She walked the several blocks to Byers and Martin, noting the world of difference between her two story office building, which was slightly seedy and aging, and the six-story Byers and Martin building, which gleamed with all the accouterments that servicing the Santa Barbara's financial elite could buy.

What a lot of brass and glass, she thought, as the automatic doors slid silently open and she walked into an air conditioned space that was cooled perfectly to keep the occupants composed and dignified in their plush setting. How did Brian feel working there?

Kristi had opted to wear a sundress because of the hot weather instead of her usual jeans and T-shirt, but she still felt hopelessly underdressed.

She rode the elevator to the second floor with two willowy women so well maintained that she had no idea how old they were. Both wore pressed linen blouses and skirts, not a strand of their styled platinum hair out of place. She stopped herself from reaching up to self-consciously smooth her own unruly curls. Giving the ladies a polite smile, she tried to stand taller in an attempt to appear more confident and self-possessed. Their faces remained expressionless.

When the bell dinged at the second floor, the two pairs of remote blue eyes followed her out of the elevator. The instant the doors closed, she heaved a sigh of relief. Though she wanted to be a bold and intrepid PI like Sue Grafton's Kinsey Millhone, who was she trying to kid? She walked down the hall to the estate attorney's office, mad at herself for being such a wimp.

"Thanks for seeing me on such short notice, Mr. Montclair," she said when the attorney waved her inside the spacious room that had views of the Santa Barbara Opera House.

"You have my ear until 10 o'clock, Miss McCormick." The man took a seat behind the large mahogany desk. He was middle-aged, with a receding hairline, horn-rimmed glasses, and a conservative navy business suit and tie. Like his outfit, his expression was polite and formal.

She handed a business card across the desk to him. "I'm a PI working on the Catherine Cole murder case with Brian Castillo, an attorney here at Byers and Martin."

"How may I be of assistance?" Blue eyes behind the horn-rimmed glasses studied her with detachment.

"I'm gathering background on Ms. Cole and how she spent her money." She gave him a friendly smile, hoping to breech his wall of formality. "How a person spends their money can reveal a lot about them, right?"

His face remained noncommittal. "I suppose, but you must understand that I am limited by confidentiality in what I can tell you about Miss Cole's financial affairs."

Kristi hadn't expected him to say anything different. Keeping the friendly smile on her face, she adopted a more formal tone, though she wished she was wearing something more professional than the bright blue sundress. It probably made her look even younger than she was. "I'm not asking you to violate your ethical code of conduct, Mr. Montclair, but may we speak in generalities?"

"Such as?"

"For starters, do you know if Miss Cole kept an itemized list of her jewelry?"

"She did."

"Do you have a copy of the list?"

"I do."

It was a long shot that he'd answer, but she had to ask, "Are there are any diamond earrings on the list?"

"I don't have the list in front of me, but regardless, Miss McCormick, I wouldn't be able to tell you if I did." He glanced at the gold boxed clock sitting on the desk and then picked up a pen, tapping it lightly against the desktop in a nervous gesture.

"Understood." She nodded and hurried on. "What about her spending habits? I don't need to know any dollar amounts or anything, but were there any unusual changes recently, maybe some large withdrawals in the last couple of months? And what about payees? Maybe there was someone new she was doing business with?"

At her volley of questions, Montclair shook his head. "I'm sorry, but Miss Cole received a monthly disbursement from her trust and conducted all her transactions in cash."

Cash? Kristi looked at him in surprise. "She didn't use credit cards?"

"No. All her transactions were conducted in cash."

"She paid everything, like her utility bills and mortgage and stuff in cash? What about checks? Did she at least write checks to do some of her banking?"

Montclair shook his head again. "As I said, she conducted all her transactions in cash. I have no record of where her money went."

"Why would she do that?" Could she have been hiding something?

Montclair shrugged. "I don't have a degree in psychology, Miss McCormick. It's not my job to understand my clients' motivations. For what it's worth, Miss Cole's assets were bound up in the irrevocable trust her father established for her when he was alive. It severely limited her access to the capital."

Kristi tried to make sense of what he said. "Wait, so she didn't have a lot of money she could actually use?" Was that why Catherine had given Eduardo jewelry instead of cash?

The attorney gave a small smile. "Let's just say she had sufficient funds for her lifestyle."

Kristi wondered exactly how much money he was talking about, but she knew he wouldn't tell her. Instead, she said, "Can you describe that lifestyle?"

His lips pursed. "I was only Miss Cole's trustee and estate attorney, nothing more. I couldn't possibly hazard to speculate about her lifestyle." His eyes went to the gold boxed clock again. "I'm sorry I can't be of more help, Miss McCormick, but it's time for my next appointment."

Kristi left the attorney's office more puzzled than ever over Catherine's money habits. Maybe she could talk to Brian about it. She rode the elevator up to the fifth floor. Unlike the opulent furnishings of the lobby and the attorney's office, Brian's floor housed a myriad small offices with glass walls and doors, which gave the place an overall fishbowl effect. A small army of people were hard at work inside the offices, some on phones, others on computers, still others poring over law books. The worker bees that powered the Byers and Martin legal machine, Kristi thought, as a receptionist not much older than she greeted her.

"I'm looking for Brian Castillo," Kristi said.

"I'm sorry, but he won't be back for a few hours. Do you want to make an appointment?"

"No thanks. I'll catch up with him later."

29. The Will

The sun beat down on Kristi's bare shoulders as she walked back to her office. When she passed the building manager's office, Haddon looked up from his TV and spotted her. Her heart sank when she heard the heavy plod of his steps following her up the stairs. She quickly unlocked her office door and stepped inside, hoping to shut and lock it before he got there, but she wasn't fast enough. He shoved his way into the room, his belly straining the lower buttons of his cheap polyester shirt. She was glad he was so busy ogling her that he left the door open behind him.

"Well, well, well, Miss McCormick, don't you look nice today." His squinty eyes took their time crawling down her sundress and focused way too long on her cleavage.

Ugh, what a lech! She resisted the urge to cross her arms over her chest and glared at him. "What do you want?"

"Well, for starters, where's the rest of your rent money?"

"I paid you last week."

"A half month's rent doesn't cut it, honey. I need it all."

"I'll pay you later today. I've been busy." This time she wasn't lying.

He moved closer, his eyes still on her body, as he smacked his lips in a disgusting manner. "You should dress like that more often. I like how it displays your tits."

Abruptly, he lunged for her. She jumped back, but one of his fingers hooked under a dress strap and tore it loose. She shoved his hand away, but the damage was done. One side of the haltertop fell forward and exposed her breast.

At the same instant, Brian walked in through the open door.

"Brian!" Angry and embarrassed, and all too aware of both men's eyes on her, Kristi fumbled to cover herself.

"What's going on here?" Brian had the good grace to keep his eyes on her face.

She wanted him to think her competent and not some damsel in distress, so she downplayed the situation. "Just a little accident." With one hand awkwardly holding the two pieces of fabric together, she hurried to her desk and pulled open the top drawer with her free hand, hoping to find a safety pin to fix her top.

Brian turned to Haddon and his lips turned downward in distaste. "You were here the other day. Who are you?"

Haddon tapped his chest with his thumb in a self-important manner. "I'm the building manager of this establishment, Mike Haddon." He cocked a thumb toward Kristi. "And she's behind on her rent."

"That's not true! I paid through the middle of October," Kristi said, relieved when she located a safety pin in a box of paper clips.

"Well, you need to pay it all. That's what the contract says." Haddon's eyes shifted back and forth between Brian and Kristi, but his eyes kept dropping rudely to her haltertop. She really, really wanted to go over and kick the guy in the crotch, but first she had to pin the torn strap back together.

"I am Miss McCormick's attorney." Brian crossed the room and positioned himself in front of her.

She realized gratefully that he was shielding her from Haddon, and though she couldn't see his face, she could see Brian's hands clenched into fists at his sides.

"If she is in violation of your contract, then you must notify her in writing as per the laws of this state. From what I am seeing here, however, I believe we have grounds to charge you with sexual assault. Wouldn't you agree, Miss McCormick?" He spoke in a forceful voice, made all the more powerful by the contained rage in it.

"Now, now, now, mister." The building manager's pale, fleshy hands shot up in a gesture of surrender. "No need to get legal. It was just a little misunderstanding. Right, Miss McCormick?"

"Hell, no!" Kristi's fingers were shaking so badly that she dropped the safety pin.

Brian stared down the building manager, who was starting to look like a hunted animal. "I think you owe Miss McCormick an apology."

"Sorry!" Haddon mumbled as he sidled out the door.

Brian went over and firmly closed it. "What a loathsome man."

Kristi located the safety pin under her desk and tried again to fix the haltertop. "Dang it!" she swore as she stabbed her finger with the pin. She really needed three hands: two to hold the pieces together and a third to pin them.

"May I help you with that?" Brian's gray eyes met hers.

"Yes, please." Her heart gave a little skip as she handed him the pin.

"Has Haddon done something like this before?" His voice was deep and low, practically against her ear, and his breath whispered across the sensitive skin on her neck as his long fingers worked to fasten the safety pin.

Butterflies fluttered up inside her and she swallowed. "I stopped him last time."

"That's not the point. I'm going to see about getting him fired."

"Please, not on my account. I'm going to find another office space as soon as I can afford it."

Brian gave the strap a tug to test that the safety pin would hold. "There, I think I fixed it."

"Thanks."

When his eyes lifted to hers, she was suddenly aware again of how much skin the sundress exposed. She tried but failed to tear her eyes away from the magnetic pull of his. Memories of how he'd kissed her hand at the beach and the electricity she'd felt zinged through her.

As if sensing her thoughts, his gaze dropped to her mouth. What would it feel like if he kissed her now? The thought made her lips go dry. She moistened them with her tongue.

His eyes shot to hers and he stepped back abruptly, as if burned. Letting out a deep breath, he ran his hands through his hair and turned away.

Kristi stumbled on quivery legs to the seat behind her desk and sat down, unsure of what to do or say.

When Brian turned back, his lawyer face was back in place. "Rose has been arrested."

"What?" It took a moment to shift gears and process what he said. "Why?"

"I don't know. Eduardo called me when he was released, but he didn't have the details." Brian turned and walked over to the small office window. Tension radiated from him as he looked out. "There's something else you should know."

Kristi got up and walked over to him. "What is it?"

"Catherine's will leaves Rose almost everything."

"What?"

"I just found out. That's why I came here to tell you. Catherine changed the terms of her will a month ago. Rose stands to acquire assets worth upwards of fifty million dollars."

"Oh." Kristi stared at Brian and felt like she'd been punched in the gut. What a windfall for Rose...what a motive for murder... "Was that why Rose was arrested?"

Brian was still looking out the window, but she could tell he wasn't focused on the lousy view. "Maybe, but I doubt it's sufficient probable cause. More likely, the police have found something truly incriminating."

"Wait, what about the other people in Catherine's will? Did she leave Lorenzo Bianchi anything?"

"Not much compared to Rose. Same with the other people, including her niece. Anyway, I need to go and see what they've got against Rose."

When he turned back from the window, he was standing so close to her that she could smell the appealing scent of his aftershave. His eyes caught hers again, and her thoughts about Rose and the case skittered away.

All she wanted to do was reach up and smooth the tension from his face, run her fingers over the high cheekbones and down the strong line of his jaw, trace the firm line of his lips. Somewhere in the distance, a car horn honked.

She swallowed, her hands clutching the soft fabric of the sundress. Something subtle shifted in his eyes, and as if reading her mind, his hand came up and gently cupped her face. When his thumb traced the curve of her mouth, lightning awareness arced down her body and she gasped.

"Kristi?" His thumb paused on the full swell of her lower lip.

She felt she was teetering on a precipice about to fall, her heart hammering a hundred miles an hour. It was all she could do to breathe the one word, "Yes."

His eyes shot dark and he curled an arm about her waist, pulling her against him. She gave a little sigh of pleasure as he lifted her upward, her body curving to fit the long line of his so well she felt dizzy with the steel-like strength of him. He bent to kiss her, and when their mouths fused, her thoughts winged away.

The kiss deepened and reason fled. She forgot everything but the feel of him kissing her, holding her. He wanted her. She could feel it in how he kissed her, in how his body moved against her. Putting her arms around his neck, she sank her fingers into his hair and urged him closer.

The phone rang.

When he started to pull back, she clung to him. "Don't stop."

He started to kiss her again as the answering machine clicked on.

"Hey, babe. It's me, James. Sorry for not getting back to you sooner, but work got hectic. Call me. I want to see you."

James' voice was like a drenching bucket of ice water. Kristi stared at Brian in shocked dismay. How could she have forgotten James?

Brian released her and stepped back, his face dark and conflicted, his breath heavy in his chest. "I'm sorry, Kristi. That wasn't supposed to happen."

Kristi's legs were trembling so much she could barely stand, and before she could gather her wits enough to reply, he spun around and was gone.

She collapsed into her chair, her body and mind whirling. No one had ever kissed her like that. Not James, and certainly not her few, inexperienced high school boyfriends. She let out a long, shaky breath and dragged her hands through her hair. They should keep their relationship professional. Of course. But wow.

The light on the answering machine was still blinking. Kristi really wanted to go outside and take a walk to clear her head, but she wasn't ready for another encounter with the building manager.

Instead, she got up and paced the room. She needed to call James back, but guilt as well as something more complicated twisted inside her. It wasn't just that she couldn't imagine talking to him while the feel and taste of Brian were still fresh on her lips but that she was realizing her feelings for Brian went way beyond a business relationship.

He was so very different from James, not merely in appearance, but in everything about him, from his family and the way he grew up to the fundamental essence of his personality. If she was honest with herself, she had to admit she found him much more relatable. James had attracted her because he was from a world she knew little about, a world that seemed glamorous and luxurious, and one that part of her hoped to enter one day. Her parents, too, held hopes that James would be a step up for her. She doubted her dad would be nearly as enthusiastic about Brian.

The light was still blinking. She picked up the receiver and listened to the dial tone as she deliberated what to say to James. Glancing down, her eyes landed on the notepad where she'd jotted down Lorenzo Bianchi's phone number the day of Catherine's funeral.

And then she remembered: Rose had been arrested. Why? She dialed her uncle at the Santa Barbara Police Department but got his answering machine.

Staring at the notepad, she thought about what Brian had said. With Catherine changing her will so recently and in such a way as to make Rose the primary beneficiary, Kristi had to admit it looked suspicious. Still, when she recalled her encounters with Rose and what other people said about her, Rose didn't strike Kristi as capable of murder.

She looked again at Lorenzo Bianchi's number. She needed a lead on other possible suspects and calling him would be a lot easier than calling James. She dialed the number. The phone rang and rang. About the twentieth ring, a deep baritone voice came on the line.

"Yes?" The man sounded distracted.

"Is this Lorenzo Bianchi?"

"Yes. You are—?"

She reminded him of their meeting at Catherine's funeral. "Is there any chance I can meet with you, maybe tomorrow? I promise it won't take too much of your time."

"Tomorrow for lunch. One o'clock." He rattled off an address in Pismo Beach and hung up before she could reply.

She pulled out a AAA map from her desk and spread it out. If she was going to drive way up north to Pismo, she might as well stop in Santa Ynez and interview Beverley and Ridley if she could.

Having met the couple, she suspected she'd have more luck with Beverly. She found the woman's number and address in the phone book. Kristi considered simply interviewing Beverly over the phone but then decided that, if she could, she should see where the party took place and reenact the drive Catherine took to Montecito. That way she'd have a better sense of the timing of events that fateful night.

"Why I'd be happy to talk to you about the party, Miss McCormick," Beverly said when she picked up. "However, I'm quite busy the next few weeks with wedding preparations, and my schedule is tight."

After some discussion, they agreed that Kristi would go to Beverly's place the next day at 5 o'clock.

Kristi dropped the phone on the receiver and looked at the list of people named in Catherine's will. After Lorenzo came Anita Walker. Kristi tapped her pencil on the notepad, remembering the stylishly dressed dark-haired woman who'd spoken at Catherine's vigil. It hadn't sounded like she'd been all that close to her aunt, and the police hadn't treated her like a suspect, which implied she had a solid alibi. On the other hand, the woman might know something useful. Besides, Kristi still wasn't ready to talk to James.

Anita answered on the first ring. Kristi launched into her spiel. "Hi Ms. Walker, I met you the other night at your aunt's service."

"What's this about?"

"Like I said the other night, I'm a PI. I'm working on a few leads associated with her death."

"What leads?" Anita's sharp voice sounded harried.

"Why don't we start with the night your aunt died. Where were you—"

"Where was I? That's none of your business."

"I know, but—"

"But nothing! As far as I'm concerned, the case is closed. Don't call me again." The phone slammed down on the other end of the line.

And you'll inherit all that lovely money, Kristi thought, if Rose was arrested. The woman's words drove home the hard fact that if Kristi didn't find out who the real killer was, Rose was as good as done for.

She picked up the phone and made more calls from the list. Sara Grice owned a bookstore in San Luis Obispo and arranged to see her tomorrow morning. She had much less luck tracking down Tabitha Tyson. No one seemed to know where the mystery writer lived, and when Kristi tried calling her publishing company, they told her that Tabitha Tyson preferred to live in anonymity and that her contact information was not available to the public. Kristi hung up the phone, doubting Tabitha could shed much light on the case. Catherine had undoubtedly left the mystery writer money because she was a fan of Tabitha's books. There was no one else on the list and the light on the answering machine was still blinking. Time to call James.

When James picked up, Kristi forced a chipper, casual note into her voice. "Hey, James, it's me, Kristi."

"I've been worried about you. How you holding up now that your client's in jail?"

"Why did the police arrest her?"

"They found Catherine's jewelry in her car, but let's not talk shop. I want to see you."

"Wait, Catherine's jewelry was in Rose's car?" That didn't make sense. Rose wouldn't be dumb enough to keep stolen property in her car, would she?

James was still talking. "Look, I've gotta go, babe. Things are slammed over here. How about lunch tomorrow at the club?"

Kristi remembered the appointments she'd just made. "I'm booked tomorrow. Can we make it Wednesday, instead?"

She heard him flipping the pages of an appointment book on his end of the line. "Ah, yes. I've got a big block Wednesday afternoon. Bring your suit and maybe we can squeeze in a swim."

When he'd taken her to lunch at the club before, he'd never invited her to swim. The attractive pool with its ocean and mountain views had always beckoned to her and the thought of swimming in it was very appealing. Besides, it sounded like he really wanted to see her. Despite the conflicted state of her feelings about him and Brian, she was flattered. "Thanks, that sounds nice."

"Great. See you then."

He signed off before she could say anything more. She hadn't asked him about the long blond-haired woman or why he hadn't called her back all weekend, but she'd do that later. What mattered now was what he'd told her about the jewelry in Rose's car.

Kristi jumped to her feet and paced. It seemed obvious: the person who broke into Rose's car hadn't stolen anything; they'd put it in. Kristi thought of the sports car the subletter had seen. There was also the sports car Catherine's neighbor had seen. Finally, there was Rose's claim about an intruder. Kristi's instincts told her these weren't coincidences but connected to the same person. Who?

She tried calling her uncle again. This time, he answered. "Hey, Uncle Pete."

"Krissy, what's up?"

"You didn't get my message?"

"No, I just got back and I've gotta leave again in a few."

"OK, I'll make this fast. How did the police know to search Rose's car for Miss Cole's jewelry?"

"We got an anonymous tip." Pete exhaled. "I'm sorry about your first client."

"An 'anonymous tip'?" She thought of her theory about someone planting the jewelry. "Sounds like she's being set up."

"That's a stretch."

"Maybe, but answer me this. If Rose killed Catherine, why bother stealing the jewelry, since she was going to inherit almost everything anyway?"

"She may not have known the exact terms of the will, but it doesn't matter. I'm sorry, Krissy. The jewelry was in her possession. You should know that's grounds for arrest."

"I understand, but I just can't imagine Rose would be stupid enough to hide stolen property in her car."

"People do stupid stuff all the time, especially under duress. Like Schmidt's attempt to deflect blame by inventing that intruder."

"What if there actually was an intruder?"

"As I said the other night, there's no evidence to support her claim. I mention it simply as an example of how someone can crack under pressure. Schmidt's desperate to cast blame somewhere other than herself, now that she's been arrested."

"Come on, Pete." Kristi tried to keep her voice calm, but the way he was talking about Rose was starting to sound like James, and it was making her mad. "Just because you haven't found evidence doesn't mean it isn't true. I mean, what about that anonymous tip? How did the person even know about the jewelry? Isn't it possible that it was the intruder trying to frame Rose? Maybe he put the jewelry in her car when it was broken into the other night."

"Look, we've found absolutely no credible evidence to back up her intruder claim." Pete sighed. "Don't go reaching, Krissy. This has been one of the highest profile murder investigations our fair town has seen in a while. I can certainly imagine why someone with pertinent information would want to remain anonymous if they could. I'm sorry, but I've got to go."

"Wait, is there any chance you can get me in to see Rose?"

"I'm sorry, but she's already been sent over to County for processing."

"Please, Uncle Pete, I really need to talk to her." She had to run her theory by Rose and ask Rose about Catherine's will.

"No can do, Krissy, but you're part of her defense team. Brian should be able to get you in. Good luck." He hung up before she ask anything else.

30. Some Answers and a Clue

It was after 3 o'clock when Kristi took the freeway west to the Santa Barbara County Jail. Pete was right. Brian was able to arrange an interview for her with Rose, and she really hoped Rose could provide some answers to her many questions. The air conditioner in her beater sedan was on the fritz again. Sweating, she rolled the window down and let the desert-hot air stream inside, blowing her short blond curls every which way. She didn't care. She doubted Rose would, either.

When she exited the off-ramp, she was surprised to discover that the jail was in the same general neighborhood as Rose's low income condo. The area was off the beaten path, where no money had been spent to make things beautiful with the Spanish Mission architecture so prevalent in the touristy areas of town. The jail was big, boxy, and industrial-looking building, with surveillance and security measures boldly proclaimed everywhere Kristi looked. Uniformed sheriffs and other county personnel surrounded her, and she felt a little too naked in her sundress, as she entered the facility, especially when several grungy-looking men being booked whistled and catcalled, until they were silenced by one of the officers.

After an unpleasantly long wait in the booking area, which, though not crowded, was still too hot and stuffy for comfort, Kristi was guided by a female correctional officer through several sets of corridors and associated locking doors to a private visitation room. Unlike the booking area, it was refreshingly air conditioned. Kristi sat down at one of the two chair, and a minute later, Rose was brought in.

Kristi hadn't seen her since Catherine's vigil, but she hardly recognized her. Rose seemed tiny and shrunken inside the over-sized orange jail suit, and her complexion had an unappealing tinge of yellow in it under the harsh fluorescent overhead lights. Deep circles pooled under her eyes.

Kristi gave her a sympathetic smile. "I'm sorry you were arrested—"

"There's something I need you to do," Rose interrupted, her dark eyes desperate behind the thick glasses. "Can you help me?"

Intrigued, Kristi asked, "Sure, what is it?"

Rose's words came on a long, quiet gush of breath, as if she'd been holding them in for so long they just had to come out. "There's an envelope in my mail cubby at the Education Station. I didn't know where else safe to put it, not after my car was broken into. Please, can you get it as soon as you can and keep it for me? Please. It's really important. There's a necklace inside. It was Catherine's."

"A necklace?" Kristi looked at Rose, an unpleasant sinking sensation in her stomach. "Shouldn't we turn it over to the police?"

"No!" Rose clenched her shackled hands together on the table so tightly that her knuckles turned white. Her dark eyes sought Kristi's again. "I'm sorry I can't explain. Please, just promise me you'll keep Catherine's necklace safe, OK? It needs to be kept secret."

"Why? Did you steal it?"

Tears suddenly burst from Rose's eyes. "It wasn't like that. I'm sorry. I'm so sorry. I took it for Catherine."

"You took it for Catherine? What does that mean?"

Rose swiped at the tears with her hands, the handcuffs jangling against her wrists. "I'm sorry, but I can't tell you."

Kristi had no idea what Rose meant, but there was a more pressing question. "What about all Catherine's jewelry the police found in your car? You take that, too?"

Rose shook her head violently. "Of course not!"

Kristi proposed her theory. "Someone put the jewelry in your car. I think it was when they broke into your car. I think they planted it to set you up."

Rose's flushed face blanched. "The intruder must know who I am." Her face crumpled and she started crying again. "He killed her, but it's all my fault."

Kristi stared at her in confusion. "What do you mean?"

"I could've stopped him. I should have. But I froze. God, why was I such a coward? Catherine wouldn't be dead, except for me."

"Didn't you say the intruder pushed Catherine down the stairs? He's the responsible one. He should be in jail, not you."

Rose kept shaking her head, sobbing. "I should've done something. I should've, but I froze. It's all my fault."

Kristi realized Rose was too upset to think rationally. She tried another approach. Gently, she said, "Can you tell me why you froze?"

Rose drew a deep, shuddering breath. She took off her glasses and wiped her eyes awkwardly on the sleeves of her jail suit. When she finally looked at Kristi again, her eyes looked haunted and strangely bruised. "My family wasn't a happy one. Not just my parents, but my aunts and uncles, cousins, grandparents." She spoke in a quiet, controlled monotone, reciting facts without feeling. "We lived out in the back woods of Wisconsin, where there was no hope and no jobs, and we were surrounded by generations of despair and frustrated dreams. My father was a big guy, really big, and he was powerful and strong, but he felt weak. That doesn't excuse what he did, but it explains him."

Kristi listened, unsure where this was going and aware the clock was ticking down on their interview. "Let's get back to Catherine and the intruder."

"Sorry." Rose seemed to shrink even more into the over-sized orange jail suit. "What I'm trying to say is that my dad beat on my mom, and us. I was the oldest. I was supposed to protect my little brother Billy, but I couldn't, not when the rage took Dad. He killed Billy, but I didn't stop him." She let out a deep sigh. "When I heard the man and Catherine fighting—" She broke off and stared at her shackled hands.

Kristi leaned forward, hopeful she'd finally get the truth from Rose. "What did you do?"

"I didn't know what to do. I couldn't understand why Catherine was at home, or why she was so angry. I was in the kitchen and Catherine and the man were shouting somewhere upstairs. I was so scared. When I finally worked up enough nerve to go down the hallway to the foyer, that's when I heard the most terrible sound, thudding, falling, like when my dad..."

"Yes?"

Rose gulped. "There was this awful silence. It went on and on. I knew something horrible had happened. I could feel it, but I was so afraid." She wiped her eyes again and then let out another deep, shuddering breath. "I peeked around the corner into the foyer. Catherine was lying at the bottom of the stairs. The man ran down the stairs and out the front door."

"You said before he was tall with light-colored hair. Can you remember anything else about him? We really need to find that man."

Rose bitterly shook her head. "I've tried to remember, but I can't. I'm sorry. I should've stopped him, but I froze. I should've checked on Catherine sooner. I should've called the police. I should've done something! But I didn't. It's my fault she's dead. Just let them lock me up."

"How can you say that?" Kristi was outraged. "The guilty man should pay for his crimes."

"It's better this way," Rose said in a resigned tone.

Kristi frowned. "Did you know Catherine changed her will and made you primary beneficiary?"

"Brian told me." Rose nodded, tears starting to stream from her eyes again. "Oh poor, poor Catherine! I don't deserve such generosity."

"You won't get any of the money if you're convicted of her murder." Kristi studied her client. "Why did she change her will? Were you and she in some kind of relationship?"

"It was nothing like that!" Rose looked at her, shocked. "I house sat for her and we were friends. I loved her, but we were friends. Just friends!"

"Then why are you willing to go to jail for her?"

"I told you. It's my fault she's dead."

Rose was obviously suffering from massive guilt, but was it because she'd actually killed Catherine as James and her uncle said, or was she punishing herself for having failed Catherine, and her little brother?

The only way to know for sure was to prove there had been an intruder. Kristi glanced at her watch that they were almost out of time. She remembered one of her questions for Rose. "Was Catherine holding anything in her hand when you went to check her pulse?"

"Why're you asking?"

"Ink and paper fibers from an airmail letter were found on her right hand, but the police didn't find it in the house." Kristi had an idea. "Did you take it?"

"No!" Rose's face went white. She gave a sharp jerk of her head. "There was nothing in her hands. Nothing."

"Come on, Rose. Talk to me. You obviously know something." If Rose hadn't taken the letter, then the intruder must have. Kristi went out on a limb. "Was Catherine arguing with the man about a letter?"

Rose nodded slowly. "They were arguing about some letters. They belonged to Catherine, but the man wouldn't give them back to her. They were struggling over them."

Kristi tried to rein in her excitement. "What were the letters about?"

Rose looked down at her shackled hands resting on the table, her face crumpling again into sadness. "It doesn't matter. Not now. Poor Catherine."

"It does matter!" Kristi fought to keep her voice calm. "It sounds to me like that argument and those letters were the reason she was killed."

Just then, the uniformed police officer came back into the room. "Time's up, Miss McCormick. Come along, Miss Schmidt."

Rose looked over her shoulder at Kristi. "Don't forget to get that envelope."

Kristi watched Rose shuffle out of the room, wanting to gnash her teeth in frustration.

Why wouldn't Rose tell her what those letters had been about? Their contents would likely reveal the intruder's motive for murder and could potentially exonerate Rose. And what about the necklace she wanted Kristi to keep secret "for Catherine"? What secrets did Catherine have?

As Kristi left the county jail, she realized she now had a few answers. She now understood why Rose had been so afraid to talk to big men like Brian and Pete, and a life-time of guilt about her little brother's death explained why Rose felt so guilty about Catherine's death and why she was willing to take the murder rap.

Still, what of the missing letters? Had the intruder also removed a photograph from Catherine's bedside table? There hadn't been time to ask Rose. Driving out of the county jail parking lot, Kristi kept wondering. Who was the man? How did Catherine know him? Letters and secrets made it seem like blackmail somehow factored into Catherine's murder, but how? The first thing was to get a hold of that necklace and see if it offered any clues.

Kristi drove to the Education Station, worried about the ethical implications of what she was about to do, considering she was about to enter private property with the intent of removing something that had been stolen and was possible evidence in a murder case. What if she got caught? Pete would be so angry. She doubted Brian would approve. More importantly, she'd be arrested and lose the chance to get her PI license.

Should she just call Pete and tell him about the necklace so the police could take over? But what was so important about the necklace and why had Rose insisted she keep it a secret? Kristi would never know if she didn't check it out. Besides, she told herself, as she went into the school, Kinsey Millhone and the other PIs she'd read about didn't always stick to the strict letter of the law.

The last time she'd been to the Education Station, she hadn't been up to anything illegal. Now, she was overly aware that the hallway and common areas were crowded with dark-haired Asian students and that she stood out like a sore thumb with her blond hair. What if someone asked what she was doing there?

Spotting a display of information pamphlets, she had an idea. She grabbed a pamphlet and pretended to read it, hoping that by avoiding eye contact with the other students, she'd escape detection. The pamphlet was a tourist brochure advertising kayaking excursions around the Channel Islands. Looked like fun, but the price tag was well beyond anything she could afford.

Tide of people carried her along to the large common area at the center of the school. Surreptitiously, she noted that the same middle-aged woman she'd asked about Rose's teaching schedule stood at the counter. The mailbox cubbies Rose had told her to look for were housed in a wall behind the counter. Kristi couldn't just waltz over there, scan the mail boxes for Rose's, and grab the envelope, not with that woman standing guard. What to do?

She ambled over to the wall closest to the mailboxes and kept her back to the woman, which put her mostly outside the woman's line of sight. The mailboxes were arranged alphabetically. Rose's was not more than six feet away from her, near the bottom of the array.

Several white envelopes protruded from the open box. Kristi's heart rate jumped as she glanced over her shoulder. The woman was still talking to the students. It was now or never.

She shoved the pamphlet in her purse and sidled over to the mailbox, grabbed the collection of envelopes, and turned to make her escape.

"Excuse me, what are you doing?"

Uh oh, the woman had spotted her.

She didn't want the woman to ID her, so she kept her back to the woman and pretended not to hear, rushing away into the crowd. She had no idea if the woman was hot on her heels, not with the loud chaotic conversations all around her, so she pushed through the crowd as fast as she could, smiling and muttering, "Excuse me."

Fighting the urge to break into a guilty run when she got outside, she made herself walk in a fast but purposeful direction to her car.

31. The Locket

Kristi's heart was still pumping fast when she got back to the safety of her office. Thank goodness she hadn't identified herself during her first visit to the Education Station or the police would be on their way to pick her up right now.

Locking the door securely behind her, she went to her desk and sorted through the envelopes she'd taken Several looked like personal notes from students; there was an official-looking one that might be a paycheck, and there was one that was unlabeled. Unlike the others, it had something heavier in it than paper.

Opening it carefully at one end, Kristi tipped the contents onto the desk. A pendant slid out. She recognized it. It was the necklace Rose was wearing the first time they met. She sat down and examined the pendant.

It formed a slim, circular gold disk about an inch in diameter and a quarter inch thick. She'd originally assumed the shiny bits on its face were rhinestones, but were they actually diamonds? Pulling her magnifying glass from her purse, she examined them more closely. Each stone's facets were perfectly cut. They had to be diamonds, she thought, and admired the intricate pattern they formed, which was as beautiful as it was complex. The thing was obviously valuable and of a different era, but Kristi had no experience with antiques. Was it Victorian? Older?

She turned it over. On the other side, the letter "M" was written in an old-fashioned script. Who was "M"? As she started to turn the pendant over again, she noticed a tiny thin line running around the edge of it. Did it open? She picked up the magnifying glass again, when a knock sounded on the door.

Putting down the necklace, she went and stood by the locked door. She doubted it was the building manager, not after Brian's threat of a lawsuit, but nonetheless, she opted for caution. "Who's there?"

From the other side, a woman's voice said, "It's me, Reb."

Kristi unlocked the door.

Her red-haired friend from the library came in, holding two cups of coffee and a paper bag. "What's up with the locked door?"

Kristi shrugged. "Good to take security precautions."

Reb handed her one of the cups."I have a half-hour break and I was jonesing for a cup of coffee. Thought you'd like one, too. I also brought some brownies."

"Yum, brownies! Thanks." Kristi was eager to get back to inspecting the necklace, but she always had time for a brownie.

Reb sat down in the chair across from her and yawned. "I love being a librarian, but the afternoons are a killer to get through. Speaking of killers, how's it going with your case?"

Kristi munched the brownie. Though they were old high school friends, Reb wasn't nearly as close to her as Carla and the rest of the Cota Club. She wasn't sure how much she could trust her. "OK, I guess."

Reb's curious eyes were on the pendant lying on the desk. "Nice necklace. Yours?"

"No." Rose had asked her to keep the thing a secret but had provided no reasonable rationale, not as far as Kristi was concerned.

"It may be a clue," she said, putting aside her unfinished brownie. She picked up the magnifying glass again. Yes, the pendant did have a seam! Using a fingernail, she traced along the narrow side of the pendant and felt a slight protrusion on the pendant's edge. She gently pushed it, and the pendant popped open. "It is a locket."

"Cool! What's inside?" Reb came around the desk as she pried open the two halves.

One side featured a tiny color photograph of a woman with short blond hair, perhaps not much older than herself.

Rose pointed. "Who's that?"

Was it a young Catherine? Kristi grabbed the magnifying glass and looked. Nope. The hair was too straight and the face too round. "I don't know."

A tiny dried flower had been mounted on the other half of the locket. She didn't recognize it. She looked up at Reb. "You know anything about flowers?"

"That looks like a wildflower of some sort. I've got a friend who's a member of the California Native Plant Society. He could probably identify it, if you want." Reb's intelligent blue eyes were keen interest and she looked eager to help.

"Sure, but it's more important to ID that woman." Kristi put down the open locket and finished the brownie. "I'm sorry I can't go into all the details, but maybe you can help me with a little mystery. See the letter 'M' engraved on the back? I'm guessing the woman's name begins with the 'M.'"

Women's names beginning with the letter 'M' popped into Kristi's mind. Maria, Mary, Marsha, Mathilda, Michelle, Monica...there were a lot of women's names that began with 'M.' Rose must know, or why would she have taken the locket and said to keep it secret? Did the secret have something to do with the intruder and the letters he took from Catherine?

Aloud, Kristi said, "I'm pretty sure 'M' was someone very important to the murder victim but that her identity had to be kept a secret."

"A secret?" Reb's eyes sparked with curiosity. "What kind of secret?"

Kristi shrugged. "That's the thing, I don't know. My guess is it had something to do with the reason the victim was killed."

"Blackmail?"

"Maybe, but blackmail about what? The only thing I can think of is 'M' was her lover or her child."

Reb looked up from the locket. "Catherine Cole was a lesbian?"

Kristi thought of Lorenzo Bianchi and shook her head. "There's no evidence to suggest that, not from what anyone has said, but she never did marry."

Rebecca chuckled. "Hah! That doesn't mean anything. Look at me. I'm still waiting for my Prince Charming." Her bushy red eyebrows scrunched together as she studied the photo in the locket. Finally, she said, "My vote is that 'M' was her secret child."

"Secret child? Sounds like the plot of a cheesy novel." Kristi laughed, but the woman in the photo looked like she could be related to Catherine, and there was what James' grandfather had said. Had Catherine's youthful wildness gone so far as to have an illegitimate child? Catherine's conservative family would surely want to hide such a scandal. Maybe someone had found out.

Her friend's voice broke into her thoughts. "Look, it's just a theory, but think about it. If this woman was a secret child, then there's a father out there somewhere. Could he play a role in the blackmail scenario?"

"I don't know." Kristi shook her head. "Why would the killer, whether he was the father or not, want to kill the victim, especially if she was paying him money to keep her secret?"

Reb shrugged. "There could be a myriad motives, but if you boil them down to their most essential ingredients, I'd say they almost always involve love or money."

Kristi heard an echo of something James had once said. "What about their opposites? Wouldn't hate and poverty be more likely to motivate someone to kill?

"People don't hate in a vacuum, and poor people don't just go around killing people."

Reb had a point. "I don't see how love or hate could've driven the people I've spoken with to kill her, so the motive must be money."

"Sounds logical." Reb glanced at her watch, then finished her coffee and tossed the cup in the waste bin. She stood up. "My break's over. Time to get back to the library."

Kristi watched her friend head for the door when she remembered another question she had. "You ever read any Tabitha Tyson mysteries?"

Reb turned and arched a brow at her. "Of course. Hers are historical and all set in a convent in Medieval England. One of her favorite themes is the idea of self-sacrifice for a higher purpose." Reb glanced again at her watch. "I've really gotta run now."

Kristi locked the door after Reb hurried down the stairs. Id didn't sound like Tabitha's mysteries were her cup of tea. She wasn't a fan of historical stuff.

She went and picked up the locket again, her brain spinning with Reb's theory about a secret child. Lorenzo Bianchi had spoken about Catherine with such feeling at the vigil. Could he have been the child's father? Had he found out and been angry enough to kill? But what about the airmail letter? Who'd sent it, and how did Africa factor in? Had someone else found out about 'M' and been blackmailing Catherine? Why hadn't Catherine left 'M' any money in her will? Had 'M' died?

Kristi hazarded a sip of the coffee Reb had brought her. It was now cold, but still tasty. Maybe it was the caffeine working on her brain, but Kristi realized Rose must know 'M's identity. That's why she'd been so insistent about hiding the necklace. Kristi picked up the phone and called the county jail.

32. Blackmail?

Unfortunately, the county jail refused to let Kristi speak to Rose without prior authorization from Brian, and she didn't hear from him until much later that night, when he finally returned her call. It was after dinner, and she was lying on her bed reading the latest Sue Grafton mystery, when her mom knocked on the door.

"It's a man. Says his name is Brian Castillo?"

Kristi had talked to her mom in general terms about the case but had never mentioned Brian for the very reason there was that question in her mom's eyes. It didn't help that she kept reliving the last time she saw Brian and the kiss they'd shared. Boy would her mom not approve, not with her dating James.

Closing the book, she got out of bed and tried to squelch the guilty flush moving up her cheeks. "He's my client's attorney."

"Kind of late for a business call, isn't it?"

"He's returning my call." Though Kristi was eager to talk to Brian, she was sick and tired of being interrogated about her personal life by her parents. Trying not to sound impatient or irritated, she said, "Mom, PIs work odd hours." She held out her hand for the phone.

Her mom's eyebrows shot up, but she did as Kristi asked. When she'd gone, Kristi closed the door firmly behind her. "Hey Brian, thanks for getting back to me." She went back to her bed and lay down, trying not to remember the kiss.

"Sorry to call you at home and so late. I hope I'm not interrupting anything?"

"Not at all." A thrill ran through her at hearing his deep voice, but she tamped it down, remembering what he'd said about maintaining a professional relationship. "We've got a lot to talk about."

He cleared his throat. "I'm sorry. I shouldn't have kissed you."

So much for keeping things professional. Her lips tingled. She tried to sound casual. "As I recall, it was a mutual thing."

Did the silence on his end of the line mean he was remembering the kiss, too? Was he calling her from his office, or was he maybe lying on his bed like she was?

At the intimate image, she rushed on, trying to cover the tense silence. "Besides, you already apologized. Anyway, that's not why I've been trying to reach you. When I met with Rose at the jail, she told me Catherine had a secret, which she's been trying to protect."

"What secret?"

"Rose wouldn't tell me, but I thought maybe she told you, maybe when you met with her after she was arrested this morning?"

"No."

"Did she mention any letters?"

"Letters?"

Kristi filled him in on the details of her interview with Rose and the revelation that Catherine and the man had been fighting over some letters.

She considered mentioning the locket and the mysterious "M," but she didn't know how to do it without revealing that she and Rose had broken the law. If she figured out how the locket factored into the case, then she'd tell him about it.

In the meantime, she simply said, "Blackmail may have been the motive for the murder and not simply greed."

"Blackmail? How do you figure that?"

"I'm still trying to connect the dots." She wished she had something more definite to tell him. "But I want to know what was in those letters. It must've been something really important. Why else was Catherine willing to fight to the death for them?"

Brian yawned. "Why didn't Rose tell me about them, since I'm her defense counsel?"

"Maybe it had to do with why you hired me." Kristi rolled onto her stomach. "Rose didn't feel safe opening up to you, and I found out why today. Turns out she isn't comfortable dealing with big men. Her father was a big guy and abused his family so badly he ended up killing her little brother while she looked on, unable to stop him. That's why she freaked when she heard the intruder fighting with Catherine. Too many bad memories."

"Poor Rose. I had no idea."

"Yeah." Their conversation made Kristi think of her own dad. Though he was strict, he was a pussycat, and he loved her.

Brian spoke again. "Let's get back to those letters. Does Rose know where are they now?"

"No, but the blackmailer must've taken them."

"The 'blackmailer'?" Brian blew out a long breath. "Kristi, I appreciate how hard you're working to exonerate Rose, but the blackmail angle doesn't make sense. Think about it. If the intruder was the blackmailer, killing Catherine would mean losing his money stream. More likely, he'd kill her because she was blackmailing him, but really? Catherine a blackmailer? There's no evidence to support it."

Kristi sighed, rolling onto her back and staring blindly at the ceiling. "You're right, it doesn't make sense, but why was the intruder there that night? From what Rose said, it sounds like the letters were the reason. She also said Catherine had a secret she was trying to hide. It seems like more of a stretch that the letters were completely unrelated to the secret Catherine was hiding. If you connect the dots, doesn't it seem like blackmail must've played a part in the intruder's motives?"

"I don't know." Brian yawned again. "I'll ask Rose about Catherine's secret, but without those letters, there's no tangible evidence of blackmail, and even the letters may not be enough to prove your theory."

"Yeah." Kristi doubted Rose would tell Brian. "Did Rose ever mention anything to you about a woman who's name starts with the letter 'M'?"

"No. Is she important?"

"I don't know." Kristi considered telling him her theory that the blackmailer had planted the jewelry in Rose's car to deflect suspicion, but she knew it, too, was purely conjecture at this point. She moved on. "Tomorrow, I'm going to interview several people mentioned in Catherine's will in the hopes of turning up other possible suspects."

"Don't bother. The police have essentially closed the case at this point, and it's likely to go to trial. I need to build Rose's defense with the information I already have."

"But we still don't know who the intruder was."

"I know, but I took Rose's case pro bono, and the funding has run out." Brian sighed. "I wish I had the money to push the investigation further, Kristi, but I don't, plus I'm swamped with other work from paying clients. It's unfortunate, but that's the way things go sometimes."

Maybe for the legal system, but not for her. No way. Kristi sat up on the bed. "So you can't pay me. I get it, but I don't care about the money, Brian. I need to know the truth."

After they hung up, Kristi revolved the case in her head. The letters and Catherine's secret had to be connected. So, too, did the intruder. But Brian was right, the likelihood that Catherine was a blackmailer seemed unlikely, which meant the intruder was the blackmailer. So, why would he kill Catherine and take those letters?

Kristi thought again about the locket and Reb's theory of a secret child. If Catherine had an illegitimate child she wanted to keep secret, maybe the father was also someone prominent, who didn't want the child's existence to be revealed. Maybe they both had a secret they didn't want made public... Maybe he'd taken the missing photograph from Catherine's bedside table because it would've exposed his identity...

Tired and confused, Kristi yawned and rolled over. Maybe she'd find out more on her road trip tomorrow.

33. Sara Grice

Tuesday morning, Kristi set out early for her interview with Sara Grice. The heat wave was finally over, and she enjoyed the cool foggy air blowing in through the open window as she took Highway 154 north over the Santa Ynez mountains. Her car whined in complaint as she gunned it up the steep climbs and tortuous turns, the steep drop-offs reminding her of what the local news station called the road: "the Highway of Death." Every year, a car or two fatally crashed along the dangerous route.

It was a relief when she finally crested the mountain range at Camino Cielo and passed over the top. The descent was much less windy and offered dramatic views of the Santa Ynez valley and the more distant and remote San Rafael Mountains, but now the ocean fog was a thing of the past, and everywhere baked under the mercilessly hot October sun.

As Kristi drove, she thought about her upcoming interview with Sara Grice. The woman spoke at Catherine's vigil and had been one of the few people at Catherine's interment. Catherine had also left her a bequest in her will. These facts suggested that Sara and Catherine had been close. Kristi wondered if Sara could shed light on the mysterious "M".

Arriving in San Luis Obispo, Kristi was glad to find it not as hot as the Santa Ynez Valley, despite being some distance from the ocean. It had been a while since she'd been there, and the town was smaller than she remembered, a more relaxed feel to it than Santa Barbara, probably because it was farther away from the dense population of Los Angeles.

Kristi took Marsh Street to the downtown area and a short while later entered the narrow storefront of Sara's bookstore. Three cats snoozed in the glass window, curling their bodies between a book display featuring local authors. Sue Grafton's latest mystery was there, as well as one by Tabitha Tyson.

Going over to it, Kristi picked up Tabitha's book, remembering what her friend Reb has told her about Tabitha's genre. The cover featured a medieval-looking cathedral and a woman in a nun's habit.

Not my cup of tea, Kristi thought, flipping the book over. There was no author photo, and no mention in the author blurb of where Tabitha hailed from, but she had to be local if her book was in the display.

Kristi put the book back and walked along the towering rows of bookshelves until she found Sara at the back of one row, unpacking books from an open cardboard box on the floor.

The woman wore a shapeless woodsy brown dress and dark green low-heeled shoes. Between the no-nonsense outfit and short straight hair framing a face free of makeup, Sara seemed the epitome of spinster cat lady.

Kristi handed her a business card and introduced herself. "As I mentioned on the phone yesterday, I'd like to talk to you about Catherine Cole."

"I'd better mind the store while we talk," Sara said. She put down the book she was holding and marched her soldier-straight body to the front of the store. Once behind the sales counter, her brown eyes were sharp and shrewd behind the large, black-framed, cat-eye glasses. "What did you want to ask me?"

"You and Catherine were friends?"

"Yes, we were. What else do you want to know?"

"She left you money in your will, so you were pretty close, right?"

"Like I said, we were friends." Sara started to fuss with the arrangement of postcards and other stationery knickknacks beside the cash register.

Kristi didn't understand why Sara looked vaguely irritated. "Aren't you sad that Catherine was killed?"

Sara's face stiffened. "My private feelings are irrelevant to this conversation and to your investigation." She had the hint of an underbite, which became more pronounced when she scowled.

Her attitude was as no nonsense as her appearance. Kristi decided not to beat around the bush. "When was the last time you saw Catherine alive?"

"Two weeks ago, when she came to visit."

"That was the week she died, right?" Kristi looked at Sara in surprise. Was that why Catherine had asked Rose to house sit?

"Yes." Sara aligned one last knickknack on the counter and moved on to sorting the currency in the cash register.

Geez, the woman was difficult to question. Kristi plowed on. "Do you remember what day of the week?"

"Tuesday."

"You didn't see her that Thursday?"

A bitter smile twisted Sara's thin mouth upwards. "You don't need to fish for my alibi, Miss McCormick. I hosted a poetry reading here at the shop that night. Here." She untacked a flier from the posterboard behind the counter and dropped it on the counter, as if to avoid any accidental physical contact with Kristi.

Kristi didn't bother to pick it up. "Look, Sara, I'm not here because I think you had something to do with Catherine's death. I'm trying to find out who killed her, and it's got to be someone she knew. You never met my client, Rose Schmidt?"

"No."

"Catherine never mentioned her to you?"

"No. Catherine and I only ever talked about cats and books."

"So you don't know of anyone who might have held a grudge against her?"

"I have no idea." Sara gave the slightest of shrugs.

Boy was she not one for polite chitchat, and forget speculation. Kristi got to the point. "There may have been a man in the house the night she died, a man who may have killed her. You ever hear of Lorenzo Bianchi? He lives in Pismo Beach."

Sara shook her head but then paused, her gray brows drawing together with the effort at recall. "Years ago, I do remember there were a few times she came in here with a man."

"How long ago was that?"

"I met Catherine when I first opened the bookstore four years ago, so it would've been about then, but I have no idea who the man was."

Kristi felt a beat of excitement. Had it been Lorenzo? Someone else? "Was he Italian? Were they a couple?"

Sara gave her a quelling glance. "I am not a gossip, but I assume they were a couple. He was just some man, and it was a long time ago. Catherine did not introduce him to me."

Was he the blackmailer? But four years was a long time ago. "Did she ever come to the bookstore with anyone else, maybe more recently than that?"

"No." Sara turned her back on Kristi and started rearranging the books in the glass window display.

Kristi let out a quiet, frustrated breath. "Let's go back to that Tuesday before Catherine was killed. Did she say where she was going after visiting you? Maybe to see other friends while she was up this way?"

"No."

"Did she mention that she was going to a fundraising party that Thursday night?"

"I already told you, we only talked about cats and books."

"What about Tabitha Tyson's books?"

Sara's tight, controlled face relaxed a smidgen. "Tabitha was Catherine's favorite mystery writer. She collected all her books."

It was clear Sara was a book-lover, and there was something in the way she spoke that made Kristi ask, "Besides being a fan, was Catherine also friends with Tabitha?"

Sara nodded. "They were."

Kristi pointed to the book display. "Do you know Tabitha?"

"She's come to the store to do readings on occasion."

That gave Kristi an idea. "Do you have her contact information?"

"I do, but I doubt she'll talk to you. She values her privacy. "

Kristi shrugged. It was probably a long shot, but she was in desperate need of clues. "Look, I really need to talk to her, if she's willing. If you give me her number, maybe you can let her know that I'm going to be in contact ahead of time, so she won't be caught unprepared when I call?"

"I can do that." Sara pulled a small book from under the counter and recited Tabitha's number.

Kristi jotted it down on her notepad. "Thanks."

A customer came into the store and approached the counter. Sara started to turn away.

"Wait! Do you know if Catherine ever had a child?" Kristi hastily pulled the Catherine's necklace from her purse and sprung the secret latch. She held the locket toward Sara. "Do you know who this is? I think her name starts with the letter 'M.'"

Sara glanced at the photograph. "No. If you'll please excuse me." She turned from Kristi to help the customer.

Kristi left the bookstore with a sense of frustration. Sara hadn't helped her learn anything about the male intruder or "M".

What about the man Sara had seen four ago? Lorenzo? Male friend? It couldn't have been Catherine's brother. Kristi remembered reading that he and his wife had died five years ago in a car accident.

As Kristi took the 101 south toward Pismo beach, she kept thinking about the man. No one except the Judge seemed to know much about Catherine's past love life, and even he didn't know much about Catherine's life after she became so reclusive. Had there been someone more recently? Did it matter? If "M" was Catherine's child, given her age, it seemed likely the father was Lorenzo.

In thinking back on how her conversation with Sara ended, Kristi wondered. When Sara had said, 'No,' had she meant that Catherine hadn't had a child, or that she, Sara, didn't know? Did Sara know more than she'd let on? What had been going on behind those Sphinx-like eyes?

Kristi sighed as she exited the freeway at Pismo Beach. At least Sara had given her Tabitha's contact information.

34. Lorenzo Bianchi

Kristi was pleasantly surprised when Lorenzo Bianchi met her at the door of his beach front condo at Pismo Beach. Where Sara had been taciturn, everything about her controlled and constrained, except perhaps for her love of books and cats, Lorenzo was the opposite.

He greeted her with a friendly smile. "Delighted to meet you, Miss McCormick." He spoke with a lilting Italian accent.

"Thanks for agreeing to see me, Mr. Bianchi."

"Please, call me Lorenzo." He wore a polo shirt and slacks, but despite the preppy clothes, his gray hair flowed to his shoulders and he wore flip flops, which made Kristi think he might once have been a hippy. Had Catherine in her wild youth shared in that free love culture?

He waved her inside. "It is rare that we are spared fog or dramatic weather here at the beach. Today is so beautiful, I thought we could converse over a light lunch and perhaps a glass of wine."

"Sounds great." They could get down to business later, plus she was starved.

He guided her through an airy living room where landscape paintings of all sizes dominated the towering, two-story walls. The impressionist play on light in each of them reminded her of his paintings in Catherine's house.

She paused in front of one depicting a rugged coastline beneath rolling, grassy hills. The way the sunshine was painted turned the hills to liquid gold, and the crash of the surf was captured in a violent contrast of stark whites and blues.

He noticed her admiring the painting and smiled with pride. "I could not part with that one. It has always been one of my favorite compositions."

"It's really striking. It's distinctive style reminds me of the paintings I saw at Catherine's house."

"Ah, Catherine." Lorenzo bowed his head and placed a hand over his heart, sighing. "She was my greatest patron."

Kristi followed him across the living room and through a slider to a small patio. A lunch of sandwiches, salad, and a bottle of white wine sat on an Italian-tiled bistro table. With an old world charm, he pulled back her seat.

"What a fantastic view!" Kristi exclaimed.

A wide swath of golden sand swept down to where the surf churned, a powerful, endless force of energy at the edge of the ocean, which today stretched a solid slate blue to the horizon.

Lorenzo smiled and poured the wine. "It is one of my sources for inspiration."

They made small talk about Pismo Beach and his life as an artist over lunch. When he attempted to pour her a second glass of wine, she put a hand over the top. "You've been a wonderful host, but we need to talk about Catherine."

He poured himself another glass of wine. "I still cannot believe she is dead. Killed!" A deep sadness dragged the features of his face downward and made him fully look his age. "I hope they—how do you say—throw the book at that young woman for her crime."

Kristi shook her head. "I don't think she killed Catherine. I have reason to believe a man killed her."

His eyes met hers and widened with shock. Putting down his glass, he tapped his chest dramatically with both hands. "Are you accusing me? I could never have killed her. Catherine was the love of my life!"

"I'm not here to accuse you, Lorenzo," she said hurriedly, hoping he was innocent. "I'm hoping you can help me find Catherine's killer."

Lorenzo placed his hands on the table and leaned toward her, his dark eyes intense. "Tell me how. I would do anything to avenge her death."

He seemed so earnest, Kristi wanted to believe him, but he was tall and had gray hair, which fit Rose's description of the intruder. "The man may have been blackmailing Catherine. Can you think of any big secrets she had?"

"Secrets? I do not know." His brown eyes didn't shift or look away as he spoke. Either he was telling the truth or he was a superb liar.

Kristi opened her purse and took out the envelope with the necklace in it. "Do you recognize this?" She lifted the chain and the locket swung free, rotating in the light breeze, the diamond facets shooting sharp shards of light in the sun.

Lorenzo nodded. "It was Catherine's. She often wore it."

Kristi's heart kicked up a beat. Popping open the locket, she held it up to him. "What about her?"

He put down his wineglass and took the open locket, holding it close to his face to better examine the small photograph. He shook his head.

"You sure you don't recognize her? Her name starts with an 'M.'" Kristi pointed to the engraved 'M' on the locket's cover.

Lorenzo shrugged. "As I said, I do not know this woman." He handed the locket back to Kristi. "I once asked Catherine about the necklace, but she merely said it was an antique that she liked." He rose to his feet and began stacking the lunch dishes. "Perhaps you would like a coffee before you go?"

"That would be nice. Thanks." Kristi closed the locket and secured it again in the envelope. As they went to the kitchen, she thought of the airmail letter. "Do you know anything about Catherine being involved with a relief organization in Africa?"

"Was she?" He looked up from where he expertly prepared a stovetop espresso maker. "I didn't know, but it wouldn't surprise me. She was very generous with her money. Do you take cream or sugar?"

"Just milk, please."

He poured the espresso into small ceramic cups and handed her one. It was hot and strong and the caffeine sizzled like lightning straight to her brain, erasing the wine. Time to pursue her main question. "Do you know if Catherine had any children?"

His dark eyebrows arced upwards, as if surprised to consider such a thing. "No, not that I know of."

Had Catherine borne his child but never told him for some reason? If someone else found out, that might be worth blackmailing Catherine for. "Tell me about Catherine. When did you first meet?"

Lorenzo leaned a hip back against the counter and sipped his espresso, a distant look in his dark eyes. "More than forty years ago."

Kristi did some quick mental math. The chronology worked! Catherine and Lorenzo could have had a child.

Lorenzo smiled at her. "Forty years must seem like an infinite to someone so young as yourself. You remind me a little of her all those years ago. She was radiant and bright and so filled with energy and vitality. She was like a shooting star across the dark canvas of my life." He gestured with a broad sweep of his hand.

"Your relationship didn't last?"

He gave a toss of his head, his gray hair sweeping his shoulders as his eyes returned from the past to focus on her. "Oh, but it did. She became my patron, as I've said. I would be nowhere today without the support she offered me. She helped me buy this condo, and she was even kind enough to include me in her will."

He put his cup down on the counter with such force that coffee sloshed over the edge. "What a tragedy! Who would do such a terrible thing?"

"I don't know, Lorenzo. That's why I'm here. Do you have any idea who might've wanted to hurt her?"

"No. It makes no sense." Like a deflating balloon, the anger went out of him, leaving him old again. He picked up a kitchen towel and mopped up the spilled coffee.

Kristi remembered what Sara had told her. "Did you ever go with her to bookstores in San Luis Obispo?"

Lorenzo glanced at her, puzzled. "No."

"Was Catherine dating someone about four or five years ago?"

"I do not know." Lorenzo rinsed his cup and put it on the drain rack. "It has been many years since Catherine and I shared confidences about anything other than art, but I do know she changed over the years. She used to be so free and happy, but then she became quiet and reserved. I'd even say sad, as if she had suffered some great loss."

"Did you ask her about it?"

He shook his head. "I did not know how to do it without causing her more pain."

The priest and James' grandfather had said Catherine withdrew from society about ten years ago. Had Catherine's child died then?

Kristi wanted to ask Lorenzo more questions about when and how Catherine changed, but she saw him glance pointedly at his watch. She had to bring the interview back to the day of the murder before she ran out of time. "When was the last time you saw Catherine?"

"She came two weeks ago."

"What days?"

"Tuesday and Wednesday. Do you know where she went after her visit with you?"

Lorenzo shook his head. "No, but it was late in the afternoon when she left, so maybe she went to her ranch."

"Ranch?" No one had ever mentioned Catherine owning a ranch. Chagrined, Kristi realized that she'd never thought to ask. How naive about money she'd been! It had never occurred to her until now that Catherine might own several properties.

Lorenzo's next words pulled her out of her thoughts. "It's in Santa Ynez. Catherine invited me to paint there whenever I wished. It has many beautiful vistas."

"Did Catherine spend much time there?"

"I do not know. She wasn't often there when I painted, but the ranch manager was very nice."

"Ranch manager?"

"Miss Annie Masters. She and her husband, Ray. They take care of the ranch and the many horses and animals. It is a big job."

From what Lorenzo said, it sounded like Catherine spent her last Thursday at the ranch. "Do you have their phone number? I'd like to talk to them."

"Of course."

Lorenzo went to a small desk tucked into the far corner of the kitchen. Unlike the rest of the tidy condo, the desk was a mess, piled high with papers, folders, and loose sheets of paper, which from what Kristi could see over Lorenzo's shoulder, looked to be invoices for artwork, bills, and account statements. He opened the Rolodex, spun through it, and copied down the number in a scrawling scribble that, for such a good artist, was surprisingly illegible.

She followed him back through the living room to the front entry, wrestling with how to ask him the last unpleasant question she still had to ask.

He opened the front door for her, but she didn't go through it.

She looked up at him. "I'm sorry to have to ask you this, but where were you that Thursday night?"

"The night she was killed?"

"Yes."

"Here."

"Can anyone back you up?"

Nodding, he gave a rueful look. "I had dinner with several friends from my golf club that night."

"I'm sorry, but I did have to ask." Kristi gave him an apologetic smile and then held out her hand. "Thanks for the delicious lunch. You've been more than generous with your time."

Lorenzo's grip was firm and warm as he shook her hand. "I bid you good luck with your inquiries, Miss McCormick."

Kristi drove out of the beach condo complex thinking about Lorenzo. She could go about verifying his alibi, but she had a feeling it'd check out. Judging from their conversation, he really didn't seem to know if Catherine had ever had a child, and even if he was lying, why would he blackmail and kill Catherine if she was already paying for his house and his paintings?

So was "M" Lorenzo's child? Had "M" died, maybe about ten years ago, when Catherine became reclusive and sad, as Lorenzo had described her? That would explain why "M" hadn't been in the will. If the child were dead, her blackmail theory was completely wrong. Still, what about the intruder? What about those letters? And if the intruder wasn't Lorenzo, then who was the man who really killed Catherine?

35. A Lead?

If she could search Catherine's ranch, she might turn up something useful, so before getting on the freeway, Kristi pulled into a gas station and used the pay phone to call the phone number Lorenzo had given her. "Annie Masters?"

"Yes?"

Kristi explained who she was and the purpose of her call.

"Why sure thing, Miss McCormick. Anything to help find Miss Cole's killer." Annie spoke with the slow drawl that might have been Texan, though the only Texans Kristi had heard were in the TV Westerns her dad sometimes watched on Sunday afternoons. Annie gave Kristi directions and said she'd see her in about an hour.

Getting back in her car, Kristi spread out the road map on the passenger seat and traced the route to Catherine's ranch and from there to the Beverly's place. She had two hours between appointments. She'd make it, but time would be tight.

She took the 101 south and turned off near the tiny rural town of Los Olivos, heading southeast through rolling grassy hills, dried yellow by the scorching sun, and dotted with dark, shadowy clumps of California live oaks. The cool ocean breeze of Pismo Beach was long gone, and the wind blew in through the open windows, furnace-hot in the peak afternoon sun.

Her car bumped off the pavement onto dirt when she turned onto the ranch property, and she had to slow way down. The breeze coming in the windows dropped to nothing, and the heat inside the car cranked up to boiling point.

By the time she pulled up to the ranch house, sweat was running down her cheeks, and her T-shirt and jeans were sticking horribly to her skin. Cursing as she got out of the car, she vowed to buy a car with decent air conditioning as soon as she had enough money.

The house was a low slung adobe with a dusty pickup parked out front. Chickens squawked somewhere behind the house.

A thin middle-aged woman dressed in cowboy boots and jeans came out the front door. "You must be Kristi McCormick. I'm Annie Masters, assistant ranch manager. 'Segundo' as we cowboy ranchers like to call it. Pleased to meet you."

They shook hands and she led Kristi into the thick-walled building.

Kristi sighed in relief as she looked around the Southwestern-themed living room. "It's nice and cool in here."

"Nothing like real adobe. The thick walls work great as insulators. The Spanish knew what they were doing when they invented the stuff. Would you like a drink? I have fresh lemonade."

"That sounds heavenly," Kristi smiled, her mouth parched.

She took a seat on a couch upholstered with Navajo-inspired patterns and checked her watch, dismayed to find it was already after 4 pm. She'd have to make this quick.

Annie came back, handed Kristi a tall glass that was ice cold and beaded with condensation, and then took a seat in a large wooden rocker across from Kristi.

Her clear gray eyes swept Kristi with open curiosity. "Why I must say, Miss McCormick, you don't look anything like that detective on Colombo."

There was no insinuation in her tone of voice, so Kristi didn't take it personally. Smiling, she sat up a little straighter on the couch. "Private investigators come in all different shapes and sizes—and ages."

Annie returned her smile. "You said on the phone there's a chance Rose Schmidt isn't guilty. If that's true, does that mean Anita Walker won't get the ranch?"

Kristi shrugged. "I'm a PI, not an estate attorney, but that seems reasonable."

Annie's face sharpened. "I'm sorry, but Catherine's niece is a holy terror. If she inherits the ranch, it's all over for me and my husband. Why, she just called over here today and told us to give her a head count of not just the cattle but all the livestock, and the horses, too. Seems like she's already got dollar signs dancing in her head with the idea of selling off this place." Annie shook her head. "I still can't believe Miss Catherine's gone."

"I'm sorry for your loss," Kristi said politely. For a "recluse," Catherine sure seemed to influence a lot of people's lives.

"Thank you, kindly. You're a sweet girl. You think Miss Schmidt will want to sell the ranch, that is, if she gets out of jail?"

Kristi shrugged. "She's a teacher who works harder than anyone I've ever met. I doubt she knows anything about ranches, and I doubt selling off Catherine's ranch would be a top priority. "

Annie sat back in the rocker and smiled, rocking at a firm, strong rhythm. "Well, then, how can I be of help?"

"How long have you worked here?"

"Going on four years ago. Pretty much since Miss Catherine bought the place."

Only four years? From Lorenzo's comments, Kristi thought it had been longer. "Do you know why she bought the ranch?"

"I have no idea, but I'd have bought it, too, if I'd had the money. Wide open spaces, beautiful views, room to range and ride. What's not to love?"

Kristi took another sip of the cold, tart lemonade, and wondered if Catherine's mysterious trips away from Montecito had simply been to come here. "How often did she visit?"

"Early on in the first year or so, she spent a lot of time here."

Kristi wondered again about Catherine's trips. "Do you know if she owns any other property besides this ranch and her place in Montecito?"

"Not that I know of."

"Did a man ever accompany her?"

"There was that artist friend of hers. He's come to paint a few times. Italian fella and a real sweetheart. Asked me my opinion on the best views around the ranch."

"Lorenzo Bianchi." Kristi smiled. "He is a nice guy. Was he the only man you ever saw here with Catherine?"

Annie shrugged. "I don't know."

Kristi was confused. "What do you mean?"

"Catherine always stayed over at the guest house, but that's a good ways from here. She could've had any number of visitors, and we wouldn't have known. There were times she came over here to talk about ranch business, but that was none too often. Mostly, we just talked on the phone. She was a nice lady, told us she trusted us to take care of things. Mostly, she just kept to herself."

Kristi wondered if the man Sara had seen with Catherine four years ago was Lorenzo, or someone else. Lorenzo had said he and Catherine had ended their romantic relationship decades earlier. Too bad Annie couldn't confirm if there'd been another man.

Time to get back to the main reason she was here. "Do you know if she was here two weeks ago?"

"You talking the week she was murdered, right?"

Kristi nodded.

"Yeah, I saw her on Thursday afternoon, when I was on my way to the Farmer's Market in Solvang."

"Was anyone with her?"

Annie shook her head. "I don't think so. I waved at her, but I'm not sure she saw me, 'cause she was already going down the side road to the guest house."

"I'd like to take a look at the guesthouse now."

"Sure thing." Annie gave her directions and handed her a key ring with a silver and turquoise Navajo thunderbird dangling from it. "It's a bad business, whoever killed Miss Catherine. She was sweet and kind, Miss McCormick. A real lady. You find her killer, you hear?"

"I'll do my best, ma'am."

A short while later, Kristi pulled up beside another low adobe building. It was smaller than the main ranch house, but not by much. Unlocking the front door, she hurried in. The place had the closed, slightly dusty smell of a place long unoccupied.

Over the couch in the living room hung a large landscape painting, depicting a solitary California live oak standing on a brilliantly green rolling hillside under a cloudless blue sky. It must've been painted in spring, because that was the only time the hills ever looked that color, Kristi thought, as she went over and confirmed Lorenzo had painted it.

Bookshelves stood on either side of the brick fireplace but with far fewer books than in Catherine's bedroom in Montecito; at least half the shelves housed decorative knickknacks. Kristi quickly scanned the spines of the books and noted several by Tabitha Tyson.

Pressed for time, she hurriedly took in the living room and ranch style kitchen and saw nothing of interest. Both were impersonally neat and tidy.

Moving quickly, she went down the hallway and found two bedroom suites. The first was obviously for visitors, also hotel-neat. She hit pay dirt in the second bedroom. It was laid out almost identically to the first with a queen bed, dresser, bedside table, and Navajo rug on the floor, but unlike the other bedroom, this one had several framed photographs on the bedside table. Kristi rushed over to take a look.

The big one was a copy of the same one she'd seen on Catherine's bedside table in Montecito: a formal family portrait of the Cole family when Catherine was young and her mom was still alive. Her adrenaline kicked in as she studied the two smaller photos.

Keeping her hands carefully behind her back, she bent to take a closer look. The first pictured a young blond-haired woman with short, straight hair, who stood mugging for the camera with a tennis racket in her hand. The second portrayed the same woman, perhaps a little older, dressed in an outfit much like Kristi would wear: jeans and a red T-shirt. She sat on a bench under a large tree, a book open in her lap, her expression distant, as if the photographer had caught her by surprise, and she'd looked up suddenly from the book.

The woman looked hauntingly familiar. With shaking hands, Kristi took out Catherine's necklace and opened the locket.

The woman in the locket and the photographs were the same! Kristi compared the young woman with the young Catherine in the Cole family portrait. They looked very much like they could be related. Both had short blond hair and both were trim, though "M" seemed more athletic-looking.

Recalling Lorenzo's face, Kristi tried to superimpose his aging good looks over the young woman in the two small photographs. If there were any similarities, she couldn't detect them, but considering their differences in age and sex, Kristi wasn't surprised. They could still be related.

So was "M" Catherine's daughter?

Kristi put the necklace away and pulled on the latex gloves she kept in her purse. She laid the first framed photo face down on the wood floor and eased off the stiff backing to see if anything was written on the rear side of the photo. Yes! Someone had written the letter "M" in blue cursive and a date, just over fifteen years ago. Kristi followed the same process with the second photo. It, too, had the letter "M" with a date from a little less than ten years ago. Where was "M" now? Had she died? If so, the timing fit with what Lorenzo had said about when Catherine changed.

As Kristi put the photographs back together again and placed them on the bedside table, she looked at the markings they made in the dust. The markings looked similar to what she'd seen on Catherine's bedside table in Montecito. As she searched the room for any sign of airmail letters or anything from Africa, she wondered if there was any connection between the photos here and the ones she thought might've been taken from Montecito.

Her search turned up only one thing importance: a formal invitation embossed on expensive, heavy-weight paper, inviting Catherine to the political fundraiser that Beverly Carlyle and Ridley Niven hosted the night she was killed. Had Catherine left the ranch and gone directly to the fundraiser that night? And why had she left the party to drive back to Montecito?

The clock on the dresser caught her eye: 4:45 pm. Time to go.

36. Beverly Carlyle and Ridley Niven

The afternoon had grown hotter as the sun sank in the southwest over the Santa Ynez mountains, and inside Kristi's car was broiling. She rolled down all the windows and then pulled checked directions to Beverly's house. No way could she make it by 5 o'clock. Cranking her car, she shifted into gear and drove as fast as she dared over the bumpy dirt road back to the highway, but by the time she pulled into the long sweeping drive of the Carlyle estate, she was almost twenty minutes late for her interview.

The enormous boxy mansion was done in some style Kristi guessed might be Italian. Or was it French? Whatever it was, it certainly wasn't the Mission style common in Santa Barbara. A huge fountain with a larger than life nymph and cupids spouting water served as a central roundabout for the main parking area, where a couple of luxury sedans and a low slung silver sports car were parked.

Kristi hurried out of her own beater, not bothering to check her appearance, and rushed up the granite flagstones to the entry. She rang a doorbell encased in an ornate frame of marble carved with vines and grapes.

When Beverly answered, she rushed out an apology. "Sorry I'm late, Ms. Carlyle." She felt a trickle of sweat running down the side of her hot cheeks, but she resisted the urge to wipe it away. It was bad enough that she was wearing a sweaty T-shirt and jeans, when Beverly looked like a fashion plate. So much for coming across as a cool, calm, and collected PI.

Confusion registered on Beverly's face. "May I help you?"

It was Kristi's turn to look confused. "I called you yesterday about Catherine Cole and the fundraiser you hosted two weeks ago. We set a 5 o'clock time today to talk." She rooted around in her purse and dug out her business card.

Beverly took the card. "Miss McCormick! I must apologize, but our meeting completely slipped my mind. Perhaps we should reschedule, as Ridley and I must leave shortly."

Kristi looked at Beverly in dismay. "I promise I'll make it quick. Please, I just have a few questions."

Graciously, . "Of course."

She led Kristi into a mansion that was completely unlike the understated wealth of Catherine's Montecito home. The place screamed money. Maybe this is the difference between nouveau riche and old money, Kristi wondered, as she took in the pendulous crystal chandelier in the grand foyer, and the abundance of marble and fine art lining the floors and walls of the cavernous great room beyond.

Like the house, Beverly exuded money. Diamonds dangled from her ears, a huge solitaire adorned her left ring finger, and she was sheathed in an ice blue silk dress that looked like it had been custom made to fit her small, yet perfectly shaped figure.

A tall, thin man came into the foyer with a wrap draped over one arm. Kristi recognized the steel blue eyes and meticulously clipped white mustache hugging his upper lip. Ridley Niven.

He came over to Beverly's side and slid an arm about her trim waist, his blue eyes sharpening when he turned and scrutinized Kristi. "You're that impertinent young private investigator. What are you doing here? We're about to go out."

Beverly swept a hand over her hair and cast a distressed look at him. "Ridley, dear, I'm so sorry, but with all our wedding preparations, I forgot I made arrangements for Miss McCormick to speak with us about Catherine Cole. Perhaps we can spare a few minutes for her?"

When Ridley looked down at the tiny woman, his face was transformed by the love that glowed openly in his eyes. His mouth softened into a tender smile. "Of course, my darling."

"Thank you for your time," Kristi said quickly. "I'll get to the point."

Ridley and Beverly turned their attention back to her. "Yes?"

"You invited Miss Cole to the party, so I take it you were friends?"

Beverly smiled, her small teeth snow white. "I would like to think everyone is my friend. Before he died, Catherine's brother, Richard, was a good friend of my poor Mason. They both were in banking, don't you know."

Catherine's younger brother had died five ago, but who was Mason?

Kristi's confusion must have registered on her face, because Beverly said, "Mason was my husband. I am a widow."

Her words reminded Kristi of the society page she'd seen in the library and that the party Beverly and Ridley hosted was a pro-marriage political fundraiser.

She glanced at Ridley. "Didn't you announce your engagement at the party?"

"Indeed, we did." Ridley turned back to the tiny woman at his side. "I can't wait to marry you, my darling, and sanctify our love in holy matrimony." He raised Beverly's hand with the diamond engagement ring on it and kissed its back in a courtly fashion.

"Oh, Ridley." Beverly looked up at him with such a saccharine smile that Kristi cringed.

Ugh. Such lovey-dovey behavior seemed totally fake, yet considering how old they were and their political views, maybe it was real. Kristi cleared her throat. "Congratulations. So, the night of the party, did you see Miss Cole?"

Beverly shook her head yes; Ridley shook his head no.

Interesting. They hadn't noticed each other's contradictory responses.

"I saw her when she arrived, but at the time, we were greeting Judge Roberts." Beverly looked up at Ridley. "You spoke to Catherine later, right dearest?"

Ridley smiled at her slowly and then nodded. "Yes. Now I remember."

"What did you talk about?" Kristi asked him.

"Oh, I don't recall. I talked to so very many people. We had over two hundred attendees that evening, and after our announcement, we were even more swamped with well-wishers." He smoothed his mustache with a self-satisfied air.

"Ridley's right. It was such a to-do, we had our hands full. Why, I don't think I had many conversations beyond a 'How do you do.'"

Beverly looked at Ridley again, and her penciled eyebrows rose. "I forgot to ask, why were you and Catherine arguing?"

"Arguing?" Ridley chuckled and patted Beverly's hand. "We didn't argue." He glanced at the heavy gold wristwatch on his arm. "I'm sorry, Miss McCormick, but we must be off or we'll miss our reservation."

He helped Beverly with her wrap and then gestured for Kristi to precede them to the front door.

Civility demanded Kristi leave, but who was telling the truth, Beverly or Ridley? Had Beverly misunderstood what she'd seen, and had Ridley simply forgotten about speaking to Catherine? Or was Ridley lying?

"I understand you're in a hurry, Mr. Niven, but if you didn't argue with Miss Cole, what did you talk about? It could provide an important clue, since as far as I know, you're the last person to speak to Miss Cole alive."

"Goodness gracious, Miss McCormick." Ridley gave a dismissive shake of his head. "We simply exchanged a few pleasantries. Now, I really must insist." He opened the front door.

"If I have any more questions, may I call you tomorrow?"

"Of course, of course. Any time." Ridley tucked one hand under Beverly's elbow. With the other, he waved Kristi out the door. "Good evening, Miss McCormick."

Kristi went to her car and watched Ridley escort Beverly carefully down the steps. The small woman teetered a bit on her high, narrow heels, and she seemed delicate, almost frail, beside Ridley, who moved with the fluid assurance of an athletic man. The couple got into the silver sports car, and the powerful engine roared to life. The taillights flared as the car shot down the drive, gravel flying in its wake. Kristi's own beater followed at a much slower pace, though her mind was racing at 100 mph.

If Ridley had actually argued with Catherine, denying it was suspicious. He also drove a light-colored sports car like the one she kept hearing about. But how could he have killed Catherine, if he was hosting a party in Santa Ynez? Wouldn't Beverly have noticed if he disappeared?

And if he was the blackmailer, how had he gained access to Catherine's secrets and why blackmail her? Catherine had apparently walked in the same social circles as Ridley, but Kristi had found nothing to indicate they were more than casual acquaintances.

As she drove back over the Santa Ynez mountains in twilight, the deep shadows shrouding highway 154 made her think of the shadow hanging over the case. What secret was hidden in that shadow, a secret Rose had been willing to go to jail for and that Catherine had apparently died for?

Lorenzo had openly admitted Catherine and he were lovers in years past, but he seemed to have no idea if Catherine had borne him a child. The photographs of "M" at Catherine's ranch sat beside the other family portrait and were of the same woman pictured in Catherine's locket. "M" could have been Catherine's child, but what had happened to her, and why did no one seem to know anything about her, except Rose, who wouldn't say?

Kristi had a gut feeling the answer she was looking for had to be somewhere in what she'd learned, but it all felt so tangled. How to find the key strand that would release the knot and let the her see the truth? The discrepancy in what Ridley and Beverly said pointed to the first possible lie she'd encountered in the case. She needed to find out more about how Ridley knew Catherine. Unfortunately, however, her road trip had not yielded anything useful as far as helping Brian prepare Rose's defense,

37. Wednesday Morning

Wednesday started on a down note. Kristi overslept, and then, when she went downstairs, she found her dad in the kitchen still finishing breakfast. She so didn't want another go around with him about her career choice.

He looked up from the paper. "Good morning, stranger. You haven't been around much lately. Busy on your case?"

"Yup." If she had the money, she'd grab a bite out, but she didn't, and she was starving. She poured some cereal in a bowl.

"It says here in the paper that the Catherine Cole murder case is wrapping up. Is that good news for you?"

If only. Kristi felt his eyes following her as she went to the refrigerator for milk. "I'm sorry, Dad, but I can't really talk about it. Client confidentiality and all that."

She stood at the counter to eat, feeling the need to maintain a physical as well as an emotional distance from him.

"The defense attorney took the case pro bono. Not a lot of money in that." He looked up from the paper. "You have any other cases lined up, or are things getting pretty tight financially?"

The hope in his voice grated on her. She knew he wanted her back at his company because he loved her, but bottom line, it also meant he wanted her to fail at the one thing she wanted most.

Stalling, she ate more cereal and tried to think of how to respond without outright lying. Finally, she said, "Don't worry. I've got things covered."

He was still looking at her. "You sure about that?"

"Yeah," she said, unable to stop the defensive tone and wishing she was a better liar.

It grated on her even more that he'd hit so close to the mark. The money was gone, and she had no other cases lined up. The cereal turned to sawdust in her mouth. If something didn't happen soon, he'd get his wish. She'd have to kiss her dream goodbye and go back to his boring insurance company.

Fortunately, he didn't push any further, but gave a small sign and turned back to the newspaper. Kristi sighed, too. They used to be so close. She hated the awkward, adversarial feeling that had sprung up between the two of them since she'd left his company, but she didn't see a way to fix it, not as long as he refused to accept that her career path wasn't the one he wanted for her.

A few minutes later, he looked up from the paper again. "I guess Pete's moved up the food chain over at the Police Department. Lead detective on the Catherine Cole murder investigation. Pretty impressive. You see much of him these days?"

"Um, yeah." Kristi glanced at him in surprise. She couldn't recall the last time he'd mentioned his younger brother, much less asked her about him.

He ran a hand through his thinning hair. "How's he doing?" When his eyes met hers, there was a vulnerability in them she'd not seen before.

Kristi didn't need to temper her smile. "He's doing great, Dad. He's a good cop and he's been an invaluable mentor to me." She paused and then couldn't help adding, "You know you could call him and ask him yourself."

"He's got a phone and our number." The old obstinate look came back on his face as he got up and came over to put his dishes in the dishwasher. "How's James?"

"Fine." She wasn't about to elaborate. It was bad enough getting grilled by her mom, and the whole thing with Brian just muddied the waters.

"I heard you went with him to that big lawyer shindig over at the seaside resort Friday night. That's good news, right? You two taking things to the next level?"

"Um, not really." She loaded her bowl in the dishwasher with clumsy haste. It was time to get out of there.

Her dad ran his hand again through his hair. He didn't look any happier than she felt, his gray brows creased and his expression dark. "I heard something through the grapevine about a national insurance firm courting the Roberts family. I was just thinking that with you and James dating..."

That was too much! She glared at him. "What, that if I get more serious with James it'll somehow make your business more secure? I'm sorry, Dad, but I won't be pimped out." She marched to the door.

He called after her, "Honey, that's not what I meant."

Kristi paused on the threshold and looked back at him. "I hope you keep the Roberts account, I really do, but what goes on in my personal life is just that. It's personal."

She rushed out the door, feeling self-righteously angry. If only she didn't care, but she did. As she drove to her office, she thought about how neither her personal relationship with James nor her professional relationship with Brian were going as planned, let alone her PI business. The anger deflated, and she sighed. It sucked that her dad didn't approve of her choices.

Things didn't much improve when she arrived late to work and heard the phone ringing as she ran up the stairs to her office. Fumbling for her keys, she dashed inside, only to catch her uncle's last words as the answering machine clicked off.

She hurried to the desk, put her purse down, and pressed the "Play" button.

"I was hoping to catch you before I head out into the field on a new case. Anyway, I wanted to keep you in the loop. Rose's arraignment has been set for tomorrow. 'Kay, gotta go."

Rose was going to be charged so soon? Kristi dropped into her chair in dismay. She'd hoped for another day or two to find evidence to clear Rose. Now, she had less than 24 hours to do it.

Picking up the phone, she spent the next hour trying but failing to reach the people she hoped might provide leads. Neither Ridley nor Beverly picked up at their respective homes. She tried James' grandfather in the hopes that he might have remembered something else about the night in question. His secretary took her message, but Kristi doubted he'd call her back. He probably didn't have the time and must know Rose was in custody. She tried Catherine's ranch manager to ask about a potential connection between Catherine and Ridley, but failed again, reaching an answering machine.

On the upside, she reached Tabitha Tyson, who agreed to see her later that afternoon. On the downside, the mystery writer lived in a remote cabin in the Malibu Mountains, which meant another long drive and more money for gas.

What else could she do? Maybe Rebecca at the library could help her find out more about Ridley and how he might be connected to Catherine. Reb might also have some other ideas about how to track down "M." Kristi grabbed her purse and hurried off to the library. Unfortunately, the day kept getting worse. When she got to the Reference section, there was no sign of Reb.

The other reference librarian was at least in her sixties, with a cap of tightly permed gray curls. "She's got the day off. Said something about hiking up near Little Pine Mountain."

Kristi explained who she was and what she was looking for. The upshot was that a short while later, she found herself seated in the microfiche section of the library, scanning through the society section of endless back issues of the local paper.

There were dozens of photographs going back more than a decade of Beverly with her first husband, Mason, and Catherine's banker brother and his wife. Mason died just a year ago, and the paper made a big deal of describing Beverly as a wealthy widow. The first reference Kristi found to Ridley was five years ago, when he purchased a sizable ranch outside Santa Ynez. In many of the accompanying photographs, he posed with a woman on his arm, mostly different women in each picture, all of them beautiful and obviously wealthy.

Kristi thought about how he'd treated Beverly when she'd interviewed them. Both seemed very much in love, but was he in love with the woman, or the money? No question Beverly was crazy rich. Could Ridley be a womanizer on the hunt for a rich wife? Had he gone after Catherine?

Kristi went back and scanned the endless tiny black and white smiling faces, looking for Catherine, but no luck. If Ridley was on the hunt for a rich wife, did that mean he had money troubles? That might be an incentive for blackmail. Kristi again scanned the microfiche, trying to find out more about where Ridley's money came from. Again, no luck.

Rubbing her tired eyes, dry and irritated from having stared for too long at the illuminated screen, she turned off the machine. She headed back to ask the librarian for more help tracking down Ridley's finances but then noticed the time. 11:30. Her questions would have to wait.

38. Lunch with James

Kristi was in a bad mood when she set off for Montecito and her lunch date with James. The time in the library had gotten her nowhere helpful, and though she'd been looking forward to seeing James and swimming in the gorgeous pool at the country club, her appointment with Tabitha meant there wouldn't be time. Worse, she kept thinking about Brian. She tried to tell herself they'd only one kissed once and that she could be forgiven a momentary slip up, but just the thought of it made lightning sizzle through her again. She turned up the drive to the Montecito Country Club with guilt eating at her.

The club sat on a hill, its ocean view only slightly diminished by the roar of the 101 Freeway in the foreground. Kristi found a space in the crowded parking lot between a late model white Mercedes and a black Porsche, their bodies immaculately clean and sparkling in the sun compared to her own car. With the drought, she hadn't bothered to hose it down, and she couldn't afford a professional car wash, much less a detail. Yesterday's trip to Catherine's ranch on the dirt road hadn't helped, either.

Flipping down the visor, she checked her appearance in the mirror. She didn't look much better than her car, she thought, trying to smooth down her wild hair and blot the smudged mascara. Ah well, she'd never win in the sophisticated department.

She got out of the car and was treated to the savory smell of grilling meat wafting across the parking lot.

"Hey, Kristi!" James came from his BMW parked several cars over. Under the bright noonday sun, his hair shone almost white.

She'd forgotten how very blond he was. So unlike Brian. She felt another twinge of guilt at comparing the two guys. She wasn't a two timer or a player, no way. And James did look great in a navy designer suit and emerald green tie that complimented his surfer blond complexion. He carried himself with that smooth authority she still found irresistible.

"It's been too long." He dipped his head and kissed her.

The kiss was familiar, pleasant, but it held none of the—

Stop it! Kristi tried to control her unruly thoughts but felt hot guilt creep up her cheeks.

"Hi James," she said, relieved that her voice came out calm.

Fortunately, he didn't seem to notice her inner turmoil and escorted her to the club's restaurant. The outdoor patio was busy with well-dressed ladies who lunch. He'd brought her there two other times, but she still felt out of place, painfully aware of her T-shirt and jeans and of the ladies watching them move to the table James had reserved.

He gallantly pulled back her chair, but Kristi wasn't able to appreciate the million-dollar ocean view as she sat down. She hadn't seen him since the cocktail party last Friday. So much had happened since then.

"Cat got your tongue?" James asked after the waiter took their order.

She took a sip of ice water and decided to start with the simple stuff. "How was the surf trip on Saturday?"

He grinned. "We had some fantastic swells. It was great."

"I'm sorry I missed it." She thought of how he hadn't returned her calls after that. "What did you do the rest of the weekend?"

"Worked. We had to prepare for Schmidt's arrest."

"Of course." A sailboat was headed for the harbor, its sail billowing white above the sparkling blue water. She wanted to appreciate the view and lunch at a classy place with a gorgeous guy, but how hard could it have been for him to return her calls, even just to tell her he was working?

The tuna nicoise came, and James ordered another glass of wine. He gave her a sympathetic look. "I'm sorry about your client, but we're going to encourage the judge to consider a first degree murder charge."

Kristi choked on the salad. First degree murder? No way could she imagine Rose lying in wait and killing with premeditation. She was stretched too thin. Killing in desperation, maybe, but not cold-blooded murder. That took a kind of calculation Rose didn't have. "Someone else could've done it."

He crossed his arms over his chest and regarded her skepticism. "Oh yeah, who?"

Kristi stared back, thinking. James walked in Ridley's circle. Maybe he knew something helpful. She decided to air her theory. "Ridley Niven."

"Ridley Niven?" James stared at her for a moment, confused, and then laughed. "My God, you're grasping at straws. The guy's harmless."

"Is he?" She gave him a challenging look. "I have a witness who saw him argue with Miss Cole the night she was murdered. Why would he?"

James shrugged. "I have no idea. The old man's a bit of a womanizer, but like I said, he's harmless."

"Is he harmless? Maybe he and Catherine had history, and maybe that caused complications now that he's planning to marry Beverly Carlyle."

James put down his wineglass. "You can't be serious."

"Well, were Catherine and Ridley ever involved?"

"I have no idea, but I don't see how, considering how what a recluse Catherine was."

"Why would a recluse go to party?"

James reached across the table and took her hand. "I know this is your first case, babe, but you can't force facts to fit together the way you want them to."

"I'm not!" Kristi shoved his hand away, aware that the commotion caused the well-mannered ladies seated around them to look over, perhaps with the same amused condescension on James' face.

An unpleasant truth crystallized inside her. James didn't take her PI work seriously. It was her dream, her passion, but he didn't think enough of her to trust her competence. A tiny voice inside whispered that Brian had always respected her profession and her feelings.

James suddenly rose to his feet. "Olivia."

Kristi had been so caught up in their conversation that she hadn't noticed the woman approaching their table. She was statuesque with long golden hair, and like James, her outfit shouted money, the silk business suit tailored to hug every curve of her model-perfect body, its short cut showcasing her long, long legs. She looked like the woman Kristi had seen driving with James in his convertible last week, but Kristi couldn't be sure.

"I hope I'm not interrupting?" The woman addressed James.

"Of course not. Kristi?" James glanced down at Kristi.

"Sure, why not?" Kristi said it with a polite smile, but she hated how dwarfish and unsophisticated she felt compared to the two of them.

James stepped behind the woman and pulled out a chair for her. Was this the woman James had talked to at the cocktail party, the one Brian had said left with him?

Olivia slid smoothly into the chair. Her blue eyes moved to Kristi, but she spoke to James. "And who's this?"

Kristi bristled. She didn't need James making introductions for her. Squaring her shoulders, she sat as tall as her five foot three inch frame would allow. "I'm Kristi McCormick. I'm owner of Eye Spy Private Eye."

Olivia's perfectly plucked eyebrows rose in a graceful arch. She sent James another amused look. "This the girl you were telling me about?"

Kristi wanted to shout, I'm no girl! Instead, she glared at Olivia. "How do you know James?"

Olivia glanced at James, and their eyes held a beat too long.

"Olivia and I went to law school together." James was still looking at Olivia. It was obvious they had history.

Kristi suddenly wondered, had he really been working over the weekend, or had he been with Olivia? Her lunch turned to acid in her stomach as she realized she didn't trust him. And he didn't seem to care enough about her to even pretend to be trustworthy, not with someone like Olivia around.

She wanted to throw down the cash for her lunch and get the heck out of there, but she didn't have the money. Instead, she pushed back from the table and launched to her feet.

Ignoring Olivia, she pointedly turned to James. "Thanks for lunch, James, but I think it best if we break things off with each other. Consider this good-bye."

"Goodbye?" He looked up at her in surprise, but then he glanced over at Olivia, who had started to laugh. Then he was laughing, too.

Whatever she'd expected from him, it wasn't laughter. Did he really share Olivia's disdain for her? Kristi was furious, but it also hurt, and the pain stabbed deeper as she stared down at the two of them. How naive she'd been to think he really cared for her! She turned and walked on stiff, shaky legs away from the picture perfect couple, fighting back sudden tears.

39. Tabitha Tyson

The drive to Tabitha Tyson's place in the Santa Monica Mountains was as tortuous as Kristi's own feelings. She was still furious at James, but she was also sad to think that any chance of something with him and the life he represented was over, and forget the fancy lunches. She also wasn't looking forward to telling her parents. At the same time, another part of her was relieved. Now she was free and didn't have to feel guilty about Brian.

Enough! She told herself as she drove up the long winding road. The tight curves felt like her case, with no way to see around the bends, and having to slow her pace to a frustrating crawl. As a result, she was half an hour late when she finally reached Tabitha's remote mountain cabin.

She knocked on the door of the rustic wood cabin and immediately launched into an apology when Tabitha opened the door. "Sorry I'm late. The drive took longer than I expected."

Tabitha greeted her with a friendly smile. "That's OK. I forgot to mention the drive."

Kristi had never met a mystery writer before, despite all the mysteries she'd devoured over the years, and she looked at Tabitha with open curiosity. The woman was a lot older than Sue Grafton, with long white hair that flowed over her shoulders. She wore a floor-length, brightly flowered muumuu in shades of blue and white. Deep lines bracketed her mouth and creased her eyebrows, indicating that she'd spent a lifetime of smiling and frowning a lot.

She led Kristi into a living room, whose walls were covered from floor to ceiling with packed bookshelves. More books lay in stacks on the coffee table, the couch, and around the room on the floor.

Tabitha lifted a stack of paperbacks off the couch to make room for Kristi to sit. "It's not often I have visitors."

"Your place is pretty remote."

"Yes, but I love how beautiful it is."

Through a large picture window, the sun blazed in the west beyond the mountains, and fog blanketed the distant ocean in a sea of white.

Tabitha settled herself into an old-fashioned wicker chair. "I still can't believe Catherine was murdered. I've been following the investigation in the paper. Everything seems to point to your client."

Kristi shook her head. "I believe Rose is being railroaded for something she didn't do. That's why I'm here."

"I thought it was a simple matter of money and a desperate woman."

Kristi shook her head again. "Think about it. Would someone who had just killed and robbed an old lady be dumb enough to keep the stolen jewels in her car? And who gave the anonymous tip to the police? There's also the question of the intruder Rose saw. The police haven't pursued that line of inquiry, because they're convinced she's guilty and made up the story."

"You think there really was an intruder?" Tabitha leaned forward, the wicker chair making crackling noises. "I love a good mystery. Who do you think it was?"

Kristi ran her hands through her hair. "That's why I'm here. I to broaden my search for suspects. Any chance you know who'd want Catherine dead?"

Tabitha shrugged. "I wish I could help, but like I said, Catherine and I haven't been close in years."

So much for that angle. Kristi tried another. "I heard that Catherine left you money in her will."

"She always supported my writing." Tabitha smiled sadly. "She was a big fan."

"Catherine's will left my client most of her estate. Do you think Catherine would be that generous with a house sitter she'd only known for a year?"

Tabitha considered Kristi's words. "Catherine was always generous, perhaps to a fault. She liked to help people. If what I've read about Rose's circumstances are true, it sure sounds like Rose would benefit from the money."

It was probably a long shot, but Kristi pulled Catherine's necklace from her purse, popped open the locket, and handed it to Tabitha. "Any chance you recognize her?"

Tabitha took the locket and stared at the photograph for a long moment. A sad, faraway expression moved across her face. She closed the locket gently, her fingers wrapping around the delicate piece of jewelry. "This necklace was Catherine's."

As she handed it back to Kristi, the pendant spun in the dim room, the sun sinking toward the foggy horizon.

Time to air her theory. "Was 'M' Catherine's daughter?" Kristi felt a surge of hope as Tabitha's eyes widened in surprise. "She was, wasn't she?"

Tabitha kept staring at the spinning pendant.

Kristi wasn't going to hold anything back, not if Tabitha could help. "Blackmail may have been the reason Catherine was killed."

Quickly, she summarized the clues she'd uncovered, from Rose giving her the locket and telling her to keep it secret, to Lorenzo's confession of having once been Catherine's lover, to the ink and paper fibers on Catherine's hand, and finally, to the photographs on Catherine's bedside table at the ranch.

When she was done, Tabitha gave her a gentle smile but shook her head. "You've created quite a case for the existence of a secret daughter, I'll give you that, but you've got it all wrong."

"Why?"

Tabitha's expression grew perplexed. "I just don't see how Miranda fits into Catherine's murder."

"Miranda? Is that 'M'?" Kristi sat forward on the couch. Finally, she was going to uncover the mystery of the locket.

A look of indecision creased the lines on Tabitha's face as she scrutinized Kristi. "I respect how hard you've worked to clear your client, despite the overwhelming odds against her, and I want to help you if I can. I'm just not sure that Miranda's relevant."

She broke off, her eyes still on Kristi. Finally, she nodded, as if to herself. "As a private investigator, you're discreet, right? If I tell you something, you'll keep it in confidence?"

"As long as it isn't something illegal, which I'd have to disclose if I were subpoenaed."

"Of course." Tabitha switched on the floor lamp beside her chair, the bright light accentuating hollows and shadows on her face, aging her. "Miranda wasn't Catherine's child. She was the love of Catherine's life."

Kristi stared at Tabitha in confusion. "What about Lorenzo Bianchi? He said Catherine and he had been in love. Was Catherine bisexual?"

Tabitha made a moue of displeasure. "I dislike labels. They have a way of forcing people into artificial constraints that restrict their freedom."

"Sorry, but I'm trying to make sense of who Catherine was."

Tabitha shook her head. "Love doesn't always make sense. It isn't an emotion of the brain but of the heart. Catherine was a woman of immense heart. Love guided her life."

Kristi tried to process what Tabitha said. "Where's Miranda now?"

"She was killed in Africa six years ago. Catherine was devastated."

"Africa?"

Tabitha nodded. "Miranda worked for a NGO over there."

That explained why Catherine had left money to a charity in Africa. Those fibers from an airmail letter must have been from Miranda!

Kristi studied Tabitha. "How do you know so much about Catherine and Miranda?"

Tears clouded Tabitha's eyes. "I doubt what I'm about to tell you will help your client, but it may help you understand Catherine's motivation for willing her the money, as long as you promise me to keep what I say an absolute secret. Do I have your word?"

"I promise." Kristi crossed a finger over her heart.

"Catherine and I were once in love."

Kristi tried not to let the shock show on her face. "When was that?"

"Oh, more than twenty years now. Long before Miranda." Tabitha pushed a stray strand of long white hair over her shoulder and sighed. "Perhaps your generation doesn't understand how hard it was for us back then. We couldn't be open about our relationship, not even with our own families. It was especially difficult for Catherine. Her family was so prominent, and she herself was such an active member in her church. My own career, too, was taking off and launching me into the public spotlight. We couldn't afford to be indiscreet. I lived here and wrote my novels. Catherine stayed in Santa Barbara."

"It must've been hard." Kristi's own love life was hard enough, but then she thought about her uncle and Catherine's vet, Josh. Maybe things still hadn't changed that much for gay people in prominent positions.

Tabitha continued. "It was a difficult way to live, always having to maintain that secrecy."

"Who ended it, you or she?"

Tabitha chuckled. "The instant we met Miranda, I knew Catherine was lovestruck."

"Weren't you angry or jealous?"

"I loved Catherine and wanted her to be happy. I knew she still loved me and would always love me, but her love for Miranda was

243

something bigger, something all-consuming." Tabitha looked out the window at the setting sun.

"What happened?"

"Perhaps it was folly and a tragic destiny in the making."

"What do you mean?"

"Catherine felt she couldn't live without Miranda by her side."

Kristi still didn't grasp what Tabitha was getting at. "I don't understand."

"Miranda went to live with Catherine at her house." The sad expression was back on Tabitha's face. "I don't know all the details, because after that, I fell out of touch with Catherine. I gather that they sequestered themselves on her estate and lived together in secret. I did hear that Catherine dropped out of public view and stopped attending church."

Kristi nodded. That jibed with what the priest had said. "She became known as the 'Recluse of Montecito.'"

Tabitha shook her head. "Grace Teller's reporting does have a flair for the melodramatic, but it was true about Catherine, especially after Miranda died."

"How did she die?"

"As I mentioned, she worked for an NGO in Africa. That's how Catherine and I met her, at a charity event for the organization. Miranda was killed during some kind of political incident in the country where she was working." The wicker chair crackled again as Tabitha shifted in her seat. She regarded Kristi with a troubled expression. "But I don't see how any of this helps your client."

Kristi thought of Ridley and what Tabitha had said about Catherine living a life ruled by love and her heart. "After Miranda died, do you know if Catherine was involved with a man named Ridley Niven?"

Tabitha shrugged. "I don't know. I only saw her a handful of times, when I was doing book signings up at Sara's bookshop in

SLO." Tabitha paused. "Come to think of it, there was one time I saw her with a man. It was a few years back, but I remember the occasion, because Catherine looked happier than I'd seen her since Miranda's death."

"Was he in his 50's or 60's, tall and handsome, maybe with a mustache?"

"Perhaps. To be honest, men don't interest me much, and that day my attention was wholly focused on my fans and on seeing Catherine again. I don't remember what we talked about, but I know she didn't mention the man. She certainly didn't introduce him to me."

"Why not?"

Tabitha shrugged again. "Catherine's love life was her own. I respected her. I've always respected whatever privacy she felt she needed." She gave Kristi a meaningful glance. "You will respect my privacy, too?"

"Of course. Thanks for telling me about Miranda." Kristi stood up. It was getting dark outside and way past time to hit the road. "One more thing. Do you know if Catherine and my client were involved?"

"I have no idea. Until I read about Rose in the paper, I'd never heard of her."

As they walked to the door, Kristi asked, "Do you think it's possible?"

Tabitha smiled. "As a mystery writer, I speculate all the time about people and their possible motives for murder, but we're talking about real people here, and about love. That's different." She opened the door to the night beyond, an unhappy expression lodging on her face. "I suppose I should wish you good luck on your case, but if Catherine was killed because of Miranda, I'm worried my own history with Catherine will come out."

Kristi stepped out into the cool night air. "Twenty years is a long time. I doubt you have to worry, and I sure won't say anything."

40. Brian at the Beach

A myriad questions burned in Kristi's brain as she headed back to Santa Barbara. Tabitha's revelations meant blackmail remained a distinct possibility in connection with Catherine's murder, but it had nothing to do with a secret child. Miranda had been Catherine's lover. Had Catherine also been involved with Rose, even though Rose denied it? Was that why she'd left Rose the bulk of her estate?

When Kristi reached Highway 1, she drove into a thick fog bank. Switching on her headlights, she scowled at the dark landscape as she thought about love. What did she really know about it, anyway?

Beyond loving her family and Carla and Gwen, she'd only ever read about love in books. Of course in many murder mysteries, love could switch to violent hate, given the right ingredients. A niggling voice that sounded unpleasantly like James' piped up. Maybe Rose had lied, and she and Catherine had been involved and had some kind of falling out. The same voice continued: wasn't it most likely that Rose had made up the intruder story in an attempt to deflect suspicion from herself, and wasn't it also just as likely that Rose had been the blackmailer?

James' casual disregard for her feelings still stung. Kristi considered the counterarguments. If Rose had been blackmailing Catherine, where was all the money? Why would she still be living in such squalid circumstances and working her ass off? And why would she tell Kristi anything at all about the locket? No, it didn't add up.

Kristi was starving by the time she finally reached Santa Barbara after the slow foggy drive. Her emotions were still raw about James, but as far as her stomach was concerned, her lunch with him was a distant memory. She needed food, but she also needed gas, so she headed to the cheapest gas station she knew about. As the dollar signs on the meter tick off, she winced. It would've been cheaper to pay with cash, but she didn't have any. Not anymore. Living on credit, her dad would so not approve.

No question, money was starting to become a real problem. If only she could solve this case, maybe the publicity would send a few new clients her way. She glanced at her watch: 7:30 pm. Time to update Brian. She went to the payphone and tried his number, doubting he'd still be in his office at such a late hour.

"Castillo."

Her pulse jumped. She hadn't expected him to answer, especially not on the first ring. "You sure are working late tonight." She couldn't stop thinking that she was a now a free agent. And so was he.

He yawned. "Sorry I didn't return your call this morning. It's been a long day."

"Mine, too." She exhaled. "There've been some developments I need to tell you about. You wanna get some dinner?"

It was just an invitation to talk shop, but her heart was pounding too hard in her chest, and she found herself holding her breath as she waited for him to respond.

"Sounds great. I've been so jammed at work, I missed lunch."

At his words, she smiled, but then worry crowded her mind. She'd been so distracted by the thought of asking him to dinner that she'd forgotten about her money problem. Dating James had spoiled her. She doubted Brian would want fast food, and there was no way she could afford a sit-down restaurant. She remembered a cheap soup and salad place on Milpas. "I'll grab some takeout. You wanna meet at the beach?"

"Sure. Where?"

"How about East Beach where we went swimming last weekend?"

He chuckled. "Kind of late for a swim, isn't it?"

She bit her lip to stop a nervous giggle. "No swimming. Just dinner. There's a lot to talk about." Anticipation flitted like butterflies through her and erased the tension that had dragged down so much of her day.

A short time later, she carried a bag of hot soup and crusty bread along with the towel she kept in her car to the beach. At night, the place was devoid of beachgoers and tourists. She'd been so distracted talking to Brian that she'd forgotten about the fog. Shivering in her cotton T-shirt, she realized she was dressed totally wrong for such a night and wished she'd suggested meeting somewhere warmer. Too late now. Brian was approaching from the boardwalk.

"Hey there." He still wore his lawyer's business suit, but he'd ditched his shoes and tie. His collar hung open at the throat, and his hair no longer lay flat and combed. It curled up unruly about his head, as if he'd been running his hands through his hair. Despite the dim light, she could see the fatigue on his face, but rather than detract, she found the sign of his humanity endearing. James never looked anything but picture perfect.

She held up the bag of takeout. "I've got food."

"Great. Here, let me help."

He took the towel from her, unfurled it, and laid it out on the sand. The towel wasn't quite big enough for the two of them, so that when he folded his long legs under himself to sit down beside her, his shoulder and knee touched hers. He didn't move away. "What did you want to talk about?"

She tried to focus on his words, but heat radiated through his clothing, and his body teased her with memories of their swim together, their kiss. Her stomach grumbled. "How about we eat first and talk later." She handed him one of the cartons and a spoon.

They ate in silence. The fog thickened, closing around them, and made it feel as if they were the only two people in the world. Despite the hot soup, Kristi shivered.

"Definitely not a good night for swimming, is it?" He said when they finished.

"More like bundling up and staying warm." She laughed, but it died in her throat as she imagined doing just that with him. Hastily, she put the empty cartons and spoons back in the bag and told her hormones to shut up. "I've learned something that might help Rose."

She quickly summarized her meeting with Lorenzo and Sara, and explained how Sara had led her to Tabitha Tyson. Tabitha's plea for confidentiality played in her head. She glanced at Brian. "As an attorney, you're bound to maintain your client's confidentiality, but what I have to tell you is particularly sensitive."

"OK." The way he said it made it sound like a question.

"I discovered that Catherine had a prior history of romantic relationships with other women, including Miranda and Tabitha. It's possible something was going on between her and Rose, considering she left most of her estate to Rose, even though Rose denied it."

"Huh. That could pose a problem." Brian shifted beside her. "I was going to argue that Rose was simply an innocent woman caught in the wrong place at the wrong time, and that the evidence against her is predominately circumstantial. If what you say is true, however, my argument falls apart, and Rose seems even more guilty." Frustration tightened his voice.

She wanted to reach over and touch his hand. Instead, she wrapped her arms tightly around herself, shivering again. The foggy night felt colder.

Brian shrugged out of his jacket. "You look like you could use this."

"Don't you need it?"

"I'm not cold."

"Thanks." She all but purred as he settled it over her shoulders, the fabric warm from his body. "There's still the issue of the intruder."

"We've already discussed that. The prosecution will argue that it's nothing but hearsay based on the biased testimony of the prime suspect, and we don't have any evidence to counter it."

"True, but think about it. Catherine had a secret she was desperate to hide, so much so that she was willing to forswear her Catholic faith and abandon her public life. For longer than a decade, she lived like a recluse as a result of that secret. I bet she'd pay any price if someone threatened to expose it. Maybe the night she died, she and the blackmailer had a confrontation."

"You know that everything you're saying is conjecture, right?" Despite the implied criticism in his words, she took heart from his empathetic tone, which sounded nothing like James' when he'd talked to her about the case.

She forged on, speaking quickly to explain her reasoning, and told him about her trip to Santa Ynez and her interview with Beverley Carlyle and Ridley Niven. "So you see, the night Catherine died, we have a witness who saw Ridley arguing with Catherine."

"What did they argue about?"

"I don't know. Yet." Kristi wished she had something more definitive to tell him. "Ridley claims Beverly simply misunderstood and that there was no argument, but he'd already tried to deny even talking to Catherine."

"What are you getting at?"

"I think Ridley's lying. He's the only person I've found who's argued with Catherine. Not only that, but it was on the very night she was murdered, and he tried to deny it. I also think he's the intruder Rose heard arguing with Catherine, which means he's the killer."

Brian shifted again beside her, his knee no longer touching hers. "Your linking two incidents that may have no connection and certainly don't prove your conclusion. How well did Ridley know Catherine?"

"Well enough to invite her to that party."

Kristi's mind spun with questions. The fundraiser had supported a pro-marriage agenda that was tacitly homophobic... Maybe Ridley had somehow found out about Catherine's history with Miranda and was blackmailing her. Considering his political views, however, why would he want to publicly associate with her? More puzzling was the question of why Catherine would attend such an event.

Aloud, Kristi said, "I've been trying to arrange another interview with Beverly and Ridley, but it's hard to get a hold of them. They're due to be married soon and are very busy with wedding preparations."

Brian ran a hand through his hair. "I don't see how Ridley could be a suspect, not if he was hosting a party the night Catherine was killed. Motive is a problem, too. Why would a wealthy man blackmail one of his friends? And as I said before, it doesn't make sense that a blackmailer would kill his source of revenue."

Kristi wanted to groan. There was nothing to say to counter him, because he was right. The heat from his jacket had cooled and she shivered.

Brian leaned on back on his elbows beside her and unfolded his legs, stretching them out. "I'm sorry, Kristi. I know you were hoping to uncover something that would prove Rose innocent. I was, too, but unfortunately, the case against her is pretty damning. Assuming it goes to trial, I'll try to argue circumstantial evidence for what the prosecution throws at her, but I doubt that'll be enough to persuade a jury."

Kristi's legs were going numb from sitting cross-legged, so she copied Brian and lay back on the towel. Renewed warmth stole into her from the long length of his body stretched out beside her, but the pleasant sensation was dampened as she thought about what he'd said. James had said as much at that horrid lunch. She could still hear his and that woman's condescending laughter.

Aloud she said, "Don't people care about the truth? I can't stand the idea of Rose being railroaded."

"She's not being railroaded. There simply aren't any other plausible suspects."

Kristi wanted to argue that Ridley was still a loose thread, but even if he were guilty, he'd simply deny it. The only way she'd could prove it was with hard evidence. Had Catherine kept any personal records showing payouts to Ridley?

She looked over at Brian. "Any chance you could get me in to take another look around Catherine's?"

Brian shook his head. "At this point, I'd need a judge to agree that we have probable cause for a search warrant. Why?"

She doubted the judge or Brian would think her blackmail theory sufficient probable cause. Looking out into the foggy murk, she said, "Forget it."

The night felt colder, and she grew aware again of how alone they were together on the dark beach. There was something intimate about lying just inches from him. Her teeth started to chatter. She clenched them together as a new tension gripped her. "I told James I don't want to see him anymore."

"You did?" Brian stated the words without feeling.

"Today at lunch." Kristi wished she could see his expression in the dim light.

"Are you OK?"

"Yes. No. Actually, it sucked."

"I'm sorry it didn't go well."

At his empathetic tone, she started shivering again. He was caring and considerate, nothing like James. How had she been so naive as to confuse James' good looks and his money with what really mattered?

Brian voice came quiet in the darkness. "I'd be lying if I said I was sorry you're done with him."

A new joy suddenly swept through Kristi. Impulsively, she reached over and laid her hand on his. "I'm not sorry, either."

"Your hand's cold." He rotated his hand so that their palms touched.

"Yours is so warm," she said, unable to stop her teeth from chattering as she interlaced her fingers with his and felt the electric tension sparking between them.

"Sounds like the perfect combination." His voice was a deep resonance that vibrated all the way down to her toes.

He inched closer until their bodies touched all the way down. He felt so warm and strong and good, she nestled even closer. Needing no further encouragement, he slid an arm under her shoulders and brought her more fully against him.

And then they were kissing, deep and passionate. All cold was gone, replaced by fire. It burned hot and bright, and soon kissing wasn't enough. Not nearly enough. Placing her hands on his chest, she pushed him down and climbed on top of him, humming with pleasure when she felt how his desire matched her own.

"Heh, heh. Whatcha doin' there?" A scruffy voice broke the moment.

Brian rolled Kristi off him, quickly and smoothly. Shielding her with his body, he sat up and faced the man. "None of your business." His usually even-tempered voice growled, rough and dangerous. "Move along."

Kristi jerked upright and peered around his shoulder. In the foggy darkness, the lumpy shadow of a homeless man wearing several coats lurked nearby. Rather than do as Brian said, the man put down his garbage bags and started rustling around inside them.

"Let's get out of here." Kristi grabbed the takeout bag and launched to her feet. She was shivering again, her body shaking with frayed nerves and the cold.

Brian gathered the towel and took her hand in his, its warm strength reassuring as they crossed the cold sand to the pavement. When they got to her car, he slid his arms around her again. She leaned into his warmth and listened to the steady, solid beat of his heart.

"I wish I had a place of my own where we could go," she murmured.

He chuckled, his voice rumbling against her ear. "I've never wanted one until now. Things moved pretty quickly back there. You OK?"

She smiled. "I am now."

41. Trespassing

Kristi tried not to think about Brian as she drove to the Magic Shop. She needed Carla's help with the plan she was forming, but when she got to the shop, she found her sister and Gwen seated at one of the display counters poring over their textbooks and cramming for their midterm exams.

When she tried to quietly talk to Carla, Izzy overheard. "You broke it off with James?"

Gwen looked up from her textbook, concerned. "Are you OK?"

Kristi scowled at her sister and Gwen. "Don't you two need to study?"

"What are Mom and Dad going to say?" Izzy obviously found her love life more interesting than math.

Carla's perceptive green eyes were still on Kristi. "Get back to work, you two."

She grabbed Kristi by the hand and pulled her over to the red Victorian couch in the Magic Shop's small reading area, which was enclosed by shelves of occult books for sale.

Out of earshot of the other girls, Carla said softly, "Nothing's stopping you from hooking up with Brian now, right?"

"Nothing except a lack of privacy. He lives at home, too." Kristi leaned back and rested her head against the plush velvet sofa cushions. It had been a long, long day.

"We could work out something here at the Magic Shop, maybe use a code or hang up a sign when you want Gwen and me outta here, so you and Brian could, you know..." Her lips turned up in a wolfish grin.

Kristi felt her cheeks heat. The beach had been one thing, but Brian alone with her here at the Magic Shop, maybe right here on the big red couch? "No way!"

Carla laughed. "No need to get embarrassed. Consider it a standing offer. You just let me know, OK?"

"Geez," Kristi groaned. She should've remembered that Carla always thought sex first and feelings later. "Thanks, but no thanks. He's still my client. Anyway, I came by tonight for help with something other than my love life."

"Yeah?" The humor on Carla's face instantly cleared and her green eyes zeroed in on Kristi with laser-like focus.

Kristi's heart ratcheted up at the thought of what she was planning to do. It went against every law abiding instinct she had, not to mention that if she got caught she'd probably be arrested and have to kiss her dreams of being a PI goodbye. "I need to do a little breaking and entering."

"Oooh, sounds dangerous! Can I come along?"

Kristi shook her head. "You can't risk getting arrested, not with Gwen still a minor."

Carla exhaled in frustration. "You've got a point."

Kristi glanced over at their two sisters. As the oldest of the Cota Club, she'd always felt responsible for setting a good example. Carla had never felt bound by such constraints. There'd been plenty of times she'd pushed the limits, especially in high school, when she fell for the golden boy, Mark Lyons, and became a pro at sneaking undetected onto his family's Montecito estate. "I need your advice about how to trespass and not get caught."

"Where are you going and when?"

"Let's just say it's a mansion in Montecito." Kristi didn't plan on getting caught, but even so, Carla didn't need to know the specifics, not for plausible deniability. Kristi glanced at the clock over the Magic Shop door. It was just past 8:30. "About midnight tonight."

Carla shook her head. "Not late enough. Go at least an hour later. You been there before, or are you going in blind?"

"I've been there once before." Kristi suddenly realized she'd forgotten to ask Brian about Tomas. Was the groundskeeper still living in the carriage house? He could pose a problem. "I'll wear black and bring a flashlight."

"You got a black cap or something to hide that bright hair of yours?"

"Good idea."

"The place have videocameras or other security?"

Kristi shook her head, but Tomas and his big muscles leapt to mind. She'd go really late, hopefully long after he went to sleep.

Carla leaned back on the sofa and clasped her hands behind her head. "That should make things easier. Obviously, you'll want to case the joint before going in, and make sure the coast is clear. You've been practicing with your lockpicks?"

Kristi nodded. "Yeah, but I'll never be as good as you."

Carla grinned. "I aim someday to be a pro. Anyway, don't forget to wear latex gloves the whole time you're trespassing, and make sure to keep your hands free and wear running shoes, in case you need to make a quick getaway."

"Why do you need your hands free to make a quick getaway?"

"In case you have to hop a fence, or fight someone."

Kristi gulped. Running away was scary enough, but fighting? "Have you had to do that before?"

"I'm just saying, it's good to keep your hands free when you're in a dangerous situation." Carla's smile reminded Kristi of the Cheshire cat.

Breaking the law was bad enough, but a confrontation, maybe with Tomas? Kristi's stomach rolled.

Carla caught her expression. "You afraid?"

"I need to find evidence related to the case I'm working on, but I don't want to get caught holding stolen property. I guess I'd better photograph the evidence."

"That could take too much time, and the camera flash could pose a problem. Better to grab and go. You have a target location, or will you have to spend time searching?"

"I'll need some time, but that's OK, because no one's there."

Carla gave a short, sharp jerk of her head. "Never assume you're safe, not when you're trespassing. It's always better to be on your guard and aim for a speedy operation. Whatever you do, be as quick and quiet as you can."

Her friend's words underscored the enormity of what she was about to do. Frowning, she shook her head. "I don't know. After everything you've said, maybe I should just forget it. If I'm caught, I could be arrested, and there's no guarantee I'll find what I'm looking for, anyway. Besides, if Brian finds out..."

Carla's green eyes glinted with challenge. "Come on, Kristi, don't be a chicken. The key is don't get caught, right?"

Rose's face flashed into Kristi's mind, the way she'd looked so sad and hopeless in the ugly orange jail suit. That image was followed by Ridley's self-satisfied smile. If he was guilty, Rose shouldn't have to pay for his crimes. The injustice of it made Kristi angry. She pushed herself off the couch. "You're right, Carla. I'll make sure not to get caught. Thanks for all the advice."

Carla also stood up. "I wish I could go with you."

"I wish you could, too." Kristi gave her friend a quick hug before leaving.

It was after 1 am Thursday morning when Kristi finally set off for Montecito. The road climbed out of the fog bank hanging over Santa Barbara and into the darkness of a moonless sky, unblemished by city lights. To the south lay the black swath of the Pacific Ocean and to the north the Los Padres National Forest, which left the Montecito foothills lit only by starlight.

Perfect for snooping, Kristi hoped, as she arrived at Catherine's property. She was tired but wired at the same time. It had been a crazy long day, and her emotions were still a wild roller coaster over her breakup with James and the kiss with Brian. What she was about to do added to the tension. Trespassing plus breaking and entering. She couldn't imagine Brian would approve, and no way did she want her uncle to find out.

She parked just outside on a gravel berm, poised for a quick escape. No way she was going to risk driving all the way up to the mansion, not after what Carla had said, and she kicked herself for letting her hormones take over with Brian. She should've asked him if Tomas was still staying at the carriage house. Too late now for regrets. Hopefully, it was late enough that Tomas would be asleep.

Gathering her supplies in her shoulder bag, she got out of the car and pulled the hood of her black sweatshirt over her hair. As she stepped onto Catherine's property, the gravel drive crunched much too loudly underfoot. Hurriedly, she moved onto the mulched berm beside road, the soft soil muffling her footsteps. The glimmering starlight was enough to see by, as long as she didn't move too fast. No way was she going to risk turning on the flashlight. Except for the occasional rustling of critters in the bushes and the distant splash of a fountain, the night was quiet, but she barely heard anything over the pounding of her heart. How she wished she had Carla's daredevil nerves, because this kind of thing was so not her cup of tea.

At the top of the hill, the mansion's hulking mass was silhouetted against the starry sky. Kristi was relieved to see no lights on in the mansion or over in the carriage house, but her adrenaline was still pumping too hard for her to relax.

She went around the mansion to the kitchen door and the two ceramic cats. Pulling on her latex gloves, she scooped up the key, slid it into the door lock, and heard the distinctly satisfying click of the bolt sliding back. She put the key back under the cat and carefully pushed open the door.

Without stars, the kitchen was pitch black. Nothing to do but use the flashlight. She pulled it out and held it low, against her side, using her fingers to dim the bright light.

The kitchen was large and surprisingly old-fashioned, with black and white checkered floor tiles and large retro appliances, which gleamed dully in the glow of her flashlight. Two sets of doors stood at opposite ends of the room.

On silent sneaker feet, she hurried to the first door and pushed aside its swinging panel. A quick sweep of the flashlight illuminated a breakfast room with a table, chairs, and buffet. No sign of anything useful. Through the other set of doors, Kristi found herself in a long, dark hallway.

As she paused there, she suddenly became aware of how quiet the house was. There was no ticking clock, no house creaks, and she couldn't hear the refrigerator hum anymore. She didn't believe in ghosts, but that didn't stop the creepy feeling crawling through her. Catherine had died in the house. Murdered. Kristi found herself again wishing that she had Carla's nerves of steel.

Get a grip! she told herself. PIs aren't supposed to get spooked. She checked her watch. 2 am. Plenty of time before daylight to search the place.

She went down the hallway to the first door, swung it open, and shone the flashlight inside. A bedroom suite. She stepped inside and did a quick search, but found nothing of interest. The next two doors along the hallway contained similar bedroom suites. Like the first, they all had the slightly musty smell of rooms long unoccupied. How many bedrooms did the place have, Kristi wondered. It was hard to imagine living in a house with so much unused space.

The hallway ended at the grand foyer. Her eyes went to the bottom of the staircase, but the markers where Catherine had died were gone. As the flashlight beam darted about, the creepy feeling came back again. The beam was too feeble to reach the second floor landing, and it did nothing to penetrate the cavernous gloom overhead. What if something white suddenly flitted across that dark space?

Gritting her teeth, Kristi brought the beam back down to ground level and forced herself to ignore the hair rising on the back of her neck. Several arched doorways led off the foyer. She passed through the closest and found herself in a large sitting room outfitted with dark Mission style furniture and a big fireplace. At the far end was a closed door.

Kristi hurried across the room, training her flashlight on the door. Halfway across, her toe caught under the edge of a runner carpet, and she catapulted forward. The flashlight flew from her hand and clattered across the tile floor, its light beam bouncing wildly, as she smashed down onto the hard tiles, banging her knees and jamming her wrists as she hit the ground.

"Ow!" she cried out, but then clamped her mouth shut, remembering Carla's advice to be quick and quiet.

Grabbing the flashlight, she got to her feet, her knees throbbing. No doubt there'd be bruises, but no time to worry about that now. She rushed to the door and turned the handle. Shining her flashlight inside, she felt a rush of elation. It was a small office, with a desk, several filing cabinets, and bookshelves, but then she saw how the filing cabinet drawers stood open, books had been pulled off the shelves and onto the floor, and the desk was covered haphazardly with paper.

What the heck? Had the police searched the place and left it like this, or had someone else ransacked it?

Kristi hurried to the desk and looked through the papers. It took a moment to switch mental gears and decipher the legalese, but she realized she was holding a property deed for the Santa Ynez ranch and paperwork associated with the purchase and sale of ranch livestock. Another collection of papers included a copy of Catherine's will.

Pushing aside the papers, she found a slim leather bound binder. She opened it and saw neat blue cursive listing dates, amounts, items, and there was a column where initials had been added.

An account book! Kristi's heart jumped with hope as she ran a finger down the balance column. Wow. She now knew exactly what Catherine's trust attorney had meant when he'd said Catherine had money 'sufficient for her lifestyle.' Her monthly allowance was more than Kristi hoped to make in a year.

Kristi looked at Catherine's expenses. An item listed as "Soil Amendment" had a "T" by it, obviously standing for Tomas, and several items were labeled "B and W" and assigned to "J," which had to correspond to Catherine's cats, Balthazar and Walnut, and their vet, Josh. One of the most recent inputs, just days before Catherine's death, was an "R" by "House sitting." The amount wasn't much, certainly not on the scale of blackmail, but considering the small size of Rose's teaching paychecks, the $100 must have been a godsend.

Kristi now also had an answer to why Catherine hadn't given cash to Eduardo. Right before Catherine gave Eduardo the diamond earrings, she'd made a $25,000 payment to "R", which had drained her balance to practically nothing. Was "R" Rose, or could it be Ridley?

Kristi pulled her camera and her beach towel from her bag. Draping the towel over her head and shoulders to hide the flash, she started snapping photos of the first pages of the account book, her excitement growing when she noted Catherine had made big payments to "R" every few months or so.

Something creaked.

Kristi froze, her heart jumping as she listened. There it was again. A distinct creak somewhere in the distance, maybe the foyer. And then again. Footsteps coming closer. Tomas?

"Who's there?" A woman called out.

A woman? The voice sounded vaguely familiar, and then Kristi placed it, remembering the sharp, distinctive tone: Catherine's niece, Anita Walker. Catherine's ranch manager had said that Anita was preparing to inherit the estate despite Rose not yet being convicted.

Darn. The woman must've already moved in.

Kristi dropped the ledger back on the desk and shoved her camera and towel back in her bag. Her eyes flew to the door on the other side of the office. She had no idea where it went, but she was a sitting duck if she stayed there. Dashing over, she swung it open, but in her haste, she pushed too hard and the door crashed into the wall. Footsteps started running toward her.

Racing through the door, she found herself in another hallway. She couldn't afford to turn off her flashlight's telltale beam as she ran full speed down the hall.

"I've got a gun!" Anita yelled behind her, footsteps pounding closer.

A gun? No way did Kristi want to confront a gun-toting angry woman.

Fear made her fly on winged feet back through the foyer and down the familiar hall to the kitchen. She made it outside, but as she started across the gravel drive, a gunshot blasted right behind her. Dropping to the ground, the sharp gravel cut into her palms and her heart pounded with terror. Glancing over her shoulder, she saw Anita standing on the kitchen stoop in some kind of red silken robe with a smoking gun in her hand.

Across the driveway, the carriage house porch light suddenly flicked on, and Tomas burst out onto the landing, dressed only in sweatpants and running shoes, the massive muscles in his huge shoulders bunched and gleaming.

He called out, "What is going on?"

"There's an intruder!" Anita shouted back at him.

"Que?"

Kristi thanked her lucky stars that Tomas' English was so bad. While Anita screamed at him in frustration and tried to explain, Kristi got up, staying in a low crouch, and ran around the side of the mansion and out of view. She didn't stop running until she got to her car.

42. Loose Ends

Thursday morning, Kristi brought a travel mug of coffee from home to her office. She hoped the extra caffeine would help compensate for the four meager hours of sleep she got after her late night trip to Catherine's place. The answering machine light was blinking, so she put her mug down on the desk and played the message.

"Krissy, we got a call about an intruder at Catherine Cole's house last night. Someone small and dressed in a dark hoodie and jeans. Was it you? If so, what the hell were you thinking? Trespassing with breaking and entering? Don't think because I'm your uncle that I'll go soft on you if you get caught. That's not how it works. I'm gonna be out of touch the next couple of days on a new case, but you be careful. Don't break the law."

Kristi sat back in her chair and tried to pull her stomach out of her shoes. Thank goodness she'd worn the hoodie last night and hadn't been more positively ID'd by Anita or Tomas. She was pretty sure she hadn't left behind any incriminating evidence, and thank goodness she hadn't taken anything.

Taking a sip of coffee, Kristi thought about what she'd found. Though she hadn't been able to photograph the entire ledger before Anita showed up, she'd seen enough to know that it appeared to track every dollar Catherine spent. More importantly, it showed that every few months, Catherine made sizable payments to "R." But did "R" stand for Ridley, or Rose?

Kristi took another sip of coffee from her travel mug and wanted to curse Catherine's secretive nature. Why couldn't she have just written out "Ridley", or at least included line item descriptions for the big payments? As it was, the house sitting payments linked "R" to Rose, but there was no proof that the big payouts to "R" corresponded to Ridley, and there was no mention of blackmail. Kristi could just imagine what James and the prosecution would argue: "R" could mean anything or anyone, including her client, Rose, and there was no indication what the money was for.

Getting up and pacing over to the window, Kristi felt her frustration mount. The morning fog made everything outside gray, the opaque sky as cryptic as the case. Even if there were love letters from Miranda and incriminating photos, and assuming Ridley was the blackmailer, how had he gotten hold of them? More importantly, even if Kristi could prove he was a blackmailer, that still didn't prove he was the killer.

The phone rang. Her uncle calling back? She let the answering machine take it. Her recorded voice rattled out its message and Brian came on the line.

She hurried back to her desk and grabbed the receiver. "Hey, Brian!"

"Good morning. You get home OK last night?"

At the quiet intimate tone of his voice, Kristi gulped, overcome by a sudden wave of guilt. "Uh, yeah."

She'd been so wrapped up in what had happened later that she hadn't thought about Brian and their relationship. She did know that until she had solid proof about Ridley, Brian didn't need to know the details of her illegal activities. Even so, she didn't like keeping things from him. "It was great hanging out last night. What's up?"

"I just met with Rose at County. After what you told me last night, I wanted to ask her about Miranda."

Kristi smiled. Brian hadn't tossed out her theory like James had but had given it enough credence to follow up with their client. "What did you find out?

Brian cleared his throat. When he spoke again, the intimate tone was gone. "Want to tell me about the locket Rose took from Catherine the night she was murdered?"

Kristi gulped again. It hadn't occurred to her that Rose might say anything. "Rose told you?"

"Why didn't you tell me?" Brian sounded impatient.

"It didn't seem relevant at the time."

"Not relevant?" Now he sounded irritated. "You're talking about additional crimes my client committed and that you didn't disclose to me, not to mention your own complicity in a crime. Kristi, this is serious."

"I know." Kristi clutched the phone to her ear. "You're right, Brian. I should've told you."

Silence on his end.

Fumbling for words, Kristi tried to fill the uncomfortable void that had opened up between them. "I'm sorry, but when the the locket surfaced, I wanted to find out if Miranda was Catherine's child, and when Rose told me to—"

"That's not the point, Kristi. Maybe our personal feelings have muddied the waters, but don't forget that I hired you. I need to know you're telling me the truth, especially with respect to my client. I can't sanction you doing anything illegal. Understand?"

Kristi cringed. He was so honorable and good. Could she measure up to his standards, especially when she hadn't told him about her trip to Catherine's? He'd probably fire her on the spot, and she'd have to kiss any hope of a future with him goodbye. Still, she couldn't outright lie to him, so she hedged. "I promise I won't hide anything from you about Rose." Before he caught what was missing from her promise, she rushed on. "When you met with her, did you find out how she knew about Miranda?"

"I did. But damn, I'm not happy just finding out now how much Rose has withheld from me."

"What do you mean?"

"Besides the whole locket thing, it turns out she wasn't simply Catherine's house sitter. She now says Catherine used to invite her for tea on Sunday afternoons, which is how they became friends and how she learned about Miranda."

Kristi frowned. "Eduardo never mentioned seeing Rose when I asked him about Catherine's visitors."

"That's because he always spent Sundays with his family."

"Why did Rose lie about her friendship with Catherine? It seems like it caused more problems than if she'd simply told the truth from the beginning."

"I asked her the same thing. She said she believed that if she claimed not to know Catherine well, she'd more easily be able to hide Catherine's secrets and thereby preserve Catherine's reputation." Kristi could hear the frustration in his voice at Rose's behavior.

"At least her intentions were honorable. It all comes back to secrets and protecting them. I need to pursue the blackmail angle."

"Forget it, Kristi. Short of proving the intruder was the killer as well as the blackmailer, we'd get nowhere in court, and I don't see how you could do that, not legally." He paused for emphasis on the last word, and she cringed again, realizing that they were at a moral impasse. He finished by saying, "I'm sorry, but I've gotta go. Rose is being arraigned today, and I've got my work cut out for me."

Kristi dropped the phone back in the receiver. Despite the moral quandaries posed by their conversation, memories of their time together on the beach whispered through her, the way the night had wrapped around them, his arms around her. Brian was right that the personal was muddling their professional relationship. He was also right about the problem of linking the blackmail theory with murder.

So why not do what he said and forget it? Let the legal process take over at this point and move onto something else... but what? That was the problem. There were no other cases, and there were still those loose threads about Ridley and the payments to "R."

No, she couldn't quit. Not yet. The first thing to do was establish that Ridley could have gone to Montecito the night Catherine was murdered. To do that, she needed to talk to Beverly Carlyle again.

It wasn't until several hours later that Beverly finally returned her call.

"The party wrapped up about 7 pm. It was just a cocktail thing, after all," Beverly said, when Kristi asked her about the timeline that night.

"What did you do after that?"

"Ridley and I drank more champagne, and well..." Beverly gave a low laugh. "We celebrated some more."

Kristi sighed. It didn't sound like Ridley could've sneaked out. "Was he with you the rest of the night?"

"Of course. Where else would he be?"

Disappointment descended on Kristi. It looked like Ridley had a solid alibi and her whole theory was nothing but wishful thinking. Still, she had to ask, "What time did you go to bed?"

There was a pause.

"Was it before or after 9:30 pm?"

There was another pause.

Kristi felt a beat of hope. "Do you remember?"

Beverly laughed again, but this time with a certain embarrassment. "After all the champagne, I honestly don't know."

"I see." Kristi managed to say the words without letting her excitement show. If Beverly passed out, Ridley could have slipped away.

There was one other question she hoped Beverly could answer, but she had no idea how to do it gracefully. "I know you're engaged to marry Mr. Niven, so this is a bit awkward to ask, but do you know if he and Miss Cole ever, um, dated?"

Beverly gave a high tittering laugh. "Well, you certainly aren't one to beat around the bush, Miss McCormick. I heard something about that, but it was a while back, maybe four or five years ago, right after her brother and his wife died. What on earth does any of that have to do with your investigation?"

Ridley had been involved with Catherine! The timeline fit with what Sara had told her about seeing Catherine with a man at her bookstore four years ago. He must've found out about Miranda while dating Catherine, and given his political views, Kristi could only imagine how furious he must've been to discover Catherine had a lesbian history.

Beverly's voice broke into her train of thought. "Miss McCormick, are you still there?"

"Sorry." Kristi scrambled for an answer. "I'm just following up some loose ends."

"Of course, but I'm sorry, I must go. I'm already running late for my golf game with Ridley."

"He's not there with you?"

"No, he's over at his place."

"I'd like to talk to him. When do you suggest I reach him?"

"The game should be over about 5 o'clock. You can try after that."

Kristi had no intention of calling him, at least not yet. She checked her watch. It was now just after 1 pm. Four hours should be enough time to snoop at Ridley's ranch before he and Beverly finished their game. If her hunch was right and she got lucky, she'd find Ridley's financial records with deposits matching Catherine's payments, and she'd find out if he'd really needed the money.

Gathering together what she'd need for her trip, Kristi gave herself a pep talk, reminding herself why she was about to break the law again, but it took some effort to quash the fear and the guilt. There'd be hell to pay, if and when Pete and Brian found out. Still, she needed to know the truth.

43. Evidence

Kristi spread the AAA road map out on her desk and checked directions to Ridley's ranch. The more she thought about her plan, the more she worried she grew. What if there were other people at Ridley's place? No way did she want another crazy gun-toting encounter.

Part of her brain told her, no way. The whole thing smacked of a harebrained scheme that might turn out pointless, if she found nothing to establish Ridley as either blackmailer or killer. That part of her brain also reminded her that if she did do it, she could forget any chance of a relationship with Brian. He'd never hire her again, not after he told her not to break the law.

At the same time, another part of her brain said, you've gotta try. What self-respecting PI would leave a crucial stone unturned, if her client was unjustly sent to prison and the guilty man got away? No way. She owed it to Rose, to the memory of Catherine, maybe even to Beverly, who was about to marry Ridley. More importantly, she had to know the truth. If Ridley killed Catherine, she'd do everything in her power to prove it. She just wished it didn't involve breaking the law again.

A tight feeling gnawed at her belly as she glanced at her watch. 1:30 pm. Brian would be on his way to Rose's arraignment. She phoned his office anyway and left a detailed message of her plan on his answering machine. If things went wrong, better him mad after the fact than for no one to know what she was up to. As an added precaution, she tucked the locket and the roll of film from her trip to Catherine's into a manila envelope, addressed it to Brian, and dropped it in the mail.

It was almost 2 o'clock by the time she got on the road. As she drove up the steep serpentine climb on Highway 154, she noticed the fog bank beginning to roll back in from the ocean, its tendrils creeping over Isla Vista and UC Santa Barbara. On the steep chaparral-covered flanks of the Santa Ynez Mountains where she drove, the sun still blazed with scorching heat.

Thursday afternoon traffic was light, and her thoughts wandered over the details of her plan. Ridley ran a horse breeding business, so he had to have some sort of office. That would be the best place to start her search. If Ridley stayed busy playing golf with Beverly until at least 4:30, she'd have almost an hour and a half to check out his place.

It was pushing 3 o'clock when she arrived at his ranch. Like the other rural properties in the area, it didn't have a gated entry, so Kristi drove right in. The place wasn't nearly the size of Catherine's ranch and smaller than Beverly's property, but it was picturesque, with white-fenced paddocks housing a few gorgeously well-groomed, grazing Arabian horses.

The house lay at the far end of the paddocks along with a horse barn and a covered riding area set off to one side. She stopped the car at the edge of the first paddock. Such a professional-looking operation must have workers and ranch hands. Squinting against the bright afternoon sun, she looked around for any sign of people. No one was in the fields, but she spotted a van parked in front of the house.

Uh oh. Were there people in it, or would the people it belonged to come out of the house and see her?

The tight feeling was back in her belly again and the heat wasn't helping. Her brain felt overheated and sweat was making her hair stick to her head.

She opened the glove compartment and pulled out a small pair of binoculars Carla had given her for Christmas last year. Adjusting their focus, she read the logo on the van's side. A cleaning service. How hard up for money could Ridley be if he could afford a cleaning service? And the ranch certainly looked well-cared for. Kristi's self-doubt flooded back. Maybe her theory was all wrong. Maybe she should just turn around and get out of there while she could.

But then you'll never know for sure, a small voice whispered. And she'd driven all the way out there.

Her eyes traveled to the barn. What were the odds it was worth checking out? She didn't know much about horses or barns and doubted there'd be an office in there, but she wasn't about to sit around and do nothing as she waited for the cleaning people to finish at the house.

Putting her car in gear, it wasn't until she'd driven past the van and all the way around behind the barn and safely out of sight of the house that she breathed a sigh of relief. Someone driving by on the road or turning onto the property would see her, but there was nothing she could do about that. She checked her watch. 3:15.

Well, here goes nothing, she thought, hitching her bag over her shoulder as she got out of the car.

The barn was big and red, painted with white trim, and reminded Kristi of every barn she'd seen in picture books as a kid. There were large double doors on each end. She headed for the closer one. Pausing outside, she listened for any indication of people, but the coast seemed clear. She stepped inside, blinking in the sudden darkness, and her nose was assaulted by the steamy pungent smell of hay and horse urine. As her eyes adapted, she counted a line of six stalls on each side. Several horses hung their heads out of the open dutch doors, studying her with curiosity.

The door at the far end of the barn and closest to the house was different than the others. It didn't have a dutch door but was solid and full-sized, and closed. Could it be an office, or was it merely a supply room?

Kristi walked quietly past the open stall doors, noting that eight of them contained horses. When she got to the closed door, she saw two locks: a standard one and a deadbolt. That was a good sign. She doubted a supply room would have the extra security. Of course, if the deadbolt was on, she'd be out of luck and unable to pick it. She stood for a moment and listened again. The only sound came from the horses shuffling about in their stalls. No sound came from behind the door. Just in case, she knocked. No response.

Here goes nothing, she thought, trying the doorknob. Locked.

Tilting her head to the side, she peeked through the crack where the door met the frame and was relieved to see the deadbolt wasn't engaged. She glanced at her watch again. 3:20 pm. Picking the lock would take time. Maybe the room had a window she could more easily access. Hurrying back outside, she went around the side of the barn. The room had a window, but it had black iron bars on it. Through the glass she saw a desk and a filing cabinet. It was an office!

Dashing back inside, Kristi pulled on her latex gloves and took her lock picks from her bag. Guiltily, she looked over her shoulder. Being caught trespassing was one thing, but to be caught red-handed picking a lock...

Her fingers trembled as she fumbled with the picks and tried working them into the lock. What if someone came now? She dropped the picks, wishing again she had Carla's nerves.

What kind of PI are you if you can't pick a darned lock, she chastised herself as she picked up the tools and tried a second time. Still no luck. Blowing out an anxious breath, she wiped the sweat from her forehead on the back of her arm and tried a third time. Click.

Elation surged through her as she hastily put away the tools and swung open the door. The office walls were lined with framed photographs of horses wearing ribbons on their halters, and in several, Ridley posed beside the horses. They were beautiful and obviously his pride and joy. Definitely Ridley's office.

Hopeful, Kristi went straight across to the bare desk and slid open the top drawer. There was a check book sitting right there on top of everything. She couldn't believe her good luck.

Eagerly flipping it open, she scanned the entries. There was a detailed tally of Ridley's bank balances covering the last two years. It was immediately clear he sank everything into his business, and at times, the balance dropped dangerously close to zero. Even better, where he listed large infusions of cash into his account, he actually wrote "Catherine."

Kristi started snapping photos, relieved to find proof of Ridley's motivation for blackmail and Catherine's payouts to him. But then she frowned. The payouts didn't actually say "blackmail." She could just imagine Ridley saying Catherine gave him the money as gifts. Catherine was known for being generous, after all. Darn. She needed more proof.

Tucking the camera back in her bag, Kristi rooted through the rest of the papers and office supplies in the desk drawers in an effort to find Miranda's letters or anything else relevant. Nothing.

She stood up, stretched out her back, and checked her watch. 3:45 pm. Still time. Letting out a calming breath, she hurried across to the filing cabinet, pulled open the drawers, and flipped through documents, but everything pertained to his horse business. It wasn't until she reached the bottom drawer that Kristi finally found something.

At the very back of the drawer, the hanging files were pushed forward to make room for a small box. It was metal, about half the size of a shoe box, and was held closed by a simple latch and no lock. She took the box to the desk and opened it. Inside was a packet of blue airmail letters, tied together in a bundle with a piece of red embroidery thread. She lifted them out gently, her pulse starting to pound when she saw who they were from. Miranda!

The shiny glass surface of something at the bottom of the box caught her eye. She picked up a framed glass photograph. In it, Catherine and Miranda stood together with their arms about each other, both smiling for the camera. The openness of Catherine's smile was unlike anything Kristi had ever seen of the woman. Catherine actually looked happy, and in love. This had to be the missing third photograph from the bedside table in Montecito. Her hunch had been right all along.

Thanks for not destroying the evidence, Ridley, Kristi thought, but she heard the sound of tires on gravel. A car was approaching. Her elation turned to terror as she glanced again at her watch. It was only 3:45 pm. Ridley wasn't supposed to be back until 5. A car door slammed.

Holding her breath, she tried to listen over the wild pounding of her heart, but all she could make out was a horse nickering in a nearby stall. What if it was Ridley?

No way did she want to get caught, but she hadn't had time to photograph the letters. She shoved the bundle and the photograph back into the metal box and slid the box into her bag. She couldn't just leave the evidence behind, not after everything she'd done to find it. Besides, technically the stuff didn't even belong to Ridley, so at least she wasn't stealing.

She rushed to the office door. The horse whiskered again, louder. Kristi cautiously stuck her head out into the barn's corridor. Her heart lurched. A man was entering the barn at the far end, the same end of the barn where she'd parked. His body was outlined against the bright backdrop of the sunny outdoors. She couldn't be sure who he was, but then he yelled, "You there, What are you doing?" and started running toward her. Ridley!

Kristi sprinted out the closer barn door. She had to get back to her car and out of there. Clutching the bouncing bag against her side, she ran around the outside of the barn, digging her keys from her jeans pocket as she went. Ridley's silver luxury sports car was parked beside her dusty beater.

She jumped into her car, cranked the ignition, and hit the accelerator, spinning gravel as she accelerated down the driveway. She didn't bother hitting the brakes, as she veered onto the road and headed for Santa Barbara and safety.

44. Showdown

When Kristi reached southbound Highway 154 over the Santa Ynez Mountains, the sun had already set behind the mountain range. The rush hour traffic coming from Santa Barbara had picked up, but there were few cars going her way. She glanced in the rear view mirror. Some distance back, a car raced uphill toward her in the wrong lane of the two-lane highway as it passed another car. It swerved back into the right lane just before a stream of downhill cars reached it.

In the growing twilight, Kristi couldn't make out its color, but she saw that it was low and had to be a sports car for the kind of power it took to pass on such a steep grade.

Kristi's heart gave a hunker. Ridley. He must have checked his office and seen what she'd taken. Why else would he come after her?

She glanced back at his car again, now certain that her suspicions were right—it had been his car Catherine's neighbor saw outside Catherine's property the night she was killed, and it was his car that Rose's roommate saw leaving the low income housing parking lot.

The timeline also fit. Ridley must have been worried Rose might ID him, and after the police interviewed him about Catherine being at his party, he probably panicked and put Catherine's jewelry in Rose's car to frame her. He then made the anonymous tip to the police to ensure Rose was arrested.

Kristi's happiness at knowing the truth was marred by the fact that he was now in hot pursuit. No question he meant to stop her, but she hoped he wouldn't be able to before she got to the Santa Barbara Police Department. Too bad her car's engine wasn't stronger.

As she drove over the pass at Camino Cielo, the car ahead of her suddenly sped up, its taillights pulling away from her on the Oceanside downhill. She eased off the gas and let gravity propel her car downward. A steady stream of headlights came uphill, commuters leaving Santa Barbara at the end of the work day. A cool breeze began to blow through the car vents, and the fog bank lay not far below her, spreading a white blanket away to the horizon.

The car ahead of her braked, its lights flaring as it slowed for a big bend in the road. She pushed on her brake pedal, but nothing happened. Her car's speed didn't slow. The other car disappeared around the bend. Her own car kept picking up speed. She pressed the brake again. Still nothing. She stomped on the brake pedal with both feet as hard as she could, cursing. Why hadn't she gotten her car serviced six months ago, like she was supposed to? Money's been tight, but...

Her eyes flew to the precipitous drop-off below the road. If she went over, she'd be smashed to smithereens on the massive sandstone boulders below the highway. Her car hurtled to the bend where the road cut into the mountainside. Clinging to the steering wheel, she took the turn way too fast. Her tires screeched and the car started to slide, but somehow she just made it around the bend.

The road abruptly straightened out again, but her relief lasted only an instant as she hit the fog bank. Her windshield instantly misted over, blinding her. Hastily, she switched on the wipers and leaned forward, desperately trying to see through the swirling gray. Somewhere up ahead, the highway went into a huge switchback, but how far ahead? She couldn't see in the fog.

The blinding headlights of oncoming cars shot out of the gloom and rushed by, much too close, separated from her by only the small double yellow line painted on the road. The fog grew thicker. Where the heck was that switchback?

Her car was picking up speed again. No way could she make the switchback, not with her car going so fast. A crash was inevitable. She could very well die.

Come on, think, she told herself, you need a plan.

But panic made her thoughts skitter around in her head. Could she stop the car before the bend? Could she do it without colliding into another vehicle? She was on the down slope side of the narrow two-lane road. Any attempt to veer to the right off the road would send her careening off the cliff.

The only option was to make a left onto Painted Cave Road, right before the switchback. She knew it veered sharply uphill and would stop her car's momentum, assuming she didn't hit an oncoming car first, but would she see the turnoff in time?

The emergency brake! She remembered something her dad had once taught her. How could she have forgotten?

Gripping the brake handle at her side, she yanked up as hard as she could. The car started to slow, but just then, Painted Cave Road emerged from the fog on her left. Now or never.

Abandoning the emergency brake, she grabbed the steering wheel with both hands, flinging it around to the left.

Her tires squealed and the car started to skid out of control as it careened over the center line, right into the headlights of an oncoming car.

Kristi screamed, clamping her eyes shut.

No impact. What?

Her eyes blinked open. The oncoming car had missed her by inches. Painted Cave Road was right there, but she was going way too fast.

She overshot the road, skidding off the pavement and onto sandy gravel. A house-sized boulder suddenly rose up out of the fog, its massive wall of sandstone bright in her headlights...

Kristi's forehead hurt. A lot. She had no idea where she was or what had happened, just the splitting pain in her head. Everything was pitch black. Something dripped down over her right eye and she realized her eyes were closed.

Opening them, she saw a spiderweb of broken glass in the dim light. She stared at it, not sure at first what she was looking at, but then everything came rushing back. Ridley, her brakes, the crash...

Through the broken glass, she saw the front end of her car smashed against an enormous boulder that formed part of a large outcropping of sandstone boulders, which jutted out from the steep flank of the mountain.

Thank God, I'm not dead, she thought, but then felt another drip fall over her eye. She wiped it and held her hand up to her face. The liquid appeared black in the dark car, and she could smell the iron in it. Blood. A lot of it. She'd read somewhere that head injuries bleed a lot.

A wave of dizziness made her lean back against the headrest, the pain in her head like a pick ax to her skull. She tried to assess the damage to the rest of her body, gingerly moving her arms and legs. Except her head, everything felt OK. She let out a breath of relief, but then got a whiff of gasoline.

Gasoline?

Her eyes shot again to the front end of her car. She'd seen enough cars explode on TV. What if her car exploded? She had to get out of there, fast.

Gritting her teeth against the clanging in her head, she shoved open the car door. It was almost night, and the fog had blown in thick and dark. The loud roar of rush hour traffic on the nearby highway filled the air, but so, too, did the acrid smell of burning rubber and the dangerous odor of gasoline.

She was about to get out when she remembered her bag and the evidence. A car fire would destroy it. No way, not if it meant Ridley got away with murder and framing Rose.

When she saw it wasn't on the passenger seat, she realized it must've fallen to the floor during the crash. A flicker of flames caught her eye, coming from the front end of the car. Panicked, she reached blindly under the passenger side dashboard, desperately groping around on the floor in the blackness. Her fingers closed over the nylon bag and the metal box of evidence inside, but her relief was nothing to the terror she felt about dying in an explosion.

Grabbing the bag, she launched herself from the car. Too late, she realized the ground beneath her wasn't level pavement or gravel, but steep rocky scree. Her left foot landed in loose sand, and she started to slide. Trying to stabilize herself, she swung her right foot forward downhill. It landed unexpectedly between two rocks.

Momentum plus gravity propelled the rest of her body downward, but with her right foot still trapped between the two rocks, she lost her balance. Her ankle gave a horrible pop as she fell down the steep slope, and her bag flew from her hand as she braced for impact. Her hands hit sand and stopped her body's descent, but her right foot stayed lodged between the two rocks. Stabbing pain shot through her ankle and up her leg.

She glanced back up at the burning car. It was still far too close. Digging her fingers into the rocky sand, she managed with difficulty to push herself back up the hill and dislodge her foot.

Unsteadily, she tried to stand, crying out in pain when she put weight on her foot. Was it sprained, or broken?

"Too bad the crash didn't kill you, Miss McCormick." A man's voice called out over the rush hour traffic.

Through the foggy gloom, Kristi spotted the shadowy form of a tall thin man about twenty feet away. He stood down on the asphalt of Painted Cave Road beside a silver sports car. Ridley. His words made her realize that, except for the cars on the highway, they were alone.

A terrible possibility crept into her mind. Had he done something to her brakes? Was that why she'd crashed?

As if on queue, he stepped off the road and came toward her. Her stomach clenched. He'd caught her trespassing. He'd chased her over the mountains, maybe cut her brake lines. No question he wanted her dead. Her eyes shot to his hands. Gun? They were empty.

She blew out a shaky breath. At least he couldn't just blow her head off. If her ankle wasn't injured, she could outrun him, or worst case fight him, but not now, and though he was an old man, she knew he was an avid horseman and unusually fit for his age.

Her eyes darted downhill to the steady stream of headlights flying by on Highway 154. She couldn't go that way. Too easy to get hit in the growing darkness by one of the speeding cars. Behind her burned her car, the engine engulfed in a bright beacon of smoky light, and behind that was the vertical wall of the boulder she'd smashed into and the sandstone outcropping.

The only real option was to head uphill to the left of the outcropping, where the mountain rose at a sharp angle of dirt, smaller boulders, and chaparral. Somewhere way up there, Painted Cave Road switched back on itself. Maybe she could climb up there. Maybe find help. She wasn't about to stay where she was and let Ridley catch her. She wasn't ready to die.

Ignoring the pounding in her head and the blood in her eyes, she picked up the nylon bag and slung its two straps over her shoulder.

Ridley called out. "I won't let you ruin my life, Miss McCormick."

Kristi bit her lip against the pain as she put pressure on her right foot and lurched uphill. No way did she want Ridley to know how hurt she was, or that he had the advantage. Talking to him might distract her from the pain and maybe slow him down. She yelled back at him. "What do you mean?"

"I love Beverly. I won't let anyone stand between us."

"Love? Don't you mean her money?" Fighting a wave of dizziness, Kristi hobbled up the rocky dirt toward a jumble of boulders, many car-sized or larger.

"How dare you! I love her." It sounded like he was getting closer.

She glanced over her shoulder. Ridley was now less than twenty feet below her, and the car fire was spreading to the neighboring chaparral. A wind had picked up, tossing embers into the air and pushing the fire uphill, smoke billowing toward them. If Ridley didn't kill her, the fire might.

Gritting her teeth, Kristi limped upward as fast as she could and finally made it to the boulder field.

"Stop," Ridley called out after her. "Your effort to escape is futile, Miss McCormick."

Kristi ignored him and climbed up a narrow gap between two boulders, the metal box of evidence in her nylon bag bumping sharply against her back.

Bracing her hands against the rough sandstone, she tried to increase her speed by leveraging herself upward and taking weight off her injured ankle, but she could hear Ridley closing in behind her. She needed to stall him, slow him down. Her brain spun frantically searching for options, but the pounding in her head made it harder. At least she could keep him talking. Maybe he'd give her some answers.

"Why did you kill Catherine, if she was paying you money to keep quiet about Miranda?"

"That damned lesbian! I still can't believe she duped me into a relationship. When I found out... Well, Catherine had to pay. I wasn't about to let a lesbian make a fool out of me." He was breathing hard as he climbed up behind her.

Kristi struggled through the sharp bushes that grew in the tight spaces between the boulders, as she sought a route upward, her eyes stinging from the smoke. It was clear Ridley was homophobic and had blackmailed Catherine, but he still hadn't admitted to killing her. "So why did you kill her?"

Ridley coughed and then gasped out, "Because when she showed up at the party, she demanded I return those disgusting letters, or she'd tell Beverly the truth."

"So, did you?" Kristi choked out the words on air now thick with the smoke of burning chaparral and plastic from the car fire.

"You'd think I'd be stupid enough to simply give the letters back?" He gave a derogatory laugh. "I demanded payment. We agreed I'd bring the letters to Montecito in exchange for the valuables she had in her safe there." He broke off in a fit of hoarse coughing.

Kristi reached the top of the boulder field, but in the smoky fog, came face to face with a dense wall of chaparral rising up the mountain above her.

Damn. She gulped down increasing panic. There was no way to get through such an impenetrable thorny wall. So much for her hope of making it to the switchback on Painted Cave Road and escaping that way.

The only option was to traverse along the top of the boulder field. It wasn't much of an option, because she knew it eventually had to end at the rocky outcropping that formed a cliff above Highway 154. Maybe if she got lucky, she'd find another way down before then.

The wind increased, blowing smoke and swirling sparks around her as she limped and scrambled as fast as she could across the boulders. The instant she reached a safe, relatively flat surface on top of one of the rocks, she glanced back. Her heart gave a violent lurch. Ridley was now within ten feet of her.

Turning, she stumbled across the top of the boulder to the other side, but then had to stop. The gap between where she stood and the next boulder was too far to jump, especially with a bad ankle. There was also no way to tell in the murky smoke how far down it was between the two boulders to the ground.

Double damn. There was no way to escape. She'd have to face Ridley. Heart pounding, she turned.

Ridley was almost upon her. His usually coiffed hair stood on end, whipped wild in the wind, and his face and clothes were dark with dirt and soot.

He held out a hand and rasped, "Give me that bag."

The bag was still hanging by its straps from her neck. She pulled it close against her side. "Why should I? You murdered Catherine and framed Rose, and I'm your one loose end. If I give it to you, you're going to try to kill me anyway, right?"

"Kudos to your powers of deduction, Miss McCormick. Now, stop stalling." Ridley took a step toward her.

Kristi held up her hand in a stop gesture, speaking quickly and lying desperately through her teeth. "The police have my written statement about everything you did. If I turn up dead, you'll be their number one suspect."

Ridley regarded her for a moment and then laughed contemptuously. "Good try, Miss McCormick, but without evidence, your words mean nothing. Besides, who's to say I'm not a good Samaritan, who stopped and tried to help an accident victim? It's my word against yours, but you won't be able to speak, not if you're dead."

He lunged for her. She tried to sidestep him, but his hand hooked the bag and jerked it from her grasp, the bag's straps still around her neck and now choking her as he tried to pull the bag off her.

She clutched at the straps, trying to relieve the pressure on her windpipe, while she shoved hard with her other hand against his chest, trying to force him back. "You'll never get away with killing me."

He seized her wrist, his face so close, she could see the murderous intent in his cold blue eyes. "Oh, but I will. Once I marry Beverly, I'll have all the money I need to buy the best defense around."

A sudden fury burned away Kristi's fear. Everything she'd done, everyone she'd tried to help, no way was she going to let it all be for nothing. No way was she going to let this horrible man destroy her and use another woman's money to buy his freedom. Enraged, she viciously thrust her knee upward, aiming to strike him in the groin.

Ridley released her wrist, trying to deflect the assault, while with his other hand, he yanked the bag off her shoulders by one of its straps.

Reflexively, Kristi's hand shot out and hooked the other strap. Pulling hard, she tried to wrench the bag back from him.

"You bitch!" He snarled. With his free hand, he swung a punch at her face.

She lurched back and avoided the blow, but too late, she realized how close they'd come to the edge of the boulder. Her bad ankle buckled.

Tumbling backward, she fell off the boulder and into the smoky chasm below, her fist still closed tight around the one strap. As she fell, she wondered, was this how Catherine had felt the moment before her death?

45. Endings and Beginnings

A week after the accident and the terrifying showdown with Ridley, the October sun shone warm over East Beach, its white sand, the shorebirds, the moving waves of the ocean. The whole world seemed to sparkle, and Kristi felt lucky to be alive, thanks to the commuters, who'd contacted 911 when they saw the car fire.

She smiled as Brian carried her across the sand. "Thanks again for bringing me here. I'm not too heavy?"

"You're perfect."

She'd almost forgotten how handsome he was, his dark face so close to hers that she could see flecks of blue in his gray eyes. She glanced down at the cast on her foot, which dangled awkwardly over his arm, and gave a rueful laugh. "I guess swimming's out?"

Brian chuckled. "We'll be swimming the buoys again soon enough."

"Six weeks? It'll be almost December before this darned thing comes off." Despite her words, she wasn't upset. A sprained ankle and concussion were nothing compared to what had happened to Ridley. She pushed the thought out of her mind. This was no place for such darkness.

"Don't worry. Six weeks will go by in no time." Brian set her down gently at the water line, where the soft dry sand met the wet. The tide was going out.

She put weight carefully on her right foot as she stood and handed him the towel she'd been carrying. "Yeah, I know, 'Patience is a virtue.'" Six weeks felt like an eternity.

Brian spread out the towel and held out a hand to her. "Let me help you sit."

"Thanks." She gripped his hand and levered herself clumsily down onto the towel, then used her hands to lift and straighten her right leg in front of her, careful not to get sand in the cast.

He dropped down and sat in the sand beside her.

She glanced over at his navy pinstripe suit. "Aren't you worried about getting your clothes dirty?"

He shrugged. "It'll wash. You need the towel more than I do."

His kind gesture reminded her again of how different he was from James, and she felt her spirits lift.

Between the days in the hospital and her family hovering protectively around her, this was the first time she'd had a real moment alone with Brian. She realized she'd missed him. She was also thankful he still wanted to see her, considering everything she'd done after he'd told her not to.

"What's up?" she asked, noticing the enigmatic expression on his face as he looked at her.

"You could so easily have died."

The sea breeze blew a strand of hair across her forehead, but before she could brush it away, he reached up and did it for her.

She had to look away from the gravity in his eyes, the concern. Blinking back tears, she willed herself not to think about that terrible night and tried to focus on the beautiful ocean glistening before them, but her head started to throb.

"I'm sorry, I didn't mean to make you cry." Brian cradled her hand in the both of his. "The important thing is, you didn't, right? You were incredibly lucky to fall the way you did. Anyway else, anywhere else, you'd have broken your neck like Ridley did."

Kristi tried to give him a watery smile, but the darkness seeped back in. She couldn't remember anything after falling off the boulder. It was only in the hospital a day later that she learned Ridley had also fallen, but to his death.

She inhaled the clean ocean air, smoke no longer clogging her nose. Why hadn't he just let go of the bag?

Pulling her hand free of Brian's, she wiped the tears from her eyes. "The thing is, now he won't have to pay for his crimes."

"At least not through the criminal justice system."

Would Ridley face a higher justice? Until her encounter with him, she'd never believed true evil existed. "I'm pretty sure he cut the brake lines of my car and that's why I crashed."

Brian shook his head. "No. The police determined the rubber tubing broke because it was old and worn out, not because of foul play."

Kristi sighed. OK, so maybe Ridley wasn't quite the villain she'd thought. A lot of her case had been like that, things not turning out to be what she'd first thought.

She looked out at the restless, moving blue water of the ocean and remembered that crazy Thursday a week ago, her desperate search for evidence at Ridley's ranch, the car chase, the showdown. "I wonder why Ridley held onto Catherine's letters and those photos of her with Miranda?"

Brian turned his gaze to the ocean, too. "Maybe he thought he could squeeze money out of Catherine's niece, once she received the inheritance. I doubt she'd have wanted people to gossip about her aunt."

"Ridley would've been disappointed. I have a feeling Anita cared more about the money than Catherine's reputation." The woman must be livid, now that Rose was out of jail and free to inherit most of Catherine's estate. "Funny how a week ago, the newspapers made Rose out to be the villain. Now, they're describing her as a hapless underdog, unfairly targeted because she's poor and didn't have the right connections."

Brian grinned. "That's the press for you. Enjoy your day in the sun, because in a day or two, the papers will move on to a new story."

"Hey, I'm not complaining. The publicity's priceless. I just got a call today from someone needing help from a 'budding young PI.'" Kristi held her fingers up and mimicked quotation marks.

The new client had been impressed by Grace Teller's description of her, and considering he wanted to hire her simply to confirm a potential business partner's identity, the new case was going to be a piece of cake.

A jogger ran by on the wet sand below where they sat, sprinting to avoid an incoming wave. Kristi watched and reflected on her first case, which had definitely been no piece of cake. "I guess I now understand the timing."

"Timing?"

"Yeah, I couldn't figure out why, of all places, Catherine would choose that pro-marriage fundraiser to demand Miranda's letters back from Ridley, but I think I now understand. She must've found out that Ridley and Beverly were going to announce their engagement at the party, and she wanted to stop him. From everything I've learned about her, I don't think Catherine would stand idly by and let an innocent person get hurt."

"Maybe." Brian shrugged. "But maybe knowing she was about to die of cancer also made her brave."

"Cancer?" Kristi looked at him in surprise.

"The final autopsy report came back today. Catherine had terminal cancer, bad enough she didn't have much longer to live. That's probably why she rewrote her will."

"Did Rose know?"

"I don't think so. She never said anything to me about it."

"Me, neither."

Kristi stared at the shorebreak and thought about Catherine and how private she'd been. Had she kept her illness a secret from everyone? Poor woman, to have no one to talk to about what she was going through.

Maybe that's why she'd gone on that trip up north to see Lorenzo, Sara, her ranch—one last visit. Maybe that's why she'd wanted Miranda's letters back, to see them one last time.

But she hadn't gotten to. Ridley had seen to that. He'd killed her before the cancer could.

Kristi's head started to throb again, and she gingerly touched the lump on her head with her fingers.

Brian glanced over. "You OK?"

"Yeah." Kristi didn't want to think about Ridley or the accident anymore. "There's been no mention of Miranda in the papers."

"They've also said nothing about Ridley blackmailing Catherine."

Kristi nodded. Catherine's big secret had been kept. Kristi bet her uncle had something to do with that. She hadn't seen Pete since he'd taken her statement in the hospital, but if anyone understood and respected a right to privacy, it was him. It still didn't seem fair, though, that some people had to hide so much.

Brian took her hand in his again and gave it a gentle squeeze. "I wish you'd trusted me enough to tell me what you were planning when you went to Ridley's."

She turned and met his gaze, willing herself to say what needed to be said. "I do trust you, Brian. That's why I left you that message."

Of course if she'd actually told him ahead of time, he never would've let her go. She didn't say the words aloud.

When Brian didn't either, but simply held her hand and regarded her for a long moment with thoughtful eyes, she felt herself falling for him. Unable to resist, she leaned over and pressed a kiss to his cheek. "Thanks."

"For what?"

"For not stating the obvious."

He grinned. "I guess we'll have to figure out a few things before we work together again."

"Will there be a next time?" She looked at him seriously, a mixture of hope and fear rising up inside her. "After what happened on this case, I'll do my best to stay law-abiding, but I can't promise you there won't be times I need to skirt close to the edge of the law."

He lifted her hand and pressed a kiss to the back of it. His eyes were warm and she saw forgiveness there. "Byers and Martin needs good PIs all the time."

"Thanks." The fear of losing him blew away on the sea breeze.

"Besides, if you break the law again, you may need my services. Your uncle won't always be able to cover for you."

Returning his smile, she said, "Double thanks."

She was also going to have to thank Pete. Her uncle had not included in the police report exactly where she'd been, before her final showdown with Ridley, which meant she'd likely escape a trespassing charge, and he'd made sure the police report did not cast suspicion on her for Ridley's death.

Rose hadn't had the benefit of such connections when Catherine turned up dead. Kristi's thoughts turned to her first case. So much had been riding on it. She'd had to save Rose from being scapegoated by a system that favored the wealthy and find out who really killed Catherine. Despite the hurdles and the steep learning curve, the red herrings like Tomas and Josh and the secret child theory, she'd actually done it. She'd actually solved the mystery. More importantly, she'd proved to herself and to her family that she could succeed as a PI and make her dream a reality.

Her thoughts went back to Rose, and she glanced over at Brian. "There's one thing I still don't understand about the case."

"Yeah?"

"Why did Catherine leave so much of her estate to her house sitter? Rose denied they were having an affair, but doesn't it seem likely?"

Brian shook his head. "Actually, they weren't. Catherine's trustee uncovered a letter she'd left Rose, which was to be opened upon her death. Turns out Catherine had come to think of Rose as the daughter she never had, and when she found out she had terminal cancer, she wanted to leave Rose a legacy."

"Quite a legacy! I wonder what Rose is going to do with all that money?"

Brian's eyes twinkled. "Funny you should ask."

"What do you mean?"

"I met with her earlier today to finish up the paperwork on her case. She told me she wants to buy a building downtown and guarantee that Eye Spy Private Eye has an office in it."

"What?" Kristi stared at him incredulously.

"She said it's the least she can do for you after all your help." Brian flicked his hand in a dismissive gesture. "Now you can say good riddance to that odious office manager. I'd still like to press charges against him."

Kristi laughed. "You're cute when you get protective."

Brian ducked his head at the compliment. "Speaking of office managers, Rose thinks Eduardo would make an excellent one, and get this, she'd like to open her own English Language school in the new building."

"She still wants to teach?"

Brian nodded. "She says that all the money in the world won't stop her from doing what she loves, though she does plan to work fewer hours."

His words led Kristi to think again about love and money, about being rich or poor, about secrets and power, and how all of it had affected Rose, Catherine and Miranda, James and Brian, Ridley and Beverly. If she'd learned anything from this case, it was to never underestimate the power of love and money. They could be such powerful forces, for either good or bad.

Brian's next words brought her out of her musing. "Rose plans to keep Tomas on, managing the estate gardens."

Kristi watched a flock of seagulls soar overhead. "I'm beginning to understand why Catherine cared about Rose. She's such a caring, good person."

He was looking at her, his eyes twinkling again. "So are you."

She loved how subtle lines crinkled the corners of his eyes when he smiled. Gazing back at him in a state of dazed wonder, she couldn't believe she'd only met him three weeks ago. Just a week ago, she'd been with James.

Aloud, she said, "I told my parents I stopped seeing James."

"How'd they take it?"

She shrugged. "I told them I met someone better."

He put a hand on his chest and pretended to look surprised. "Me?"

She grinned. "You want to come to dinner sometime and meet them?"

"I'd be honored."

"The sooner they meet you, the sooner they'll realize I've made the right choice. Even if you don't drive a fancy sports car."

"Hey, my dad's truck is very reliable."

"Doesn't he mind you driving it?"

"He walks to work. Besides, one of these days, I'll have enough money saved up to buy my own car."

"Speaking of cars, I have no idea when I'll be able to buy another of my own." Kristi looked down gloomily at her cast. "I can't drive for the next six weeks, anyway." It was probably better that her old deathtrap was history, considering what had happened.

"I'm planning on being your private chauffeur."

His words made her forget the accident, and she laughed. "Yeah?"

The blowing sound of dolphins nearby distracted her. A pod had surfaced, just beyond the break. She and Brian watched as the dolphins sprayed fine sparkling mists of water into the air, their long slick dark bodies rising and then sliding beneath the surface of the liquid blue. There was something so beautiful and yet mysterious about them.

Kristi's eyes lifted beyond them to the shadowy Channel Islands, sitting on the distant horizon, and she remembered the childhood story Brian's dad had told him about the rainbow bridge and the dolphins being like brothers to the Chumash. "Maybe you can tell me more stories about the Chumash sometime."

"I'd love to."

The brilliant sunlight burnished his hair to polished ebony, and his eyes glowed bright in his dark, intent face. He looked nothing like the stern, almost forbidding man, who had first showed up at her office asking for help.

She remembered what Carla had told her when they'd gone to Pete's for cocktails, that Brian was perfect for her. She felt suddenly dizzy to think how much had happened since meeting him. The lump on her head gave another throb.

The light in Brian's eyes shifted to concern. "You OK?"

His hand moved up to cup her cheek. It felt warm and strong, reassuring, and she leaned into him, the pain receding. "I am now." He was such a good man, so kind. When he started to pull away, she slid her arms up around his neck. "Kiss me."

He obliged, dipping his head.

The tender kiss deepened, intensified. She didn't care if it was broad daylight on the beach where anyone could see. Desperate to get closer, she pulled herself onto his lap, ignoring her ankle when it twinged with discomfort.

"Whoa!" Brian lifted his head and let out a tense breath. "We'd better cool things down, sweetheart, or we'll be arrested." He shifted her off his lap.

"I can't stand this!" Kristi shuddered. There'd been too many stolen moments that always ended too soon.

"Does that mean you won't be offended by a proposition?"

Words were hard to form around the need still gripping her. "What?" she managed to croak.

He dug into his coat pocket and held up a motel key dangling from a plastic fob. "I was thinking, kind of hoping... ?" His lips kicked up in a self-conscious, lop-sided grin. "I'm not being too presumptuous, am I?"

She was confused. "What's that for?"

"Somewhere private." His expression sobered. "I wish I could offer you somewhere more deluxe than a cheap motel—-"

"I don't care about that!" If she had, she'd still be with James. "But it's Thursday. Don't you have to go back to work this afternoon?"

He chuckled. "With the hours I've been putting in? I'm free the rest of the day. You?"

Her new client could wait. Eye Spy Private Eye was going to make it. She had the feeling that she and Brian would, too. "Let's go!"

THE END

About the Author

Lisa Frieden grew up in California, with a side trip around the world as a kid, college in Cambridge, and a few unforgettable years in Santa Barbara. She's read everything from William Shakespeare, Virginia Woolf, and Toni Morrison, to Linda Howard, Sue Grafton, and Jayne Ann Krentz. Her own books reflect this diversity, from *Dialysis: a Memoir*, to her romantic suspense books: *The Offering* and *Finding Clarity*, to her mystery, *Love and Money*. For updated author info, please visit: www.lisafrieden.com.

Read more at www.lisafrieden.com.